SHADOW BOX

SHADOW BOX

KIM PRITEKEL

SAPPHIRE BOOKS

SALINAS, CALIFORNIA

Shadow Box
Copyright © 2013 by **Kim Pritekel**, All rights reserved.

ISBN -978-1-939062-07-9

This is a work of fiction - names, characters, places, and incidents are the product of the author's imagination or are used fictitiously. Any resemblance to actual persons living or dead, business, events or locales is entirely coincidental.

All rights reserved. No part of this publication may be reproduced, distributed, or transmitted in any form or by any means, including photocopying, recording, or other electronic or mechanical methods, without written permission of the publisher.

Cover Design by Christine Svendsen
Editor Kaycee Hawn -

Sapphire Books
Salinas, CA 93912
www.sapphirebooks.com

Printed in the United States of America
First Edition – May 2013

Dedication

For my mom. Despite all you've been through, I've never seen anyone so strong and willing to see all the good life has to offer. I love you.

Acknowledgements

I'd like to acknowledge the woman who inspired this story. I can only hope she managed to get her life together and off the streets. Though I never knew her name, she will remain in my thoughts forever.

Prologue

1991 - Fort Worth, Texas

The night was swept blue and red, a small army of police cars littering the Robard property. Uniformed men came and went, radio squawks interrupting what would be a still, Sunday night in the Rockbridge Trailer Park.

Connie Robard sat on the steps of Michelle and Daniel's trailer, across the dirt road, her four-year-old daughter in her arms. Green eyes peeked out from a near-smothering embrace.

The young mother of two was crying softly, a small trail of tears making its way down her chin and onto the top of her child's head, making auburn hair even darker. She couldn't watch, closing her eyes as the stretcher was removed from her trailer, the small body dwarfed inside the black body bag.

"Jesus, can you believe this shit?" Sergeant Billy Haynes muttered, watching as the body was loaded into the coroner's van. His partner, Seth Shyly, shook his head.

"Hate it when they're that young. At least she's got the other one." The blonde cop nodded toward the sobbing Connie Robard.

Haynes nodded. "Yeah. Guess so."

"We're ready here."

Both men's attention turned at the voice of lead

detective, Bryce Martinez. He was peeling latex gloves from large hands as he walked over to them. Sighing heavily, lacing the air with stale coffee and even staler cigarettes, he ran a hand over well-greased hair. He turned to Seth.

"You wanna get the mother all taken care of? We'll run in the father." The man in question was being guided into the back of a squad car, brand new bracelets courtesy of the Fort Worth Police Department.

"Sure thing." Without another word, Seth jogged off, his fellow officers watching him go.

"Man, I remember when I had that kind of energy." Billy chuckled, seeing his long-time friend nod. Losing his mirth, the twenty-two year veteran glanced back at the trailer, lit up like a Christmas tree. He knew that through all his time on the FWPD, this case would stick with him forever. The young ones always did. "Man, what a shame."

"Crying shame."

Connie Robard's swimming eyes followed the policeman's approach. He knelt down in front of her, knees cracking.

"Mrs. Robard, I need you to come with me now, okay?" he said, voice soft. The young blonde glanced at her babe in arms.

"Can I meet you down there? I need to get hold of my mom."

Understanding, the officer nodded, getting to his feet.

The trailer almost seemed deadly silent, especially after the uproar of an hour ago. Connie walked through it, mindful not to touch anything. The nice officer told her it was still a crime scene. Making her way down the short, narrow hallway, her daughter on her hip, she couldn't allow herself to look in the bathroom. Couldn't. No! Literally closing her eyes as she passed, she hurried into the girls' bedroom. The dim overhead light bounced off cheap wood paneling, giving the room a dark, dreary feel.

Red-rimmed blue eyes took in the double bed, two identical pairs of Mary Janes nestled against the wall. Two identical Teddy Bears, both missing an opposite eye, tucked into the bed for the night, waiting for their mommies to join them.

The sob tore from Connie's throat before she could stop it. Slowly falling to her knees, she curled up in a ball, her daughter staggering backward on bare feet from suddenly being nearly thrown down.

"Mommy?" she whispered, scared and unsure. She tapped her mother's shoulder, feeling it tremble under the weight of an enormous grief. "Mommy?" the girl tried again, her voice even softer, afraid she'd make her mommy mad. "Is Jenny gonna be okay?" Green eyes looked into tortured blue as her mother looked up at her, face flaming and moist from unending tears. Connie shook her head slowly.

"No, baby. No, she's not."

Chapter One

Present Day – Northglenn, Colorado

A hand reached up, tucking light brown strands behind an ear, the fingers staying to play with the small, gold hoop that was pierced through the cartilage; a nervous tick, keeping Erin's body busy while she contemplated her handiwork. Leaving the ear alone, she grabbed the edges of the picture, nudging it to the right half an inch. Stepping back, blue eyes studied it as though the frame would magically move back on its own. Satisfied, she turned back to the other decorations she had to hang.

Anyone who didn't know Erin very well was always shocked when they stepped into her place. She had a deep love of anything sharp and pointy. Her sword collection was unusual, to say the least, but she loved it. The obsession had been with her since childhood, and she had yet to grow out of it. She bought her first piece at twenty-one, and the world would have thought she'd won the lottery, so enthusiastic was her happy dance.

One of the things Erin had loved about the new apartment was the amount of wall space. Her old place, back home in Pueblo, had offered little to nothing in opportunities to hang her beloved swords and daggers. Her blades had to battle with picture space. One day, when she bought a house, she wanted a room for nothing but her sword collection, pictures, and books. And the binders.

Looking to her bookcase, she was somewhat proud to see the thick, plastic spines, all red with neat, white labels. The titles and dates they'd been started and finished were printed in neat, block lettering. Only about half had a finished date. She would get back to the others. Someday.

Snagging a handful of the long, heavy nails, she lined them between her teeth, and grabbed her hammer. She had it all mapped out in her mind, where all the swords would go: her Viking sword – longer than the others – would go center. Straddling it would be the shorter Celtic blade, and then the replica of the sword from the Battle of Agincourt. That was her favorite, by far; simple yet elegant. Throw in a Gladius and a few double-headed axes, and she had the wall behind her couch filled.

The past year had been hard on her. Ten months ago, she had left her first substantial relationship. Mark had been everything she'd ever wanted, or thought she wanted. When she had heard a rumor at work that he'd been asking about her, she'd been beside herself, partly not believing it, and partly thrilled. Well, mostly thrilled. And then the day had come.

Working diligently at her desk at Re/Max, the pages she'd been looking over fell into shadow. Looking up to see who was blocking her light, she'd found herself looking into smiling brown eyes. The thirty year-old Realtor had said hello, the grin he was known for firmly in place. It was lopsided, but filled with boyish charm. Having no clue what to do, she had simply said hello back. When he'd asked her to go to lunch with him, she thought she'd heard him wrong.

Erin sighed, her breath coming out, along with a few curses, between the row of nail heads between her lips. The pain had subsided over the last year; the anger, too. But she'd never forget, and she'd never be the same. For a woman who already had trust issues, she was screwed.

※ ※ ※ ※

It had been such a long weekend. Ridiculously long. Erin had moved before, but never to another city. It was twice the work, twice the expense, and twice the exhaustion.

The hot water continued to pour into the tub, bubbles blooming, cool and frothy. She played with them, gathering a bouquet, inhaling their lavender fragrance with closed eyes and an appreciative smile.

She loved bubble baths. Smiling, she thought of her old house back home; it had been awful! A seventy-year-old money pit. The furnace had a spider's web of cracks in it, the heat oozing out into the attic space. Her landlord hadn't believed her at first, fifty-five degree house temperatures with two hundred dollar gas bill results.

She remembered sitting in the tiny tub, unable to lie down fully. She used to feel like a bird on a wire, sitting there, cupping hot water in her hands to drape over her shoulders and breasts. She'd started taking two and three bubble baths a day, just to keep warm.

"No more," she moaned, allowing the heat and steam to slip into every single nook and cranny of her sore, tired body. She rested her fingertips against her water-softened thighs, sighing heavily.

The decision to move out of her hometown, away from her family – and everything she'd known for twenty-seven years – was one of the most difficult decisions she'd ever made. But it had to be done.

After she'd caught Mark in another lie, she couldn't take it anymore. He refused to be man enough to admit he was cheating. Erin felt it in her heart, which had been torn in two. They'd been together for three and a half years. She'd given the relationship her all, everything she had. Mark had owned her heart, body, and soul.

Had that been wrong? Was she stupid to give it her all? Maybe she should have kept some for herself. Knowing she had to be strong, she left him and moved out of his house. Sadly, there was nothing to bury her pain in. Her job certainly didn't hold her heart, so instead she had buried herself in doubt and self-recrimination. Trying to put the tattered pieces of her life back together, she'd announced to her family that she needed a new start, a place where she wouldn't see Mark's face at every turn. In short, she needed to rebuild and regroup.

Her mother had begged her to stay in town, that she needed her family to get her through it. But Erin realized that even with her parents and four brothers around her, she felt no better. In fact, it was worse. She could count on them; they were right there to lean on. For the first time in her life, she felt she needed to do it alone. She needed to take a baby step out of her comfort zone and spread her wings to fly solo.

It had been difficult, and Erin had cried as she'd packed up her stuff, her life, everything she knew. Her home was her sanctuary, and all her precious things the guard within, the light through the storm, offering a beckoning flame of comfort and warmth, and mostly, protection. She'd forced herself to throw away so much of it, anything that reminded her of Mark, or her life before him: her quiet, lonely existence.

Erin smiled, eyes still closed, a sense of pride washing through her like a warm sip of hot chocolate. She was growing, that was obvious. She longed for things she'd never thought possible before. She needed this time and space to explore this new, expanding self. At home, under the watchful eye of four older brothers and doting parents, Erin had basked in what she had thought was a protective ray of sun. Now, arms extending into the wings that would send her flying, she realized all of it had simply acted as a mold for her to live in. Their mold, loving as it may have been. Stifling as it was.

After her brothers had left earlier in the day, Erin had looked around her new place, almost feeling like she had gotten her first apartment all over again. That wonderful fear mixed with deep pride and accomplishment. She'd felt like crying once they were gone, on her own as they drove the nearly three hours back home.

Truly alone, standing in the middle of her living room piled with boxes, she hadn't been sure what to do, where to start, and how to be alone.

Though still slightly scared – new town, new neighborhood, and not a soul to call for help – Erin felt mostly profoundly grateful for the opportunity and the courage to see it through.

※※※※※

"Oh, crap." Erin waved an apology as she got her

blue Honda Civic back in her lane again, keeping her eyes from wandering to all the stores available. She felt like a kid in a candy store! Pueblo was a large enough town – around one hundred and twenty thousand souls – but it was an old town, with small town values. The businesses there were old and small; any major shopping had to be done in Colorado Springs or Denver. The biggest thing to do was the two Super Wal-Marts. With a single-level mall that was ancient and crumbling, merchants weren't Pueblo's strong point.

As she drove down 120th, she was stunned at the strip malls and clumps of random stores and restaurants. She felt her hick roots coming back to smack her in the butt, staring wide-eyed and open-mouthed.

She kept her eyes peeled for Federal. The lady on the phone said it would be just off to the right.

"Federal!" she crowed, excited to have found it so easily. One of the craziest things about her move was she had gone sans a job. She'd cleaned out her savings account and had gone. Most spontaneous thing she'd ever done.

Looking at herself in the rearview mirror, Erin brushed a wayward strand of hair back into place, noting the dusting of makeup made her eyes really pop. She looked good and for the most part, she felt good.

The offices were nice, decorated in earth tones, subtle. Erin sat in the leather chair, doing her best not to tap her nervousness into the floor, almost having to nail her shoe to the tile.

"Erinbeth Riggs?"

Erin looked up to see a woman of about thirty-five, dressed in a navy skirt suit, standing at the entrance of the waiting area.

"Right here." Erin grabbed her coat, giving the woman a smile, which was quickly returned.

"Hi, Erinbeth, I'm Nancy Pierce," she said, holding out her hand, which Erin immediately took. As they headed down a well-lit hallway, Nancy glanced at her companion. "Erinbeth, I've never heard that before. It's lovely."

"Oh, thank you. I usually go by Erin."

"Then Erin it is. Have a seat." Nancy Pierce took a seat behind a large walnut desk, papers in neat stacks with a screensaver ball bouncing around the seventeen-inch flat screen computer monitor behind her. "So," she blew out, opening a manila folder on her desk blotter. She blindly reached for a pair of glasses, sliding them in place as she scanned the page before her, the white page reflecting clearly in the lenses. She glanced up at the nervous woman sitting across from her. "It says you're new to the area?"

Erin glanced at her watch. "Yep. Seventy-two hours new." She smiled, Nancy chuckling as she glanced back down at the pages before her.

Erin was pleasantly surprised at how comfortable she felt with Nancy Pierce, and it was certainly the most entertaining interview she'd ever had. As she walked out of the offices of Brand, Gillman, & Pierce, she felt confident, a little pep in her step and song in the cold, cold air. That was something else to get used to. The southern part of the state was much warmer, becoming more and more desert-like every year. Further north, in Denver and all her suburbs, the snow fell, winds blew and chilled the bone.

Erin couldn't keep the goofy grin from her face

as she walked back to her car, tempted to skip. If she hadn't been in the lot of her possible-new employer, she would have. As she dug her keys out of her coat pocket, she heard the chirping of her cell. She tried to juggle them both, finally managing to flip the phone open.

"Hello?" She reached up, brushing long strands of sandy colored hair from her face, only for the wind to whip it back, nearly blinding her.

"Erin, Nancy Pierce."

Erin tried to keep the hope from her heart, but it wasn't working. "Yes, hello, ma'am."

"Ma'am?! Oh no, Erin. That won't do if you're going to be working here."

"Really!" Erin couldn't keep the excitement from her voice. Her lack of a job had been the only thing keeping her excitement levels from reaching a boiling point.

"I don't know why I let you walk out of here. I like you, Erin, and I think you'd be perfect for the job. What say you get your butt back in here, out of the wind, and we get started?"

"Yes, ma'am! I mean, Mrs. Pierce."

There was *definitely* a song in the air as Erin drove toward her new home. The first interview she'd gone to, and she'd gotten it!

Reaching for the volume on her radio, she cranked the volume, her happy self singing along with Queen.

"Hell yes, we are the champions!"

༄༄༄༄

"I'm telling you, Mom, you wouldn't believe

it," Erin gushed, "You really should have come up with the boys this weekend. I could have shown you around. There are stores everywhere! Great places to eat. I'm just amazed and overwhelmed. So much to do. And, next weekend I'm going to head to the museum. God, it'll be *so* nice to actually have some culture, and like ten minutes away. There's the theater downtown. 'Phantom of the Opera' was here this year, I guess. Can you imagine?"

"I'm so happy for you, honey. Anything on the job yet?"

"Oh!" Erin stopped, laying her screwdriver on the unfinished hall table. "I got the job at the law offices." She grinned at her mother's squeal of delight. "I start next Monday. Yeah. I think it'll be nice, too. Give me a chance to get all unpacked. Oh, and I'm definitely going to have to do some shopping. It's a pretty classy outfit, so my clothes from Re/Max aren't going to work."

"And, will they be paying you for your new wardrobe?" Janice asked.

"I know. Yeah, right. I don't think any places give you a clothing allowance." Erin chuckled at the idea. "Okay, Mom, I better go. I love you and tell grandma I said hi."

The two finishing their goodbyes, Erin flipped her phone shut then stared at the half-finished table. Her face hurt from the grin that had been permanently planted there since she'd left Nancy Pierce's office for the second time in one day.

"Things are going to be okay," she said, voice soft and wistful. "It's all going to be just fine."

Looking around her apartment, Erin saw what was left to do. The majority of her boxes were unpacked, pictures and swords hung, and clothes put away. She had yet to hook up her electronics. She wasn't a huge television watcher, and as long as she had her laptop, she was fine. Glancing again to her bookshelves of binders, she felt a pang of guilt. It had been weeks since she'd written anything, but the words just weren't coming. The imagination was dry, her worries and the excitement of the move and getting ready for it effectively acting as the Sahara to her creative juices.

Table forgotten for a moment, Erin rose to her feet and walked over to her sacred binders. She felt the cool, smooth plastic beneath her fingertips, smiling as she read some of the titles, written years ago, some from as far back as high school. They were sacred volumes; never had another human being laid eyes on the words within, nor likely would they.

Pulling one randomly, she opened its stiff cover, smoothing her hand over the clean, white page within. It was an older story, written in her late teens. By the title, she couldn't remember clearly what it was about. Too many. Though she did have to smile at her young exuberance. She had created a title page, followed by a dedication page, then Chapter One.

Leafing through the bound pages, she laughed outright when she turned the binder over, seeing tucked inside the plastic covering, a descriptive back page, giving a brief summary of the story within.

"So presumptuous," she said, chuckling, sliding the binder back home. It was always such a bittersweet moment for her, staring at all her creations, bound for no more glory than to act as reminders for what would never be.

With a heavy sigh, she returned to the hall table.

At the very least, she'd finish that.

※ ※ ※ ※

Erin gasped, shooting up in bed. Her eyes were huge, trying desperately to see what had awoken her through the midnight ink of her bedroom. Heart pounding, she glanced at the alarm clock – three thirty-three. Looking back through the space, she held her breath, listening. All she could hear was her own heart pounding in her ears.

Gasping again, she tried to stare a hole through the three walls that blocked her gaze of the front door: a pounding then a scream.

"Oh my god," she whispered, saucered eyes staring at her bedroom door.

Jumping out of bed, Erin felt around desperately for the sweats and t-shirt she'd thrown off before getting into the bed in just a pair of panties. Only finding her t-shirt, she grabbed her cell phone from her dresser then headed toward the front door.

"Help me!" a woman screamed, making Erin jump.

Visions of a woman attacked, just raped, bloody, and bruised, marched across her mind's eye. Without a thought, she quickly unlatched the chain and deadbolt. Bristling cold washed over her, along with the smell of an unwashed body. At her doorstep stood a young woman, her hair wild, stiff, and a fairly putrid color of pink, as though she'd dunked her head in Pepto Bismol.

"I need to use your phone, man," she said, her voice high-pitched, tears streaming down her cheeks.

"Do you need to call the cops? Are you okay?"

Erin asked, stepping back away from her surprise guest.

"No man, no cops. I need to call a cab."

Against her better judgment, Erin took another step back in reluctant invitation. She felt obligated now that she'd opened her door. It was freezing and she didn't have the heart to throw the woman back out. The snow was starting to fall in earnest. Plus, she felt sick with exhaustion, her brain muddied and barely chugging.

After the woman stepped inside, Erin closed the door, the cold leaving in a huff, the heater roaring to life as the apartment's temperature dropped rapidly. She took a step back, looking down as she remembered she had no pants on. *Shit.*

"Um, here." She handed her cell phone to the woman, who under the light of her entryway, Erin realized just how small and petit this stranger really was.

The stranger took the phone, tears continuing to stream down her cheeks as she flipped it open.

Taking that time to disappear for a second – not wanting to leave this strange woman in her home alone for too long – Erin flipped on her light switch, finding her sweats and hopping into them as she headed back to the entryway. The woman was talking quietly. Green eyes looked over at her.

"What's the address to this place?" she asked.

Erin gave it to her, the woman repeating it into the phone. Erin watched her closely, noting a pair of very worn jeans, the right knee thin, threatening to wear through, stealing precious protection. The woman wore black boots, fairly decent condition. Her coat was thin, like a windbreaker. It looked like she wore a yellow t-shirt underneath. At the woman's feet was a light blue bag, stuffed fat with various bits of this and that that had tumbled out when she'd dropped the bag to the ground.

"Fuck!"

Erin's gaze tore up to the flustered woman's face. She was crying again, hard sobs, burying her face in her hands. Erin was at a loss. She had no idea what to do, what to say. The woman made the choice for her.

"Man, people are so fucked up, you know? I gave this guy, I saw him at the store, I gave him my last fucking four bucks to get me home, down to fuckin' East Colfax! Man, he said he would." She began to cry again. "It was all I had, man!"

"I'm so sorry," Erin said, unsure what to say. She was so out of her element. She looked closer at the woman. She looked young, maybe twenty-five. Her eyes were dilated and wild, her hands shaking, though Erin wasn't so sure if all of that was from the cold outside. "How long were you outside?"

"Man, he fucking robbed me!" the woman cried, almost as though she hadn't even heard Erin's question. "I just wanted some smokes," she whined, almost unintelligible from the cage of her fingers. Suddenly her sobs were gone, eyes looking around. "Jesus Christ, lady! You a fucking serial killer or something? Fucking Ted Bundy?"

Confused, Erin looked to where the woman was looking, grinning slightly at the swords. Good. Maybe this woman wouldn't try anything stupid.

"No. I just collect them," she said softly.

"Fucking crack pot. Goddamn!" She stomped her foot into the linoleum of the entry, a hollow thud the resounding answer. Silently Erin apologized to her downstairs neighbors. "He fucking *robbed* me!"

"Who? Who robbed you?"

"The guy!" she yelled, as if that explained it all. "He pushed me out of his fucking car!"

Erin nodded. She had no idea who this guy was, or how the woman had even met up with him, but suddenly Erin was very uncomfortable. She wanted badly to kick the woman out of her house, wondering how the hell she'd gotten herself into this in the first place.

She gave her apartment a surreptitious once over, seeing what the closest weapon was. It was a double-headed axe from the fifteenth century. The air in the apartment had shifted. The woman was getting more agitated, like a caged lion. Erin just prayed she wouldn't attack.

The woman dropped to her knees, digging through her bag, muttering to herself, and crying. She found a half crushed pack of cigarettes, shaking hands tugging out one of the sticks and sliding it between ruby red lips. The woman patted herself down then looked at Erin.

"You got a lighter?" she asked around the smoke.

Erin shook her head, never taking her eyes from the woman who still held her phone. "Uh, no. I don't smoke."

"Fuckin' figures," she muttered. Standing, she looked around, peeking her head around the corner into the kitchen. "Can I use your stove?"

"Listen, I'm really not comfort-"

"Fine. Fucking fine." The woman ripped the cigarette from between her lips, splitting it in half as she did. "Shit!" Throwing the halves on the floor, along with Erin's cell phone, she threw all of her stuff back into the bag, slinging it over her shoulder. Muttering about the high and mighty world of the rich, and without so much as a second glance at Erin, she was gone, slamming the door in her wake. Erin jumped at the crack, then again at the "FUCK!" that was yelled into the night.

Trembling badly, Erin tried to breathe, her heart pounding, sending a resounding thud to her temples.

❦ ❦ ❦

Erin stood, arms wrapped tightly around herself as she watched a pen, dwarfed by a huge hand, race across a small pad.

"Anything else you can remember, ma'am?" Officer Allan asked, looking down at the frightened woman, her sandy head shaking.

"No."

"Okay." He capped his pen, tucking it into a pocket. "We did catch up with her, ma'am, down by the 7-Eleven. Other than a pretty bad potty mouth," he chuckled, "we didn't find anything else. She has no priors, so that's good."

"Oh," Erin breathed out with relief. "That is good. I was really worried that maybe she was casing the place out or something." Blue eyes scanned over her things. "For drug money or something."

"Well, and that may be. So just be careful." The officer turned to the door behind him, tapping his finger just under the peephole. "You've got this for a reason, ma'am." With a polite smile, he headed out.

Locking up tight, Erin ran a hand through her hair, sitting down on the couch with a long, shaky breath.

"God, that was stupid," she whispered to the room. After the woman had left, she had tried to call the cab company to see if they'd picked her up yet. When they had no record of a pickup at that address, Erin freaked, calling the police.

Standing, she walked over to the sliding glass door that led to her balcony. Staring out into the night, she couldn't help but wonder where the woman went after 7-Eleven, or did the officers arrest her? If not, was she wandering around out there in the frigid chill of a Colorado winter?

Erin once again felt her small-town roots sprouting. Her naïveté could have gotten her killed tonight.

"Stupid, Erin. Stupid, stupid."

Chapter Two

"Fuck, it's cold," Tamson muttered, trying in vain to pull her jacket even tighter. Her face was beyond numb, her nose about to fall off. She was tired and felt nauseas. "Fucking Tanner. Answer your fucking phone," she hissed, as though her friend could hear her. Thank god the 7-Eleven guy had a pack of matches. She pulled another lungful of nicotine into her lungs, letting it warm her, holding it in just a second too long – liking the burn – before blowing it out. It was so cold, she had no idea which cloud was her breath and which was the ciggy smoke.

Glancing over her shoulder, she heard the telltale sound of a car. Holding her thumb out, she walked backward, watching the car's progress.

"Fucker!" she yelled as the truck passed on by, leaving her in its cold wake. "Shit!" The last place she wanted to freeze to death was fucking Washington Street. If the cops were going to bust her, the least they could do was give her a ride home. "Shit," she said again, shoving her hands in her pockets as she continued walking, eyes peeled to anything that would be helpful, a shelter, something.

Forging ahead, she felt her body coming down and reality falling on her shoulders like a five thousand pound weight. She felt sluggish and unreal. She pulled in the last drag of her cigarette, the cherry nearly burning her fingertips. Throwing it to the ground, she plodded on, nearly squealing in delight when she noticed a bakery, just starting to come to life.

Cutting across the frozen landscaping that ran along the sidewalk, she stepped into the parking lot, realizing that she could no longer feel her fingers.

"Mornin'," the man behind the counter said as Tamson stumbled through the newly unlocked door. She glanced at him, then hurried to a back booth, frantically rubbing her hands together, blowing hot air over her fingers. "Get you something?" he asked, stepping around to the seating area. Tamson shook her head, frazzled, pink hair flopping into her eyes. Realizing just how frozen she was, he hurried back behind the counter, returning with a steaming mug of coffee.

Tamson looked at the cup with hungry eyes, but knew she had nothing but a lint covered nickel and a condom in her pocket. "I didn't order that," she muttered.

"I know. Look, it's cold out there, so if you want it, drink it. If you don't, leave it." With a kind smile, he left her alone.

She eyed the coffee, almost as though determining whether it would bite her or not. Finally giving in, she wrapped her hands around its warmth, which was almost painful as it began to thaw chilled flesh. She closed her eyes as she leaned her head back against the wall behind her booth, taking a deep breath. Her stomach began to growl at the smells beginning to fill the small bakery. She thought back over her night, and what a disaster it had been. She should have known better.

Mike had called her yesterday, telling her he had a party he wanted her to work, clear up near

Thornton. She hadn't wanted to go, but needed the money desperately. She'd hopped a bus and made her way north. There'd been lots of booze, some poppers, and Tamson had seen a small group working a line, but no one had wanted her services. She'd managed to score a little candy for a blowjob, but that was it.

Wanting to head home and enjoy her candy alone, she'd managed to talk a guy into giving her a lift, for yet another blowjob. No sooner had the asshole shot his load, not even warning her, he'd kicked her out of his car. Literally. Coming down from her high and scared, no clue where she was, she found her way to that apartment complex and the frigid woman inside.

"Fucking bitch," she muttered, sipping the hot brew. "Calling the cops on me."

Glancing up toward the front of the shop, she saw the guy with the coffee emptying out the glass case, tossing the old stuff in the trash. Up like a shot, she leaned over the half door that led behind the counter.

"Hey," she said, nodding at the trashcan. "You gonna throw all that out?"

"Yeah. Health code."

"Well how 'bout I help you out, you know, less trash for you to throw out and carry." Tamson grinned at him, trying not to sound as desperate as she was.

"I'm sorry, miss, but I can't –"

"Come on, man. Who's gonna know?" She flashed pleading green eyes at him. He sighed, glancing over his shoulder at the bakers in the back room. No one was watching.

"Don't tell anybody," he whispered, handing her a handful of hard rolls.

"Thanks." Snagging them from his fingers,

nearly taking his hand with her, she scurried back to her corner, hiding all but two rolls into her bag; the others she brought to her mouth, ravaging them, one after the other, downing the coffee as she began to choke.

Leaning her head back again, she sighed, feeling halfway human. Now she just had to wait for the buses to start running again.

❧❧❧❧

1996 - Fort Worth, Texas

The room was mostly dark, save for the Care Bear nightlight plugged into the wall by the closet. Trying to stay as quiet as possible, the little girl tiptoed over to the door, pressing her ear against it. Crying. Reaching a small hand out, she turned the knob, cringing when it squeaked. Her heart was pounding in her throat as she waited, making sure she hadn't been heard. Still only the crying.

The little girl knew which areas of the floor to avoid, keeping her stealthy while hidden in the dark shadows. As she neared the entrance to the living room, she could see the buttery light of a single lamp, the one by the window. Momma had left it on when she'd gone out. Green eyes flickered to the kitchen, by the breakfast bar that separated it from the living room. There on the floor was Connie Robard, curled up in the fetal position on the scarred linoleum.

"Momma?" The little girl hurried over to the fallen woman, dropping to her knees. Connie looked through her tears at her daughter, the girl's visage watery and surreal. "Come on, Momma."

"Sorry I woke you again, Tamson," Connie slurred, her arm lifted and put around narrow shoulders.

"I'll help you to bed." Tamson grunted as she got to her feet, her mother's weight leaning on her. It was everything the little girl could do to keep her and her mother's balance. She bit her bottom lip in concentration as they made slow progress back down the hall, Connie muttering incoherently between sobs as they went. "We're almost there, Momma."

Tamson pushed her mother's bedroom door open, the smell of absinthe as strong in the air as on her mother's breath.

"Momma!" Tamson cried out as her mother slipped from her grip. The young mother fell to the floor in a heap, half crying, half laughing. The nine year old reached down, tugging uselessly on Connie's arm. "Get up, Momma. I can't pull you up."

"I'm sorry, Tamson," Connie sobbed, self-loathing in her voice. Using the converter for leverage, and her little girl's help, she managed to flop onto the bed. A moment later, her shoes were untied and pulled off, the cool night air falling over her socked feet.

"Come on, Momma," Tamson whispered, crawling up on the bed behind her mother. She grabbed her under the arms, eyes squeezed shut and checkerboard teeth bared as she used all her strength to drag the much larger body back onto the bed. Tamson panting heavily, her mother's head finally rested on the pillow. Tamson scurried around, trying to tuck Connie in.

"Baby?"

"Yes, Momma?"

"I'm sorry." Connie began to cry again, reaching

up to cup a round cheek. Tamson's eyes closed as she nodded, long auburn bangs falling across her face. "Come on. Get in here with me."

Tamson nodded again, crawling under the covers, immediately drawn into a warm embrace.

"Sleep now, Momma. It'll all be better in the morning."

Present Day

"Miss? Lady, wake up."

Tamson's eyes flew open, shooting up in the seat. Her long-empty coffee cup was sent sprawling to the floor. Looking around with frantic eyes, she saw the guy who had given her the coffee and rolls. She blinked.

"You can't sleep here," he said.

Tamson looked around the small bakery, customers glancing at her, obvious disdain on their faces. *Fuck 'em.* Scooting out of the booth, she grabbed her bag and headed outside into the new morning. The sun was already bright, the day cold, but significantly warmer than the night and early morning had been.

The bus stop wasn't more than half a block away. Sitting on the metal mesh bench, she dug through her oversized bag until she found her bus pass. The schedule posted on the plastic wall of the stop told her the bus would be arriving in fifteen minutes. Sighing heavily, Tamson placed a cigarette between her lips, sheltering the tip with her hands as she lit it. Sucking in a lungful, she released it with a sigh. *What a shitty night.*

Shaky from sleep deprivation, Tamson managed to get the door unlocked then used her body weight to push it open. Glancing around the door with the faux oak job, she saw a pile of clothes, grimacing when something scurried out from beneath a pair of disgusting jockey shorts.

Tamson shoved the door the rest of the way open, stepping over the clothes, then walked through the obstacle course of laundry, trail of empty beer cans and cigarette butts. Finding a half-smoked roach, she grinned.

"Lucky day." Bringing it to her lips, she lit the burnt tip, inhaling deeply, instantly feeling herself relax as she walked further into the pigsty, kicking aside Tanner's girly mag, though she noted the woman on the cover had nice tits.

Tossing her bag onto the floor of her closet-sized bedroom, Tamson walked over to the mattress in the corner. Sighing, she threw herself down on it, wincing as her sore and tired body groaned.

"I really fucked up, Penny." She smirked, then giggled as she took another drag on the joint, the burning end already starting to warm her fingertips. "Sure did." Sucking the last pull from the joint, Tamson crushed its remains in the small bowl next to the mattress, a small mountain of butts already dead and buried in ash.

She lay back against the pillows, flat and hard, but better than nothing. Brows drawn, Tamson sniffed then looked down at the sheet.

"Goddamn it, Tanner," she hissed, noting the large, stiff spot on the material. She smelled sex, and knew it wasn't from anything she'd done. "Fucker."

Lying back down, she allowed the effects of the marijuana to filter through her, slowing her brain down, letting her body finally relax. Eyes closing, she smiled, feeling her guardian angel with her, hovering somewhere nearby. "Nighty night, Penny," she murmured then fell asleep.

Chapter Three

"Ma'am?"

"Hmm?" Erin looked up, startled. "Oh. Sorry." Smiling sweetly at the cashier, she handed over her credit card. She watched as the man ran the card, immediately her mind returning to her train of thought to two nights ago: the woman who had shown up at her door during the very cold, very dark, and very lonely night.

"Sign here please," the man said, setting her card on the small, raised signing counter, along with the small, rectangular credit receipt.

Erin quickly scrawled her signature, tucking her card back into her wallet. Gathering the 'designer' paper bags, Erin headed out of the high-end clothing store. She'd never spent so much on clothing at one time in her life.

Returning to her thoughts, ever since that night she had the strange woman on her mind. Yes, it had been weird. Yes, it had even been scary. But it had been nine below zero that night, and Erin had thrown the pink-haired stranger out into the cold. The police had been no help. All they would tell her was that the woman hadn't been arrested, but allowed to mosey on her way. At least if she'd been arrested she would have been warm. Had she made it home, or at least somewhere safe? It was irrational, but Erin felt guilty.

As time had passed, she had tried to analyze that night and figure out how the woman had ended up so far north if she, in fact, came from Colfax, where she said she did. From her condition, the woman was obviously high on something. But Erin had a gut feeling that the woman had been a prostitute. Maybe she had given the guy what he wanted then he kicked her out before paying her. The way the woman's story kept changing, Erin's creative mind had immediately gone to work.

She slammed the trunk on her Civic Coupe, bags of new clothes stowed away inside, ready to make a brand new wardrobe for her job Monday.

Sliding into the driver's seat, she tapped the steering wheel, trying to decide where she wanted to go next. Glancing at the cross street just beyond the parking lot of the small boutique, she noted the street sign – Colfax. Chewing on her bottom lip, Erin put the car in gear and headed out. Taking a left on Colfax, the blue Civic joined the cattle drive home. A glance at the dash clock told her it was nearly five o'clock. Traffic would start picking up even more as rush hour was in full swing.

Not even sure where she was headed – or what she was looking for – Erin drove on, another bubble in an endless stream of humanity.

The further east she went the worse it got. The buildings were dark, a sense of danger oozing from empty windows, like eyes daring Erin to continue. The brick was chipped, spray painted, and mottled. Grass was non-existent, weeds and garbage choking old neighborhoods, turning them sad and begging for breath.

Erin turned off on a random street, eyes scanning

the derelict buildings and houses. A small group of teenagers stood on a street corner, eyes following the Civic. Even in the safety of her car, she felt intimidated by them and her surroundings.

A shiver working its way down her spine, Erin pressed the gas, surprised to hear her tires screeching as she shot out of the neighborhood.

Back on Colfax, Erin hung a right, heading back west. She hadn't gotten past the first traffic light before lights glanced off her rearview mirror, a quick siren whine making her jump.

"Crap," she muttered, pulling off the side of the road, stopping in front of a squat, ugly gray building. Glancing briefly at it, she turned to her glove compartment, digging for her insurance when she heard a tap on the window. Glancing at the officer waiting, she continued to dig as she pressed the button for the driver's side window.

"Evenin'," the officer said, taking a cursory glance around the inside of the car before giving his full attention back to Erin. "Got yourself a tail light out back there."

"Hi," Erin said, voice shaky. She'd never been pulled over before. "Oh. I hadn't realized. Um, here's my insurance. And um, what else do you need?"

The officer chuckled. "Just your license, ma'am."

"Oh. Right. Okay." Erin turned to the passenger seat, where her bag usually sat. "Oh, shit!" Glancing up at the officer, she covered her mouth, muttering an apology behind her hand.

"It's alright, ma'am. Just calm down, now."

"Okay." Erin took a deep breath then turned back to the officer. "Um, I was just shopping and put my bag in the trunk. I need to get it. That's where my wallet is."

"Alright." The officer took a step back, eyes focused on her, watching her every move.

Erin popped the trunk from the lever inside the car then hurried to it, digging through her shopping bags until she found her own bag. Rifling through with shaky hands, she finally found her wallet. "Here it is."

She handed the card to him, nearly dropping it. As the officer looked at the I.D., comparing the name with the insurance, Erin looked around. A small crowd watched her humiliation from the sidewalk, smirking, and walking on. One person caught her eye. Pink. Hair the color of watered down Pepto Bismol. The owner was talking to a tall, extremely thin man, who looked none too happy. He grabbed the woman's arm, bringing her in close as he bent down. Erin couldn't hear anything he said, but could see the intensity of deep-set eyes. With a cruel shove, he walked away, the woman with pink hair stumbling back at the force.

Tamson took a deep breath, trying to keep her anger in check.

"Bastard," she growled, feeling eyes on her.

Looking to her left, she saw a copper parked behind a small, blue car. A woman stood at the trunk, looking right at her. Looking at the woman – light brown hair blowing in the growing evening wind, her body all snuggled up in a nice coat and scarf – Tamson met her eyes. The woman was looking at her as though she knew her. The woman looked vaguely familiar, but not enough for Tamson to give a shit.

Turning away, Tamson stuffed her hands into the deep pockets of her fitted fatigue cargo pants, headed to work. Her mind buzzed with that asshole, Tanner's, final words to her. *I'm serious, Tam. You get the fucking candy or I'll burn every fucking thing you own.*

"Prick."

The Swagger was four blocks from the shit hole-turned fourplex where Tamson lived with Tanner. He was becoming more and more forceful, demanding either candy or money for candy. He didn't care how she got it, but she had to. Or else he would tell.

Tamson found herself becoming more bitter by the day. Her anger was building, and it scared her. She had to keep it in check, or it would happen again. It could *never* happen again.

"You're late, Robard," Henry Ortiz said, not even bothering to look up from the roster he was scribbling on the yellow Post It.

"Fuck off, Hank. Not in the mood." Tamson breezed by the manager's office, heading to the changing room, which smelled of mold and vomit.

"Someone's pissy," Melissa snickered, glancing at Tamson's pink haired reflection in the yellow, cracked mirror she was using to apply another layer of fire engine red lipstick.

"Yup," Tamson said, noncommittal. She had no desire to hear any shit from the blonde whore at the vanity.

"Hank can't get the left side speakers to work again. Try and do a good job to keep their attention, hmm?" Melissa stood, her outfit, what there was of it, falling around her body to her stiletto-heeled shoes.

Tamson watched Melissa go, her eyes narrowed and dangerous. "God, I hate people."

Walking over to the curtain that gave the girls a tiny bit of privacy while they got ready, she glanced into the hall, looking left then right. Alone – Hank having left his office across the hall – she scurried into it. Digging through the mountain of papers on his desk, she cursed softly, not finding it where she usually did. She glanced up, slightly panicked when she heard a floorboard squeaking near the office door. Still alone, she turned back to the desk. Blowing pink hair out of her eyes, she yanked open a desk drawer, a grin quickly spreading over full lips.

"Come to momma," she whispered, holding the shiny black capsule up for bloodshot green eyes to examine. Finding a small handful more, she stuffed them in one of the pockets of her cargo pants then went back for more. The mother lode! Glancing up again, Tamson knew her time was running out soon.

Bringing up her left hand – the pinky nail longer than the other nine – she quickly unscrewed the black cap of the tiny, plastic tube. Dipping her nail into the white power, she brought her face down, closing her eyes as she snorted the drug, wincing at the burn and trying to ignore the metallic taste that spread throughout the back of her mouth and nasal passage.

Sighing with relief, she dipped once more, taking the powder in before recapping the tube and shoving it back into Hank's drawer. Sniffling, she wiped at her nostrils, making sure no tell-tale signs of her deed were evident then headed out of the tiny office, nearly running smack into her boss.

"What the hell are you doing? Go get ready!" he bellowed.

Tamson grinned. "Fuck yeah!" Clapping her hands together, she hurried across the hall and back into the dressing room.

As she stepped inside, she closed her eyes, hearing the music from the main room, the beat pounding through the walls and floor and vibrating through her shoes and up her legs to pound in her stomach before working its way up. Soon Tamson's head was bobbing to the beat, her grin spreading, a long, low moan escaping her throat.

She was ready.

※※※※

The music was loud, pulsing, and *alive*. Tamson closed her eyes, allowing it to fill her. When she opened them again, she saw the crowd around the stage, yelling and vying for her attention. Grinning down at a fella with a black Stetson, she made her way over to him, tossing her hair over a bared shoulder. The club was cold, as usual, making her nipples stand proud.

"Come on over here, sugar!" he yelled, holding a fistful of bills up as a beacon.

She made her way over to him, turning to wiggle her g-string-clad ass in his face. His whoops and hollers were muffled as he grabbed her thighs, burying his face in the firm flesh.

Tamson put up with it long enough to feel the cool silk of bills sliding against her mostly naked, oiled flesh. Once she had the money tucked safely inside the dental floss holding the g-string together, she moved on to the next hard-on Jack, as they called them.

Scanning the crowded club, Tamson looked for anyone familiar, anyone she knew she could get a hit off of or a big score. Lord knew Swagger had its regulars.

As she moved on–more money filling her g-string–one bill was shoved down a little too far, the crisp edge grazing her clit and making her jump. She felt wonderful. She could dance all night, her senses soaring and vibrating with the music. The colors of the searching, pulsing lights were almost blinding in their beauty and radiance, each red, yellow, and green flying in straight from the rainbow, just for Tamson's set.

The music began to come to an end, marking her exit. For one last kick, she reached up, cupping her own naked breasts, feeling their oiled slickness against her own palms. She tweaked her erect nipples for shits and giggles–and to get even better tips on her next set–then she was gone. The chorus of excited men, and a few brave women, followed her back into the dark hallways, like catacombs under the city.

Tamson pressed herself to the wall in the narrow corridor so the next dancer could hurry past her, then headed on back to the dressing room.

Never in her wildest dreams would she have thought she'd be comfortable walking around in just a g-string. At The Swagger, modesty had no place nor any home. It was more common than not to see a half-naked, or completely naked woman, walking around, happy as day. In some ways, Tamson liked the freedom that brought. Certainly liberating. That is, she felt that way when her mind was pickled in some sort of chemical. When sober, she had a slightly different take. But in that moment as Tamson flopped down in a chair in the dressing room, she was a happy girl, looking forward to seeing just how much money her pussy and tits had made for her.

Chapter Four

Chewing on her bottom lip, Erin stared at the screen of her laptop, the cursor winking at her, daring her to stop now. Glancing up, the would-be writer watched a few minutes of the ten o'clock news before her eyes swept back to her Word document.

"What next," she murmured, reading over what she'd written. Again. "Damn it." Slamming her head to the back of the couch, she tried to think, tried to concentrate on the characters she'd created. Her mind was blank as she focused on them, their personalities. She tried to create her own psychological profile for them, pinpointing what they'd do, how they'd act, and where they'd go. "Talk to me," she whispered, eyes closed as she tried to get a mental image. "Shit," she sighed, frustrated.

Giving up, Erin hit save, then shut down her laptop. It was getting late and she was tired, nothing forthcoming but a headache anyway. Clicking the computer shut, she set it on the ottoman where her feet had rested moments before. It was time for bed.

Erin stood, stretching her body, arms over her head. She winced at the unhealthy crunch in her back as she stretched. With a heavy sigh, she stared down mournfully at her laptop, frustrated. She'd had writer's block before, but nothing like this. Her characters weren't speaking to her, weren't willing to tell their story or share their secrets.

With another sigh, Erin walked over to her bookcase, yet again looking at her bound stories. She felt a sense of cowardice and shame flowing through her, as well as a longing that was so painful it nearly brought her to her knees. *It'll make a nice hobby, honey.* Her mother's words rang through her head, over the echoes of time and a child discouraged and feeling alone in her dream. It seemed that she was the only one who believed in it, and even that belief was in frighteningly short supply lately.

Perhaps it *was* just a hobby, and best to stay that way. Hobbies were safe, something to do on a Sunday afternoon then put away Monday morning before going to a 'real' job, something that was stable, secure, a sure thing.

Erin remembered once, while wandering the stacks of the library back home, she had walked along the novels, fingers trailing over the hard, glossy spines. She had gotten to the R's: Ra, Re, Rh, Ri. Ridley, Riley. Right there, right between those two names, Riggs would fit nicely. It had been literally painful for her, seeing a blank space, left specifically for her, emptiness. A black hole like a gapped-tooth smile.

With a sigh, Erin decided she'd tortured and punished herself enough for one night. She needed sleep. That was it. It would be better in the morning.

"Disgusting." Tamson filled the Dixie cup once more, swirling the tepid, sour water around her mouth, catching her reflection in the mirror above the bathroom sink. The putrid light made her look gaunt and ghoulish. Spitting the mouthful at it, she grinned.

She also hoped the cowboy had already left. She hated how attached some of those assholes got. *One time only, dude. Deal.*

Heading back out into the hall, she was relieved to see he'd finally gotten the hint, and was gone. The payphone was free, and that was good. Tanner had busted her cell phone two weeks before, and she didn't have the money to get another one at the moment. Well, she probably did but had other things in mind she wanted to spend the money on. A mouthful for a handful of fresh money burning a hole in her hot little hand, Tamson grabbed the smooth plastic receiver, holding it to her ear.

"Tam?" Hank called from his office.

"Hold on. I'm on the phone," she called back, sliding some coins into the slot, dialing the number she knew all too well. When the deep voice answered, she grinned. "Hey, Mike, it's me. What'cha got for me tonight?" She listened to what he had to say, her grin growing. "Yeah? ... Uh huh... Okay. I'll wait outside the club."

Henry heard his most popular dancer walk toward his office, her heavy steps indicative of her state of mind. Her dilated eyes added to the picture, the green irises nearly gone.

"I need to go. What do you want?" Tamson crossed her arms over her chest, head slightly cocked to the side. The burly man didn't even bother to look up at her, a wad of bills in his hands, counting and placing the money in stacks by denomination.

"First off, you touch the Black Beauties again and I'll kick your fucking ass," he began.

"Aww, come on, Hank. It was just a few jelly beans." She pouted, still feeling their potent buzz racing through her diminutive body.

"Yeah, well stay the fuck out. Secondly." He turned in the cheap office chair, the squeal making both of them wince. "Why the fuck you still got pink hair? I told you two weeks ago to get rid of that shit."

"Fuck you, Hank! It's *my* hair." Oh, he was pushing it, now. She needed to get out of there before Mike got mad and left, which would mean Tanner would be mad, too.

"Yeah, well it's *my* fucking hair while you're working here!" the manager roared, slamming his fist on the scarred desk. "Them guys don't want to see your cotton candy head and fire red twat, you got me?"

"Jesus," she murmured, subconsciously shrinking from his ire. "Fine." Taking several deep breaths, she held her chin high, defiance floating to the surface to cover the fear that zinged through her veins. "We done?"

Hank nodded, waving her off, leaving her to stomp out of the club, shoving through the fire door.

Tamson watched her breath billow in the dim, orange security lights outside the back of the club. She bounced on the balls of her feet, trying to keep warm as she waited. Finally, the familiar blue and silver pick-up roared into the lot. Running to the passenger side, she slid across the cold, vinyl bench seat.

"Hey, baby." Mike leaned across, one hand still on the steering wheel, taking her in a hard kiss. She pulled back from him, already reaching into his coat pocket. Chuckling, he shoved her hand away, reaching in himself to bring out what she sought.

"Oh, yeah," Tamson purred, seeing the baggy filled with sickly yellowish brown crystals. The strong, nasty smell filled the small space between her nose and the candy. It didn't matter. She knew what those little babies could do. She could withstand the taste, too.

Reaching into her own pocket, she felt an old tissue. Tugging it out, she had no idea how long it had been in there, or what it had been used for. No matter as she ripped a small piece off before reaching into the baggy, grabbing enough of the crystals to bomb it. Wrapping them up in the tissue, she put the whole thing in her mouth, squeezing her eyes tightly shut as she swallowed. Beginning to choke, she took the cold can that was thrust into her hand.

Mike watched as his hot little piece of ass took a swig from the beer, her relief radiating in every fiber of her body as she relaxed against the seat, a small smile spreading over her features.

"Come on, baby. Let's see it," he reminded, tossing a few crystals back, himself. Tamson reached into her cleavage, pulling out a wad of bills. She had no idea how much was there. It didn't matter. All that mattered was that she felt the baggy placed in her hand.

࿐࿐࿐࿐

The morning light was harsh, shining in slanted torches. A groan was muffled in Tamson's hands as she rolled over, burying her face in the shag carpet she lay upon. Sniffing, she recoiled, smelling dog piss and vomit. Sitting up, she fell back to the floor, her head raging. She wanted to die, as she felt like a Mac truck had run over her.

Trying again, she used a nearby wall to steady herself as she gained shaky legs. Looking around, vision fuzzy and head filled with cotton, Tamson tried to figure out where she was. The room was bare, no furniture, save for a single wooden crate turned upside down. There was a paper plate on its top, an empty sandwich bag reflecting the morning sun.

Walking over to it, she picked it up, sniffing. The smell instantly brought tears to her eyes, so strong and potent.

"That bastard," she whispered, turning frantically to see what else was in the apartment. The only other room was also bare, save for an old pair of canvas pants and a few used condoms. A white painted door with a deadbolt stood in one wall. The bathroom held similar results. Her bag was nowhere to be found, nor were her pants; Tamson looked down at herself, gasping.

"Where are my pants?" Running back to the bedroom, she grabbed the canvas pants, looking under them, finding nothing but more dirty, mottled shag carpet, though she did find her panties on the window ledge. Throwing the pants, she became panicked as she looked through the closet then the cabinets in the kitchenette attached to the main room. Looking around desperately, Tamson tried to think. What had happened last night? How had she ended up there? And who the hell did she have sex with? Or did she? Though she was sure she had.

Thinking back over the course of the previous hours, Tamson tried to piece together her night.

Last Night

"God, this is good candy," Tamson murmured, a grin spreading across her face. Mike nodded, pulling out to join the late night party traffic. "I gotta get this

home to Tanner."

"Fuck Tanner. I know a great party. Wanna go?" Mike glanced over at his passenger before turning back to the road. He had to be careful. One more ticket and his license was gone. And if he got busted with candy in his system, two years automatic.

Tamson thought for a moment then nodded vigorously. "Yeah. Man, that sounds good. I wanna dance!" She bounced around in the cab of the truck on her butt, filled with energy and the need to move.

Mike got the truck turned around, headed to old Arvada, another suburb of Denver. The house was already rockin' by time they got there, close to three in the morning. The music pounded out of open windows and doors despite the weather, along with voices, laughter, and shouts.

Tamson took the beer that was thrust into her hand as soon as she walked in the door. Looking around at the crush of people, she thought she recognized a few, but didn't know any by name. She had seen them at other parties. Getting into the groove of the music, Tamson raised her arms above her head, moving her body. She felt alive and like she could party all night. She grinned when she saw a beautiful woman dance towards her, her blonde hair long and wild around her shoulders. She danced up behind Tamson and grinded with her, her hands moving up to cup Tamson's breasts, which she gave a playful tweak before moving off into the crowd.

It wasn't long before she had gotten herself another dancing partner. Turning around, she faced him, his hands already on her hips.

"What's your name, baby?" he asked, leaning in close to be heard over the music.

"None of your business. What's yours?" she asked, her face coy. He chuckled.

"Call me John."

"Alright, John. Call me Jane. Got any sweets?"

John grinned, pulling her into him, hands grabbing her ass possessively. He nodded, Tamson grinned.

After John led Tamson to a back room, he brought out a joint from his shirt pocket. Handing the tightly rolled joint to Tamson, he produced a lighter, flicking the tip with his flame. Tamson's eyes closed as she breathed deep, letting the drug flow through her lungs. John was watching her, chuckling.

"What?" she asked, handing him the joint. He shook his head, waving her off.

"Nah. I've had enough. Go ahead, baby."

Shrugging his loss, she sauntered past him, taking another drag. Before she could even exhale, she felt as though her head were filled with water, almost to the point of fish swimming before her eyes.

"Whoa." Stumbling into a wall, she put her hand out, watching in horror as it slid through the plaster. Bringing her hand back, she stared at it, eyes wide with wonder, fingers waving, drifting through the waves, the world an ocean of slow movement and garbled voices.

Looking around, Tamson saw the shimmering images of the other party-goers, then watched in horror and awe as a small group crowded around a table, and lines, a man falling to the floor, his body surfing the waves of the room. Tamson smiled, moving her own body in concert with his movements, throwing her head back, a cackle bursting from her throat ...

... gagging again. Blindly Tamson tried to push him away, but he wouldn't let go of her hair, forcing *her closer ...*

... then further away, then he got closer again. Tamson's head fell to the side, drips of sweat falling on her neck, a cold tickle.

... more moaning and little grunts from him then the scratchiness of an unshaven face scraping across her neck.

... words, muffled, slow, and coming from the surface of the water. Tamson tried to turn to her side from her back, the skin of her butt and shoulder blades burned from the rough carpet beneath her.

She'd managed to roll to her left side then hands were on her, grabbing her, lifting her to her feet. Tamson grunted as she was tossed over something, like a ragdoll. Then all went black.

Tamson felt her eyes beginning to sting, realization dawning on her that she'd been robbed and left. Those were the only things that had happened that she could allow herself to focus on. She had nothing. No money, no keys, and no candy.

"Fuckers!" she yelled to the empty apartment, hearing a dog beginning to bark somewhere in the apartment above her. She held her emotions back, keeping the anger front and center, letting it push her on.

Left with no choice, Tamson put the disgusting canvas pants on. They were huge and hung off her hips. Holding them up with one hand, she made one more cursory look through the dump, then walked out into the new day.

Chapter Five

Erin cruised down Colfax, keeping an eye out for familiar pink hair. Last night she'd sat on her couch, laptop in place, same open, nearly blank document taunting her. Tapping her fingers on the side of the machine, Erin became inspired. She'd hit control A, highlighting the entire document, then with a small moment's hesitation, she hit delete. She had been trying to force a story that just wasn't ready to be told. Why do that when she had a story that was just unfolding, screaming for her attention?

Slowing her Civic, she retraced her steps from the day before, looking at every passerby. She passed the squat, ugly gray building where she'd seen the pink haired woman yesterday evening. Of course she wouldn't be lucky enough to see her there again. After all, they say lightening doesn't strike in the same place twice.

Making a drastic decision, Erin decided to park her car and walk, asking around for the woman. Finding a KFC, she pulled into the parking lot, turned off the engine, and locked up. Zipping her jacket, Erin took a deep breath, trying to square her shoulders and look far more confident and comfortable than she was. On a mission, she took a left once she hit the sidewalk and began her search.

"Thanks, lady." Tamson slammed the door of the 4Runner closed, then hugged herself as the cooling air hit her bare arms. Dressed in the filthy canvas pants and the shirt she'd had on the night before, she made her way into The Swagger. She was almost glad her bag had been stolen; Tanner couldn't kill her for losing the candy, too.

At midday the club was quiet, a few of the girls wandering around, chatting, or working a new routine. A drinker or two sat at the bar, lazily watching the human trade strut around.

"Hey, Tam. Jesus! You look like shit!"

"Thanks, Manny. Appreciate that." Tamson glared at the bartender as she passed him, heading back to the dancers' private bathroom, where at least she could grab a shower.

As she stripped down, she winced, her sex sore, the muscles overtaxed. Looking down at her legs as she kicked off the pants, she gasped. Her head was clearer, though it still felt like she had a marching band practicing in it. She hadn't noticed the knot work of bruises that morning.

"Jesus," she whispered. Tugging her shirt over her head, she looked at her reflection in the unshattered part of the mirror above the sink. Not as bad as her legs, though her breasts were bruised to all hell, and what she initially thought was a bruise was actually a bite mark. "Jesus Christ," she whispered, gently fingering the wound. There was no way in hell she was going to be able to dance that night, or for the next few nights. She knew Hank was going to shit a duck.

After the third person looked at her as though she was crazy, Erin moved on. She walked down the street, tossing casual interest at the businesses she passed, bars, and trashy bookstores, mostly. She'd never seen so many neon beer signs in her entire life.

Sighing, she ran a hand through her hair, which the cold breeze was blowing around her shoulders. She stopped where she stood, glancing back the way she'd come then the way she was headed. Behind her stood a two-story brick building, its maroon trim peeling and crumbling. The sign read The Swagger. Eyes gazing at the solid wood door, painted black, she was about to move on when a woman stepped out, cigarette in hand. The blonde woman gave Erin the once over, then lit her smoke.

Swallowing, Erin decided to give it another try. Putting her best smile on, she walked over to the woman.

"Um, excuse me?"

The woman looked at her like she was a bug. Not saying anything, the woman took another drag from her cigarette. Erin figured she'd better speak fast before she lost the woman's attention. It was hard to tell what color the blonde's eyes were with the heavy eye makeup and fake eyelashes.

Clearing her throat, Erin spoke. "Do you happen to know a woman, young, mid-twenties maybe, with pink hair? I think she lives around here somewhere."

The woman stared at her for a moment, blowing her exhale in Erin's face. Erin tried not to cough it back out, but could feel her lungs burning. Suddenly the woman's face transformed, a smile slithering across the red slash that were her lips.

"You're in luck, honey. She works in there," she said, hitching a thumb toward the black door. "Just ask for Tamson."

"Oh, okay." Erin smiled and nodded her thanks.

The club was dark, filled with the smell of sweat and beer. The only real lights were along the bar. The stage was dark, a few scattered blue lights shining down on its polished, black surface. It was a big circle in the center of the room, connected to the back wall and curtain by a narrow catwalk. A brass pole stabbed through the center.

"Can I help you?"

Erin glanced over her shoulder at the man behind the bar. He leaned against its cleaned surface, white towel flipped over a shoulder.

"Yeah." She walked over to him, glancing around quickly before turning to him. "I need to talk to Tamson." She gave him a weak smile. Her confidence had melted away with every step inside the club. She was so out of her world, and felt it acutely. She wondered, not for the first time, if it had been a good idea to track the woman down after all.

The irony wasn't lost on her that these were the sort of people she used to judge so harshly. Now, standing on their turf, dressed in nice clothes with polite bearing, feeling their eyes watching her every move, she felt like a bug.

"So, what'cha want Tamson for? You a cop?" the bartender asked, shaking Erin from her thoughts.

"No," she said, amused. "I'm not a cop. I need to ask her a question."

He smirked. "What, she not give you the lap dance you paid for?"

Erin looked around, feeling exceedingly uncomfortable as a couple folks standing around snickered at the bartender's joke. "Um," she murmured. "No. Uh, lap dance, no. No lap dance. Just a quick question."

He looked her over, eyes narrowed, then he glanced at a woman who sat at the other end of the bar, nodding at her. The brunette slid off her barstool and disappeared behind a doorway, curtained off with beads.

As she waited, palms beginning to sweat, Erin gave the place another look. She'd never been in a club like it before. Assuming it was a strip joint with the stage and the way the women were dressed, she walked toward the main attraction. Glancing up at it, she tried to imagine what it would be like, everything lit up, loud music pulsing through the place. Some girl up there, shaking her wares for a bunch of horny old men. Was that how it worked? That woman outside said Tamson worked here. Was she a stripper? Waitress? Bartender, too?

"Who the hell are you?"

Whirling around, Erin found herself face to face with the woman with the pink hair, though at the moment it was more of a strange fuchsia, slicked away from her face, and trailing down her back. It looked as though it had just been wet or washed then combed back away from her face.

"Hi." Erin smiled, clasping her hands together to keep them from shaking. "Uh, my name is Erin." Tamson just stared at her. "Um." Looking around the club, seeing that they were being watched, she lowered her voice. "Can we talk somewhere?"

"We are talking. Who the fuck are you?" Tamson

eyed the woman, her pearly white teeth, clean, styled hair, and fancy clothes.

"My name is Erin—"

"Lady, I don't know who you are, so your name doesn't mean shit to me." As Tamson stared at her, recognition flashed through her eyes. Auburn brows drew. "On the street that day. You and the cop were talking."

"Yes!" Erin exclaimed, nodding with excitement. "And you were at my house that morning."

Tamson glanced around, looking a bit sheepish. She saw her co-workers' eyes on her, listening to every word. There was no way in hell she was going to let them hear about that. Turning back to Erin, she grabbed her by the arm and dragged her further away from everyone.

"Look, I don't need my business yapped out to everyone," she growled.

Erin looked at her, taken aback. She had tried to get the pink haired woman to leave, for crying out loud! Deciding to let it go, she lowered her voice. "Listen, Tamson, I've got an idea for a story." She cut herself off at the strange look on the other woman's face. "I'm kind of a writer," she explained, "and I want to do a story about you. About your lifestyle."

Tamson looked at her, brows shooting up. Her entire body language changed, going from irritated to downright offended. "My *lifestyle*?"

"Yes, well, living on the streets—"

"Forget it!" Tamson began to walk away.

Erin realized with horror that she had offended her. "Wait," she stepped forward, laying a hand on Tamson's shoulder before snatching it back as Tamson moved out of her reach. "I'm sorry. I didn't word that very well."

"Ya think? Jesus. And you say you're a writer?" Tamson looked at her, incredulous. "You got some set, lady, coming in here like this. I'm not some fucking circus freak, okay?"

"No. I know you're not. I'm sorry." Erin felt terrible, looking down at her fidgeting hands. About to make another attempt, Tamson cut her off.

"Go home, lady. You don't belong here, and I need to get to work." Her expression changed suddenly, her gaze becoming predatory and a smirk curling the corner of her mouth. She stepped up to Erin, raising a hand and trailing a finger along Erin's jaw line. "That is, unless you're here to make a little deal, hmm?"

Erin gasped, nearly falling over her feet as she stumbled backwards, eyes huge with shock.

Tamson let out a bark of harsh laughter, then without so much as another glance, she hurried from the main room, leaving Erin shaken.

Tucked safely in the tiny bathroom again, Tamson plopped down onto the closed toilet seat, her head falling until her forehead rested on her knees, the wet strands of her hair tickling her bare legs. She'd been able to find a pair of shorts in the dressing room to change into after her shower.

Despite her bravado with Erin moments before, she felt so exposed and vulnerable. Burying her face, she took several deep breaths, trying to calm herself enough to force the tears back. She didn't want them. They'd never done a damn thing for her, so why let them fall?

The drive home was a quiet one, Erin even switching the radio off. She felt terrible, her stomach roiling at the memory. Tamson's face, the shame that had settled in her eyes just before the anger washed it away. How could she have been so stupid? Treating the woman as though she was some object to put under glass and study. In truth, though she didn't want to admit it to herself, that's exactly how she was thinking of Tamson. Something interesting, different, nothing like anyone Erin had ever known.

Erin had always shielded herself from that kind of person. They scared her. She didn't understand them, their lifestyle, their need to self-destruct.

"I'm such a bitch," she muttered to the empty car with a heavy sigh. Back to the drawing board. "Shit." Erin had erased the story she'd been working on. She wondered if there was some way to get it back off the hard drive.

Thinking back to Tamson as she hit the highway, Erin wondered how she'd ended up where she was. Seeing the woman in the light of day – and seemingly sober – she realized that the petit woman was actually very pretty. She had delicate features, and beautiful eyes. Her face had been freshly scrubbed, no running makeup as it had been that night at Erin's apartment, tears and hard living destroying a work of art. At the club, without the makeup, Tamson looked almost like a young girl, barely out of her teens. Dare she say, almost innocent?

Where was Tamson from? What did she do there at The Swagger?

There was a part of Erin that felt a strange protectiveness toward her, which was ridiculous.

She'd never see the woman again. Tamson had made it clear that she was not interested in being a science project, and they certainly weren't friends material.

Running a hand through her hair, Erin wished there was something she could do. Maybe she should start looking into donating to women's shelters, or something. Some small way to help women like Tamson, if she couldn't help the woman directly. It was a thought.

Chapter Six

1999 - Taos, New Mexico

"Momma, I'm going!" Tamson called back into the house, glancing out the small front window of the apartment, seeing the yellow school bus pull up in the parking lot. No answer. Running back down the hall, she pushed open her mother's bedroom door. Green eyes quickly ducked away when she saw two naked bodies asleep, only a leg and foot covered by the sheet.

Sighing heavily, the young girl hurried back to the living room, finding her mother's purse. She dug out a couple dollars then hurried out into the bright morning, which was already becoming nearly uncomfortably warm. It was going to be a hot day.

The driver smiled down at the new rider, nodding a welcome. The small girl with the bright eyes and auburn hair smiled weakly back, climbing up into the long cab. Two rows of curious eyes watched Tamson as she made her way down the aisle, holding her purple and turquoise backpack as close to her body as she could. Finding an empty seat near the middle of the bus, she sat down, then groaned, realizing why the seat was empty.

Scooting to the side, she saw the smeared pool of what looked like spilled milk. She groaned inwardly as she felt the liquid already beginning to soak into the material of her pants. Snickers all around her colored her cheeks even more. Scooting down into the seat, she hugged her backpack even closer, praying the bus ride wouldn't be that long. She seemed to be one of the last stops, the bus lumbering along with breaks squeaking in protest each time they were applied. She wanted to cry, feeling the seat of her pants becoming wetter and wetter. Turning to her backpack, she messed with the straps, making them as loose as possible, hoping her backpack would hang low enough on her back that it might cover the seat of her worn cords until the mess dried.

Tamson walked along the sun scorched courtyard of the new school, students all around her, looking at her and sizing her up, seeing just where she'd fit and just what her weaknesses were. She kept her eyes focused straight ahead, not meeting anyone's gaze. She had no desire to bring anymore undue attention to herself. As it was, she could hear more snickers and a couple of 'whispered' comments about how the new girl had wet her pants.

Running into the apartment after school, Tamson wasn't sure if she was glad her mother was home or wished she'd been gone.

"Hey, sweetpea. How was school?" Connie Robard asked, snuffing out the cigarette she'd just finished smoking, red lipstick still staining the filter.

"I hate it here!" Tamson cried, slamming her bedroom door, her sobs only partially muffled by the paper-thin pressboard door.

With a heavy sigh, Connie headed down the hall, pushing her daughter's door open. Tamson had thrown herself down on the twin bed, face first. She was crying into her pillow.

"Hey." Connie sat down beside her, putting a tentative hand on the girl's back. "What happened?"

With a final sob, Tamson turned over to her side, looking up at her mother. "Can we please go back to San Antonio? Please?" she begged.

"Baby, you know we can't."

"Maybe Grandma won't find us this time!" Tamson said, trying to fill herself with any kind of hope. "I hate it here! They're mean!"

"Oh, Tam. Come on now, honey. Kids are cruel. That's just being a kid." Connie glanced around the tiny room, looking for anything to help bolster her argument. She smiled at her daughter. "You got your own room here, right? That's good, right?"

"Momma, I hate it," Tamson whispered. Even not sleeping on the couch as she had in the last place didn't matter. Pushing herself to sit up, Tamson could feel her anger building. "This is all your fault! Why can't we stay in one place!?"

Connie jumped from the bed as though she'd been slapped. "I'm doin' this for you, Tamson!" she raged. "It's just me. Your dad is dead. What do you want me to do?" Not even giving her daughter a chance to answer, she stormed over to the door. "Ungrateful brat."

Tamson jumped at the crack of the slamming door, a split working its way through the wood.

Tears running down her cheeks, Connie found herself sitting on her own bed, the mattress giving way under her slight weight. Looking up at the ceiling, she closed her eyes, praying for guidance. When none was forthcoming, she walked over to the tiny, curtained-off closet, sweeping the checkered material aside and reaching up, her fingers brushed against the smooth cardboard of the lidded box. Fingering the handhold, she felt the full weight of her life crash down upon her. Taking the box from the shelf, she hugged it to her, sinking to the floor, rocking back and forth as she cried.

"Momma?"

Looking up through her tears, she saw the mirage of her daughter. Setting the box aside, she reached for the girl, pulling her down to the floor with her.

"I'm sorry, baby," Connie whispered, holding her little girl close. Tamson was all she had left. She kissed the top of the girl's head, rocking them both. "I'm sorry you had a bad day."

"It's gonna be okay, Momma," Tamson whispered, tucking her head under her mother's chin.

"Yeah," Connie agreed, nodding vaguely. "Yeah. It's all gonna be okay."

≈≈≈≈

Tamson had been more than careful where she sat on the bus the next day. There was no way she was about to replay it all. Besides, she'd learned with her fellow peers that once they saw you do something stupid once, they did everything they could to get you to do it again. She had gotten particularly good at watching for pranks.

As she walked the halls of the junior high, sixth through eighth grades, she heard more snickering. It took every bit of will power she had not to run her hand over the seat of her pants to make sure they weren't wet or sticky.

"She's wearing the same shirt she had on yesterday," one girl whispered to another as Tamson passed. Tamson tried to shrug deeper into her own head, trying to ignore the comments. One in particular, though, made her blanch. "Piece of white trash."

She had been called every name under the sun, never staying long enough at a school to prove them wrong. It hurt. It hurt bad. Tamson felt impotent to do anything about it, but try to lose herself inside her own head. She felt Penny with her, walking beside her. Her guardian angel's presence was particularly strong during those kinds of days. She felt the ghostly touch of the only childhood friend she'd ever had. Penny had been with her since she'd been a baby.

When Tamson had been really young, Penny had taken on the guise of her favorite stuffed animal – the one-eyed Teddy Bear that never really had a name. Except Penny.

As she walked down the hall to her last class at Martinez Junior High, Tamson felt her head lift a little higher, shoulders straighten just enough. She couldn't let them know she was afraid, intimidated, and deeply scarred. Penny wouldn't allow it.

≈≈≈≈

The strip mall was busy, Friday shoppers getting their goods before heading home for the weekend. Tamson browsed in a woman's clothing store, fingers sampling the tactile banquet. Cotton, polyester, spandex, silk, and many more she couldn't identify. An array of color pallets met her curious gaze as she wandered through the racks of clothing.

Finding a children's clothing store, green eyes zeroed in on a lime green top. The sleeves were short, a pink flower stitched on the front. She had seen girls at school dressed in shirts like that. Glancing at the price tag, she saw that it was twelve dollars and ninety-eight cents more than the lint-covered penny she had in her pocket. She always carried that penny with her. It was the tangible link to an otherwise invisible friend.

Running shaky fingers over the smooth material, Tamson glanced around her, noting the sales girl standing near the back of the store talking to a customer. Scanning the other way, she noted the round, converse mirror mounted in the corner. She noticed her slightly distorted image, though it wasn't hard to hide that, walking around the backside of the rack she stood at.

Glancing back to the sales girl, Tamson surreptitiously removed the shirt from its hanger, carefully rolling it up and tucking it up under the shirt she wore. Her eyes never left the sales girl, her ears perked to anyone near her. The shirt completely out of view, she turned back to the mirror, stepping aside from the rack. Satisfied that the shirt couldn't be seen, Tamson quickly headed out of the store and into the bright, hot afternoon sun.

Heart pounding, she tried to control her breathing, only to have it hitch when she saw a woman walking toward her. She recognized her as a clerk from the store she'd just left. But the woman smiled politely at her then breezed past, back into the store.

Letting out the breath she'd been holding, Tamson quickened her pace, not allowing herself to run, though she wanted to so badly. She gave in to the impulse once she reached the corner of the building. Breaking out into a sprint, she reached the parking lot of the K-Mart on the other side of the highway.

Out of breath and lungs burning, she leaned

against the pole of a parking lot light. Reaching up under her shirt, she brought out the new shirt, holding it up to look at it again. Fashion quickly replaced her sense of guilt, and possibly a sense of acceptance. Pulling off the price tags and size stickers, she dropped them onto the pavement as she headed down the sidewalk toward home.

It had become all too easy. She had returned to the store three more times, each time stealing another part of what would be a complete outfit. Each piece had garnered envious looks from her classmates, which had filled a young Tamson with exhilaration and pride she'd never felt before.

When the clerk had followed her back to the fitting room, Tamson hadn't even noticed. She'd been too focused on the game of getting out of the store without being noticed. It had become a game. A game she was getting good at.

※ ※ ※ ※

Connie grinned coyly at Paul; he'd been nice enough to give her a ride home, and in thanks, she'd offered him a beer. They'd barely had their first sip of Bud when a knock sounded at the door of the small apartment.

Walking over to it, she glanced out the front window, shocked to see a police car parked outside. Brows drawn, she'd pulled open the door, a uniformed officer standing on the stoop, a firm hand placed on Tamson's shoulder.

"What happened?" she asked, pushing the screen door open. Her daughter ran past her, nearly knocking her over in her haste to get into the apartment. The officer had removed his hat.

"Are you Connie Robard?" he asked.

"Yes. What's going on?"

"May I come in, ma'am?"

Tamson lay on her bed, eyes burning with fear and humiliation. She could hear the voice of her mother steadily rise in the living room, the muted rumble of the officer mixed in. She knew she was in deep, and when her mother screamed her name at the top of her lungs, Tamson cringed. Knowing it would be worse to ignore her mother, Tamson dragged herself to her feet, shuffling her way into the living room.

The policemen sat on the couch, glancing up at her as she entered the room. Connie was on her feet, pacing. As soon as she laid eyes on her daughter, Connie was over to her in a blink of an eye.

Grabbing her daughter by the arm, she tugged her over to the officer. Face red and veins bulging, Connie pointed a finger at the man.

"Is this true, Tamson? Did you do this?" she raged, her anger almost beyond containment.

In lieu of an answer, Tamson's head fell. She winced as her mother began to scream at her, some words completely unintelligible. All she could really comprehend were the dreaded – "... grounded for the rest of your fucking life!"

Present Day

Perhaps not the rest of her life, but she had been banned from the television and couldn't so much as breathe for a month without her mother giving her permission first. The store hadn't pressed charges, instead demanding the clothing be returned and

Tamson and Connie's word that the girl would never set foot in any of their stores again.

Tamson wiped her eyes on the sleeve of her shirt from where she stood in the bathroom at the club, sniffling. They had moved on to another town after that, another school and another crowd of judgment.

"I'm not a circus freak," she whispered, staring at her reflection in the mirror above the sink. Finger combing her drying hair, she took a deep breath, readying herself to face her boss.

The club was getting rowdy, more of the girls coming in either to get ready for their shift or to get their weekly advance from Hank.

Taking a short walk around the club, Tamson got her head together. On her third pass, she saw that Hank was alone in his office, the line of desperate girls abating for the time being.

"Hank?" she said, standing in the doorway of the tiny, disgusting room. Her boss glanced up at her then turned back to payroll.

"Why you still got pink hair?" he muttered, licking a sausage-sized fingertip so he could count a stack of bills faster.

"I need to talk to you, Hank," Tamson said, ignoring his comment. Without waiting for an invite, she squeezed past his chair and slid into the only other solid surface in the room. Perched on the edge of the plastic chair, she watched him work. "I got robbed last night," she began, not sure how much to tell him. "And got kinda hurt. I got bruises."

Suspicious of just where this conversation was headed, Hank looked up at her with a sigh. He sat back in his chair, resting folded arms atop his eighth month bulge.

"I need a few days off. I gotta try and get my bag back, my keys, my money, my—"

"Why you doin' this to me, Tam? Hmm? You think I got replacement dancers crawling out of my ass?"

"No. Of course not. Hank, come on, man. I really need this time." She leaned forward in her chair, wincing at the ache in her thighs. "I haven't even been home since yesterday." She looked him in the eye, praying for his understanding.

Looking into pleading green eyes, Hank sighed, glancing at the bruised skin in front of him. "You got one day, kid." He held up a finger to emphasize his point. "*One* day. Got me? After that, I don't give a shit if you have to use makeup or whatever, but you'll get your pretty little ass back on that stage and make me some money."

Tamson nodded, knowing that was all she was going to get from the bastard. Standing, she squeezed past him again, stepping out into the hall.

"Tam?"

She stopped, turning to him. Stunned, she took the money that was clutched in an outstretched fist.

"It's only a loan."

"Thanks," she whispered, holding the money close. Without another glance, she headed toward the door at the end of the hall, back out into the afternoon sunlight.

Counting the money as she stepped into the parking lot, Tamson was shocked to see it was two hundred bucks. Shoving it all into the pocket of the shorts she'd found to wear, she took a deep breath and headed the four blocks towards her apartment. She hoped Tanner was there to let her in so she could explain. What was she going to do? She couldn't go to the cops. What would they do, anyway?

"Fuck, it's cold," Tamson muttered as she hurried home. She knew she looked like a complete idiot walking down the sidewalk in clothing not even remotely appropriate for the harsh weather conditions.

As she neared the ugly, gray building, her steps faltered. She could hear screaming from the crazy neighbors upstairs already. A few passersby glanced over at the building, inadvertently quickening their pace a bit.

The door to Tamson and Tanner's apartment was open, one hinge broken. Tamson peeked inside, just around the door, her breath catching.

The apartment was in shambles, everything overturned and torn to shreds. Dishes were broken on the floor, the TV screen kicked in.

"Oh, Jesus," she whispered, mouth hanging open and eyes wide.

Mindful of everything that lay in her path, Tamson made her way slowly through the main room. She felt nauseous. Tanner's voice screeching at the top of his lungs from his bedroom snagged her attention.

"You motherfucker! Why did you do this? ... No? Then who?!"

As there was no answer, she realized he was on the phone. Tamson felt outright like throwing up when she spotted her bag tossed in the corner, empty and deflated. *Oh god.* That bastard had her I.D. and her keys. Had he done this?

A crash made her jump, her eyes once again trained on her roommate's bedroom door. A few more crashes and he appeared in the frame, his tall, lanky body draped in wrinkled clothing, and he looked exhausted.

"Where you been?" he asked, walking over to her, grabbing her arm. "Where you been? We've been fucking robbed, Tamson! It's all gone. Everything. Every fucking thing is gone!" His unshaven face was beat red, making his blue eyes look like the summer sky in contrast. He ran a hand through stringy hair, looking around at the disaster. "Fuckers got us while I was out getting smokes this morning," he muttered, as though explaining to himself when this could have possibly happened.

"I'm sorry, Tanner," she said, her voice shaky, fear welling in her eyes. The tall man looked at her, brows drawn in confusion. Tamson shook her head, deep remorse making her tremble. "He put something bad in that joint, Tan. Something real bad. I didn't know," she explained, head still shaking slowly from side to side. "I didn't know. He took my bag."

"Who?" Tanner growled, menacing, every muscle in his body tightening into pounce mode. "What did you do this time, you dumb whore bitch?"

"We were just having fun. I swear, that's all." Tamson could already feel herself bracing, readying for what she knew was coming next. It took everything she had not to back up. That would make him even more mad. Instead, she mentally began to shrink away.

"Yeah? Well, while you were having *fun*, you little slut, that fucker broke in here and robbed us blind. You understand? *Blind!*"

"I'm sor—" Tamson stumbled backwards from the first blow, the coppery taste of blood immediately filling her mouth as she'd bitten her tongue from the force.

The second blow was just as quick and packed even more force than the first, knocking her to the ground. She didn't even hear his words anymore, her mind shutting down and all thoughts disappearing to that happy place inside, to the place where Penny was waiting for her. *Help me, Penny. Please help me.*

"Damn you! You can't even do one fucking thing right!" Tanner exploded, backhanding her across the mouth. He grinned as his hand came back bloody. "I told you to get candy, and you can't even do that!" SMACK!

Tamson groaned as the side of her head caught the edge of the entertainment center on her way down. Vision growing fuzzy around the edges, she shook her head, trying to shake the blackness away. She heard Tanner walk toward her, his heavy boot crushing a bowl beneath its heft. She had that moment, that one single moment.

Tugging herself to her feet, head and face pounding and vision still not completely clear, she hurled herself toward the door, stumbling over one of the throw pillows from the couch that had been scattered with everything else. Making her legs work, she got up again, crying out as she felt a handful of her hair grabbed, her head yanked back.

"You're not going anywhere, Tamson," Tanner growled, his upside down image the vision of a killer. Gathering every last ounce of spit she had, she hawked it in the back of her throat, forcing it out with every ounce of energy she had.

Crying out in surprise and disgust, Tanner stumbled back, giving her just enough time and space to get the hell out.

Staggering out onto the sidewalk, Tamson pushed past a group of teenage boys, ignoring their hollers as she ran.

Chapter Seven

Sucking a finger into her mouth, Erin silently cursed the piece of pepperoni. Sucker was hot! Letting the pizza cool for a minute, she headed to the kitchen to run her finger under cold water and grab some paper towels. Making her way back to the living room where her movie was about to start, she stopped, glancing at the door when she heard a soft knock.

The clock on the microwave read half-past eight. Brows drawn, she walked to the door.

"Who is it?" She heard a muffled voice, but couldn't understand. Trying to look through the peephole, she only saw the darkness beyond. "Who did you say it was?"

"Tamson!"

Startled, Erin stood there for a moment, unsure what to do. Shaking herself out of her shock and uncertainty, she unchained the lock and pulled the door open. The pink-headed woman stood on her stoop, shivering in the same shorts she'd had on earlier that day, a t-shirt finishing off her entirely weather-inappropriate outfit.

"Oh my god. You must be freezing." Erin stepped aside allowing the other woman to enter. Tamson couldn't help the sigh of relief as the apartment's warmth engulfed her. The two stood in the entryway for a moment, an awkward silence bouncing between them.

Tamson looked down, ashamed at her appearance, knowing full well she looked like the dead. She was desperate. Glancing up at the concerned woman, she took a deep breath.

"Look, uh, I need a place to stay for the night, just until morning. Um," she shuffled her feet, ready to bolt at any moment. "If you still wanna do your story, I'll talk."

Erin looked at the other woman, seeing the bruises that littered pale legs, which she'd noticed earlier. But now there were fresh wounds: her lip was split open, dried blood gathered in the corner of her mouth and a cut had stopped bleeding over her eye, but still looked angry.

Erin felt her heart break for the woman. Nodding, she stepped further into the apartment, motioning for Tamson to follow.

"Have you eaten?" she asked, moving the toss pillows from her couch to the easy chair, making room for her unexpected guest to sit down.

"I'm fine," Tamson muttered, doing her best to not stare and drool at the Papa John's Pizza box that lay on the coffee table.

"Look, it's here already and there's no way I can eat that whole thing myself. You might as well dig in. Kay?" Not getting a response, Erin decided to try an animal trick. Maybe if she left the room, the skittish woman would hurry and make a mad dash for the food.

Heading to the bathroom, she took her time gathering some peroxide and cotton balls, as well as antiseptic. Tamson was close to her size and there was no way she was going to allow her to freeze to death in shorts in the middle of December, so she gathered a pair of fleece sweats and sweatshirt from her own drawers. Loaded with goodies, Erin headed back into the living room. She couldn't help but smile when she saw that two pieces of pizza had 'mysteriously' disappeared. *Damn, she's quick!*

"Okay. We need to get you cleaned up." She set everything on the coffee table, glancing up at Tamson.

As Erin looked at her, who seemed so small to her, almost as though Tamson's body was closing in on itself, she felt a wave of compassion wash over her. Yes, she was nervous about her being in her apartment and couldn't help but wonder what huge event had made her change her mind.

"Would you like to take a shower?" She saw the uncertainty in Tamson's red-rimmed eyes. "Come on," Erin tried to coax. "Hot water, fresh towels, soap..." She saw a ghost of a smile, and Tamson's nearly imperceptible nod. "First, let's get this taken care of." Sitting on the edge of the table, Erin unscrewed the cap of the brown bottle, soaking a cotton ball. "This may hurt a bit," she whispered, bringing it up to the cut over Tamson's eye.

Tamson winced, but other than that, held still. Erin could feel the uncertainty coming from Tamson in waves. It was though she was vibrating in her own skin.

"Looks like you've had a bad day," Erin said conversationally, re-soaking the cotton ball for a second coat. Once the blood was wiped away, she was able to see that the cut was bad, but not nearly as bad as it seemed with so much blood. She didn't think Tamson would need stitches.

"You could say that," Tamson muttered, focusing

her eyes on the television as her face was cleaned. She was surprised at the gentle touch, and even more so at how comforting it was, though it made her slightly uncomfortable. Why was Erin being so nice to her? What did she want?

"So what do you do at The Swagger?" Erin asked softly, turning back to her triage table, grabbing the Neosporin and a Band-Aid. Gently applying the thick goop, she whispered an apology as her patient winced again.

"I dance," Tamson said absently.

"Oh. That's great." Erin tried to keep her voice upbeat, but visions of Tamson wiggling her assets in front of red-faced men swam before her mind's eye. She'd never met a stripper before.

Tamson rolled her eyes. *Yeah, it's peachy. God, I need a hit.*

Finished with the cut over an eye, Erin moved her attention to Tamson's mouth. That one looked painful and she couldn't help but wince in sympathy as she cleaned it.

"Sorry, Momma. Don't mean to hurt you." Tamson whispered, squinting as she tried to make sure she had all the blood off.

Connie said nothing for a moment, just bowed her head. "Give me one of them butterfly Band-Aids, honey. I'll need it on this one on my cheek."

The little girl nodded, digging one out of the nearly-empty box of bandages. Returning her attention back to her mother's face, she used the head of the Q-Tip to clean out the indention from Byron's ring. It was a deep one.

Tamson shook herself from the memory, shame filling her once again. She pushed away from Erin.

"I'm fine. I can do it from here."

Erin watched as Tamson hurried into the bathroom, closing the door soundly behind her. Confused, and slightly hurt, she gathered up all the First-Aid supplies, sighing as she tucked them all back into their packaging.

❧ ❧ ❦ ❦

Erin nibbled on her second slice of pizza, her appetite pretty much vanishing with her company's arrival, but she knew she'd regret it if she didn't eat. Absently she watched the action on the screen, not really caring what was on. It was just distraction anyway. She couldn't help it as she glanced toward the bathroom door again. Still no Tamson. Once in awhile she'd hear movement in there, the water turn on, toilet flush then silence again.

Sighing, she closed up the pizza box, tucking it into her fridge. About to grab a bottle of water, she heard the bathroom door open and smelled a burst of soap-scented steam filling the apartment.

"Feel better?" she asked, holding out a second bottle of water to her guest. Tamson took it with a soft thank you.

"Yes. Um, I appreciate it."

"Sure." Trying to keep things low key, Erin headed back into the living room, plopping down on the couch as she took a long draw from the bottle. Tamson did the same, sitting on the other end of the couch. "Feel free to move those pillows if you want. Make yourself comfortable," Erin offered.

"Oh, uh. Thanks. I'm fine." Tamson said, feeling unimaginably better. Erin had knocked on the door before she'd gotten into the shower, an armload of fresh, warm clothes waiting when Tamson had opened the bathroom door. Her gaze was drawn to soft material thud next to her. She found the remote where it had landed by her leg. Meeting twinkling blue eyes, she took it. She didn't even own a TV.

The night passed in silence, other than a random chuckle from one or the other at something on the screen. Erin was itching to talk to Tamson, had a head full of questions, but at the few side glances she'd given the other woman, Tamson seemed to be relaxed and enjoying the comfortable silence. So, she'd kept her mouth shut. She nearly jumped out of her skin when Tamson spoke not half an hour later.

"Why did you call the cops?" Tamson kept her eyes on the TV, watching as Jay Leno made one stupid joke after another.

"Because you scared the hell out of me," Erin answered honestly. She glanced at her guest. "I'm new here. Not used to someone pounding on my door at three in the morning." She smiled sheepishly, meeting amused green eyes. "Besides, I was worried that maybe you were casing the place out."

Tamson snorted. "Lady, you watch *way* too much TV. Did you think I was going to come back with my glasscutters? Climb onto your balcony and cut a human-shaped hole into your sliding glass doors?" She nodded at the doors in question.

Erin chuckled. "I guess. I was worried about you that night. It was so cold."

Tamson nodded in agreement, but said nothing. Finally, "So what do you want to know?"

"Listen, you've had a really bad day. It can wait," Erin said softly.

Tamson grinned. "Lady, I'm going to be gone in a few hours. You might as well get your questions out now then write your bestseller."

"Alright." Erin stood, walking over to the desk to grab a pad and pen. Sitting back down, she turned, her back against the arm of the couch, pulling her legs up to tuck under her. She waited, watching as Tamson snagged the remote and turned the TV off. "Okay. Well, I'm going to make an assumption that you were on drugs that night. Am I right?" Erin glanced up at Tamson, seeing intense green eyes boring into her. "I'm not a cop, Tamson. Who am I going to tell?"

Tamson looked away, suddenly looking very uncomfortable and uncertain. "Maybe this wasn't such a good idea," she muttered before turning back to Erin. "Look, lady—"

"Erin. Please call me Erin."

"Fine. Look, Erin, I grew up with great parents, happy as can be. Met a guy in high school, real asshole, got me into pot. Smoked it for a while then did more. The end." Pushing up from the couch, Tamson walked over to the sliding glass doors, unlatched it and stepped out into the cold, night air. The view from the balcony was beautiful, even at night. Lights, bright and twinkling. Lights from cars and buildings, like little diamonds in the velvet of night. She took in a few deep lungfulls of cold air, eyes closing.

"Tamson?" Erin said softly, stepping up behind Tamson, who didn't turn around. Standing in the doorway, crossing her arms over her chest against the cold air, Erin said her name again. "Are you okay? Is there anything I can do?"

Tamson shook her head, turning to look Erin. "I'm fine. You don't smoke, right?"

"No. Sorry."

Tamson sighed, turning back to the night. "Maybe this is a bad idea. I should go."

"No, Tamson, please don't. At the very least get some good sleep."

"I've intruded enough." Tamson turned back to Erin, who was backlit by the soft lamps inside. "I'll be out of your hair in a few minutes."

"You're not in my hair, Tamson. I really want to help."

"Yeah? Well then go back twenty-five years ago and help. Okay? Right now there's nothing you can do. Save your pity for someone else." Pushing through the door, Tamson almost knocked Erin over in her haste to get back inside. She tugged the sweatshirt off, throwing it to the couch, her petit body immediately beginning to shiver as she now just wore a t-shirt beneath the warmth of the sweatshirt.

"Wait," Erin said, shoving the glass door closed, trying to catch up to what was happening. "Hold on. What did I do?"

"Listen, Erin. You seem like a real nice person and all, but I'm not a charity case for you to put your cape on for, 'kay?" Tamson's eyes were sad as they took in the other woman, Erin's arms crossed over her chest, shoulders slumped.

Erin nodded, looking down at her feet. "Do what you want, Tamson. Obviously I'm not going to stop you. I don't see you as anything other than a woman who needs a little help right now. If you'd like to stay tonight, you're welcome to. I'll leave you alone." She shrugged, a sheepish grin on her face. "Guess I've always just been a bit of the nurturer."

Tamson smiled weakly, running a hand through her hair. She took several deep breaths, as though trying to calm herself. "Okay," she murmured, gaze on the floor. "Thanks." She tossed Erin an apologetic glance then returned to her spot on the couch.

❦❦❦❦

Erin lay awake for more than an hour, listening. Was that a drawer opening? Maybe a closet? Rolling her eyes, she turned to her side. She knew she was being ridiculous. Tamson was lying on the couch, exactly where she'd left her, curled up in the blankets she'd given her. Her smile was soft as she drifted off to sleep. She didn't even notice the light flickering on under her closed bedroom door.

Tamson looked around the living room. She couldn't get to sleep no matter how many sheep bah'd in her ear. Her eyes were immediately drawn to the bookcase. What was up with all the binders?

Tucking long strands of hair behind her ear, she grabbed one randomly, reading the neatly typed description: *My Year in Italy*. Expecting to see a bunch of pictures, she was stunned when she realized she'd stumbled onto a story.

Shifting her weight to her other leg, she turned the page, scanning the words, flipping through the binder until she reached the last page. Quickly reading over the short synopsis, Tamson carried the binder over to the couch with her, plopping down in her nest of blankets. Settling onto her side, she cleared her throat. Page one.

Chapter Eight

Erin stretched languidly in her queen-sized bed, a limb stretched to every corner. The sun was shining in, warming her. She almost felt like a cat purring in a puddle of sunlight.

The night before came rushing back to her, interrupting her bliss. Erin sat up in the bed and listened, wondering if Tamson was still there. She heard nothing. Crawling out of bed, she tugged on a pair of mesh shorts to go with the t-shirt she'd slept in and padded out to the living room. To her surprise, Tamson was still very much there. She was curled up on the couch, face calm and peaceful, what could be seen of it. Her entire body was burritoed in the blankets; only from her lips up was visible.

Erin would have found it adorable if not for the stacks of binders on the floor next to the couch. One binder was still open, flipped to about three-fourths the way through the story.

Anger, bright like fire, raged through Erin. She felt violated and like her privacy had been trampled on. Taking a deep breath, she called the sleeping woman's name. No answer.

"Tamson!"

Green eyes flew open, Tamson nearly falling off the couch, startled and disoriented. She looked up through disheveled hair and huge, confused eyes.

"What the hell were you doing with my work?"

Erin demanded, grabbing the binders and holding them to her chest like a shield. "These." Erin swallowed, feeling the sting of threatening emotion behind her eyes. "These are private to me. How dare you invade that?"

Stunned, Tamson just stared up at her for a moment, unsure if she'd heard right. When she saw the flush in Erin's cheeks, and welling tears in her eyes, she realized the extent of her folly, though had no clue why it was such a crime.

"I'm sorry, Erin—"

"Please just go," Erin whispered, walking over to the bookcase, reverently replacing the volumes. She couldn't bring herself to look at the other woman, so worried she'd see disapproval in her eyes. Disapproval for her work and for her time and attempt at storytelling.

Tamson got to her feet, shrugging out of the sweats and sweatshirt, pulling on the shorts she'd come in and stepping into her shoes. Looking around, she realized she hadn't brought anything else with her. She took one more look at Erin, whose back was still to her.

"Maybe you shouldn't put those in a bookcase if you don't want them read," she said, her voice soft, then she left.

Erin jumped at the crack of the front door.

Storming down the stairs of the building, Tamson angrily swiped at a tear, desperately trying to hold the others back. It was amazing to her, a first: in trouble for something she had no idea she'd done. She hurried across the parking lot, stepping out onto Washington Street, yet again.

"Cursed street," she muttered, looking around to

see who was out and about, even as she stood freezing. It was early. Too early for commuter traffic. So, hands tucked into the pockets of her shorts, she headed out again. She could waste some of the money Hank had given her on cab fare or a bus ticket. Nah. She was too angry and needed to walk it off. Besides, it might help warm her up.

Tucking the last of the binders into place, Erin looked at the bookcase. Glancing around the living room, she saw Tamson's blankets still spread out over the couch, the pillow still with the indention of her pink head. She sighed.

Hurrying to her bedroom, she tugged on a pair of jeans and boots, slammed a hat on her head, and ran out the door. She had no idea which way Tamson would have turned.

Tapping her steering wheel as she chewed on her bottom lip, she nudged her turn signal, the right blinker slowly glowing into an orange pulse. Blue eyes scanned both sides of Washington, looking at parking lots and trying to figure out what businesses were open at the early hour. *Where could she have gone?*

About to turn around and head the other way, Erin yanked the wheel to the right, pulling off into the parking lot of what used to be a Dairy Queen, but was now just a sad, empty building. Jumping out of the car, Erin called to the woman who was making quick time down the sidewalk. Tamson glanced over at her, surprised but then kept walking.

"Tamson!" Erin yelled again, jogging after her. "Please? Can we talk?" she begged.

Without a word, Tamson glared at her, head held high and chin raised in defiance.

"Come on." Erin led the way back to her car

where she climbed up onto the trunk, booted feet resting on the bumper. Tamson mirrored her position. "I'm really sorry, Tamson," she began, voice soft on the cold, morning air. She glanced over at the other woman who stared down at her clasped hands. "I've been writing since I was a kid, and it's always been my personal thoughts, dreams, fantasies, venting, whatever. In some ways it's like a diary, you know? I've never let anyone read them before."

"Why?" Tamson looked at Erin, eyes squinting in the intense rays of early morning. Erin shrugged. "You should, you know. Your stuff is really good."

"Really? You're not just saying that so I won't be pissed anymore?" Erin grinned, though it was very fragile. She still felt so very exposed.

Tamson chuckled. "No. I'm not just saying that. I was up most the night reading. I only stopped 'cause I fell asleep."

Erin looked at her own hands, absorbing this information and trying to process it and believe it. "Thank you," she finally said, unable to keep the smile from her lips. For some reason, she believed Tamson. "I really appreciate that."

"Why don't you let people read your stuff? Why hide it? In plain sight, I might add."

"Yeah, yeah." Erin shrugged good-naturedly, sighing. "I don't know. As a kid I was never encouraged to write, you know? My brothers used to act like it was a real pain in the ass if I talked about it, so one day," she shrugged again, "I just stopped."

"Yeah, well if you ever need a critic, I'm your girl."

Erin studied Tamson for long moment, seeing nothing but honest sincerity. Finally, she hopped down from the trunk. "Come on. I'll make you breakfast."

"As tempting as that might be, I need to go." Tamson sighed, meeting Erin's gaze.

"You sure?" At Tamson's nod, Erin slapped her thighs. "Okay. Can I give you a ride? At the very least, let me give you some clothes." Erin looked at the goosebumps that littered Tamson's legs and arms.

"Okay." Tamson nodded. "Yeah, I can let you do that."

"Not bad. They just about fit you. You're skinnier than I am, though." Erin walked around Tamson. The jeans were baggy, but it might have been because the woman weighed ninety pounds. "Need to fatten you up."

"Can't. My boss would kill me." Tamson tugged on the sweatshirt. Sweeping her hair free of the collar, she grinned at Erin. "He's already pissed about my hair. Ready?"

"Yeah. Let's go."

❧❧❧❧❧

Erin glanced up at the club, then over to her passenger. "Are you sure you'll be okay?"

Tamson nodded. "I'll be fine. I'll get these back to you," she said, tugging at a pant leg.

Erin waved her off. "Don't worry about it." Smiling softly, she placed a tentative hand on Tamson's shoulder. "Please be careful, okay? Take care of yourself."

"Yeah. You, too." Tamson opened the car door. "Keep writing. If you sell my story, I want half."

Erin laughed and nodded. "Hey, Tamson?" She waited until Tamson turned back to her. Erin reached across the car, to the still-open passenger door. "If you need anything..."

Tamson took the small slip of paper offered to her. She glanced at the number before tucking it into the pocket of her jeans. With a smile, she closed the door.

Erin watched as Tamson stepped out into the morning, one last wave before she disappeared into the club. With a sigh, she got the car moving and headed back home.

"Jesus, Tam. What the hell happened to your face?" Hank asked, standing from his chair, eyes pinned to the swelling bruises that had turned purple over night.

"You should see the other guy." Tamson quipped, sitting in the same chair she'd been in the night before. "I need some time off, Hank. I need to get some things straightened out and find a new place to live." She sighed, running a hand through her hair. When the big man opened his mouth, Tamson was easily able to read his growing irritation in his expression. She cut him off. "Please, man. Please. Don't fuck with me on this. I need the time."

"I was just gonna say good luck."

"Oh." Tamson grinned, sheepish. "I'll keep in touch."

The building was quiet; even the birds seemed to have taken a vacation. Tamson eyed her surroundings suspiciously. She wondered if Tanner was home. Chewing on her bottom lip, she was nervous and afraid but she had to chance it.

The apartment was a disaster. Luckily, landlord Marty hadn't asked any questions when she'd asked him to let her in. He rarely did. Furniture was shredded and toppled on its side. Clothes were thrown everywhere, cabinets hanging open in the kitchen and bathroom. It looked like Tanner had thrown a major shit fit when she'd left.

Hurrying to her bedroom, which was in even worse condition than the rest of the place, she quickly found a bag. Digging through the clothes on the floor, she found a few articles that were in one piece. She shoved them into the bag, along with her brush and toothbrush. Looking around desperately, she cursed the stubborn carpet as she tried to lift it in the corner. She could feel herself beginning to sweat from the effort, as well as from withdrawal. Finally, it gave, and she was able to get to the rotten floorboard beneath.

"Thank god," she breathed.

They hadn't found her secret stash. There wasn't much there, only a couple rocks, but it was something. Face scrunching up at the taste, Tamson swallowed, hurrying to the kitchen to drink from the faucet. Heading back to her room, she began to look around for anything else of value that was easily mobile. Spotting her CD collection, she hurried over to it.

As she knelt down, her heart began to race, a burst of energy washing over her as her candy begin to trickle into her bloodstream. She couldn't keep the smile from her lips, her mind racing as she began to finger through the small pile of jewel cases. Most had been cracked or shattered altogether, but the CDs themselves seemed to be okay.

A sense of urgency filled Tamson with panic, overshadowing the growing effects of the drugs. She shoved in the rest of the CDs, regardless of their condition. Standing, she tugged the bag to her shoulder, climbing over the mess. She wasn't more than five feet from the front door when she heard a key in the lock.

"Oh no," she whispered, not sure what to do. She knew she was trapped. It wouldn't have mattered anyway. The door flew open, Tanner's step faltering in shock when he registered who stood in the middle of his living room.

"What are you doing, Tamson?" he asked, voice deadly calm.

"I just wanna leave, Tanner," she said, trying to stay calm, even though fear was trickling up her spine.

"Yeah?" He grinned, closing the door behind him, the lock sliding into place.

≈≈≈≈

Erin closed the linen closet door, the last of the blankets folded and put away and the sheets stuffed into the hamper. The living room was basically back to normal, throw pillows in place and the floor vacuumed. It seemed amazingly empty, now.

Glancing to the bookcase, Erin couldn't help but smile. She walked over to it, pulling out *Buyer Beware*. It had been the binder that lay open on the floor. What had Tamson thought of it? Her smile broadened when she remembered that Tamson thought was a good writer.

The smile grew wider. Erin felt giddy and foolish. What was one opinion? Putting the binder away, she walked back to her bedroom to gather her laundry. As she began to sort darks from whites, reds from towels, her mind wandered. Ideas flashed before her mind's eye at dizzying speeds, almost like a neurological creative assault.

Tossing the dirty clothes to the floor, Erin hurried to her laptop, opening and booting it up. Impatient, she tapped a steady rhythm on her knee. When her desktop finally came up, she immediately opened a Word doc, fingers flying over the keyboard.

'UNTITLED' by Erinbeth Riggs.

Soon, the story of a young girl, lost, vulnerable, and deeply scarred, began to emerge. Each situation the writer put her in, Erin saw green eyes, aged far beyond twenty-five years. She felt the almost obsessive need to make things right for her character, fix everything, and teach this character how to survive.

Fingers beginning to cramp, Erin was stunned to see the shadows spreading across the room, slanted dusk creeping in between the vertical blinds of the sliding glass door. Scrolling up through her work, she was even more stunned to see that she'd written one hundred and sixty-four pages. Lord only knew the editing they'd need, but that didn't matter. They were there!

It was as though she was possessed, her character desperate to tell her story, find absolution. Erin was determined to give it to her. But, no more tonight. Her head was beginning to hurt and her stomach was rumbling. Besides, she was feeling guilty for putting the poor girl through one hellish situation after another.

Saving her work, she set the laptop aside, stretching an aching back. She chuckled to herself as she passed her bedroom and the mess she'd left on the floor, on the way to the bathroom. Never had her inspiration outweighed housework. A truly interesting experience. She felt like a slacker, but a happy one.

Dropping her pants and about to sit on the cold

toilet seat, she groaned at the sound of her phone ringing to life.

"Damnit," she muttered, galloping with pants around her ankles, snatching the phone from the kitchen counter.

She looked at the screen on her cell phone to see who was calling. A Denver number, but not one she recognized. She almost didn't answer it, but decided that maybe she'd better.

"Hello?" There was nothing, empty silence. "Hello?" Erin couldn't keep the irritation out of her voice, her bladder speaking for her. About to hang up, she faltered, bringing the phone back to her ear. There it was again, almost a whisper.

"Erin?"

"Yeah. Who is this?"

"Erin, I need your help." A quiet cough, followed by a gasp. "Please. Can you pick me up?"

"Tamson?" Immediate worry filled Erin, who flicked on her kitchen light as she looked for something to write with and then to write on.

"Please?"

"Yeah, sure. Of course. Where are you?"

More coughing. "I'm at a payphone on Sierra. It's a few blocks away from the club. Please hurry. I don't know how much longer I can hide."

"Okay. Is it a gas station? Convenience store, what?"

"Shell gas station."

"On my way."

Erin ran to the bathroom, nearly making a nasty mess before she reached the toilet. She did her business as quickly as she could then pulled her pants up, heart pounding as she found her keys. She was out the door, nearly forgetting to lock it.

"Sierra," she murmured, looking at each street she passed. She wasn't sure which direction it was from the Swagger. "Shit." Passing it, she pulled into the parking lot of a bar. Waiting for a bright yellow Hummer to pass, she pulled back out onto Colfax, turning right on Sierra. Trolling down the mostly residential street, she saw the lights of the gas station, a veritable eyesore amongst the old, squat houses.

Erin searched the parking lot and building for the phone Tamson was using. Seeing a bank of payphones, she parked next to them. There was no Tamson. Cutting her engine, she fought the urge to call Tamson's name – or the cops – instead walking around to the darkness behind the building, a small, compact car parked back there. She figured it must belong to an employee. As movement caught her eye, Erin turned to her left where she saw a huddled shadow against the side of the building.

"Tamson?" she whispered. Walking to the figure, she squatted down, Tamson's face barely recognizable in the darkness. "Hey. Are you okay?"

"Please get me out of here," Tamson whispered, struggling to her feet.

Erin gasped when she saw the gnarled mess that was Tamson's face emerge from the shadows. "Oh my god," she whispered, tears immediately springing to her eyes. She tried to hold them back. "Who did this to you?"

"Nobody. Please, just get me out of here," Tamson pleaded.

Nodding, Erin took her arm and helped her to her car. Making sure she got settled in okay, Erin trotted around to the driver's side. A quick glance around the parking lot and she climbed in, the car roaring to life.

Chapter Nine

Erin glanced at her passenger before her eyes turned back to the road. She remembered a hospital off of Federal, she just had to remember what the cross street was.

"Yes!" To her delight, the cross street was Colfax. She ran right into Saint Anthony's Central. They passed the bright lights of Emergency, pulling into a space.

Tamson opened her one good eye and looked around. Sitting up slightly, she saw an ambulance whiz by. Shaking her head, she looked at Erin.

"No. No hospitals."

"Tamson, you're hurt. You need a doc—"

"No! No doctors! No hospitals!" A small sob tore from her throat. "Please."

Erin stared at her for a long moment, stunned. Finally, she sighed and nodded. She'd respect Tamson's wishes, against her better judgment. Pulling back out into the night, she tried to decide what to do. Another look at Tamson told her that she was hurt badly and needed medical attention. Pulling her cell phone from the console, she hit Speed Dial 3.

"Answer, Alex. Please, please, answer," she whispered, glancing behind her as she switched lanes.

"Hello?"

"Oh, thank god. Alex, it's Erin."

"Hey, Erin. How are you?"

"Alex, I need a huge favor from you," she told her sister-in-law, the nurse who studied in Denver and knew lots of people in the medical community there still, even though she now lived two hours away in Pueblo.

Buzzing. Like a million bees. Light. Muted light reflecting off shiny walls. Dark walls. Wood walls. A narrow hallway. More buzzing. Screaming? Walk along the narrow hallway, prickly floor. Someone near, comforting. A light. Big light cutting across the darkness of the hallway, across the floor. Near the light. Loud noise, more screaming. Big noise! Scared! Must get away!

Tamson's eye flew open, a loud sob scraping her throat. Her heart pounding and her body panicked, she tried to sit up.

"Hey, hey," Erin said gently, a hand on Tamson's shoulder. "It's okay. We're here."

"Where are we?" Tamson asked weakly, looking around.

The clinic was dark, only a security light shining like a beacon. A silver Jaguar was waiting in the parking lot, the driver's side door opening as Erin pulled in next to it.

Without a word, a man with a full head of white hair opened the passenger side door, immediately, but gently, pulling Tamson from the passenger seat, murmuring words of encouragement as she groaned in pain. He hurried across the parking lot, the diminutive woman cradled to a barrel chest. A woman with long, graying hair, who had been behind the wheel in the luxury car, unlocked the tinted glass door of the clinic, holding it open as the large man passed, followed by a trembling Erin.

The man, whom Erin assumed was Dr. Monty Gonzales, barked out orders, the woman rushing around to follow them. Erin was asked to wait outside the examination room.

Pacing around the darkened waiting room, Erin ran a hand through her hair, looking out the large, plate glass windows into the night. It was late on a Thursday night and the streets were fairly quiet and calm. Tucking her hands in the back pockets of her jeans, she blew out an anxious breath.

What was she going to do with Tamson? She assumed whatever had happened to Tamson, and whoever had beaten the hell out of her was someone in her personal life. Was it a boyfriend? Husband? If so, it was obvious that she couldn't go back home, wherever home was. Her mind began to turn, trying desperately to think of a place she could take Tamson where she could heal and be safe. Maybe her parents' house back home? Get her into fresh surroundings, away from what was obviously a life of indulgence and self-destruction.

"Erin?"

Erin's head whipped up, ripped from her thoughts as the woman was walking over to her.

"Hi. I'm Shay, Dr. Gonzales' wife and nurse."

"Is she okay?"

Shay nodded. "She will be. Nothing life-threatening. Lots of contusions and lacerations, two badly bruised ribs and a cracked ulna, here in the forearm." Shay touched the bone in question. "She needs to be kept safe," the nurse said, dark eyes boring into Erin's.

Erin nodded. "Okay. I can do that."

"She really should go to the police. They can help her. Get her out of what is obviously a bad situation. The doctor found lots of old wounds, including a broken wrist that was never taken care of. It will always give her problems."

Erin blew out a breath. She felt a tremendous weight lowering onto her shoulders, but nodded. "I'll do what I can."

"Okay. Come on. You can see her now."

Erin followed as she was led through the darkened building, the light of the examining room sharp and bright. Tamson lay on the examination bed, a paper gown covering her nakedness. Her arm had been freshly cast from just below her elbow to wrap around her palm, fingers free, the doctor talking to her about a splint. When Erin walked through the door, Tamson glanced at her, relief flooding her face.

"Thanks, doctor," Tamson said, looking down at her arm, automatically her other hand coming up to hold it, protect it.

"How are you feeling?" Erin asked, once they were alone.

Tamson shrugged a shoulder. "I'm okay." She sighed, looking extremely worn.

"The nurse said you need to chill out a little bit. Get some rest."

Tamson nodded, looking around the sterile room. "Yeah. I'm sure Hank will let me crash on a cot in the back room."

"Who's Hank?"

"My boss."

"Tamson," Erin said, sitting on the edge of the very small bed. "Who did this to you? *Keeps* doing this to you."

Tamson shook her head. "Doesn't matter." She scooted to the edge of the bed, bare feet hitting the floor. "Will you give me a lift to the Swagger?"

Erin shook her head. "No. But I will take you home with me." She withstood the hard look from the other woman, refusing to back down. "I'm not going to let this happen to you again, Tamson."

"Erin, you're not my mother. It's not your place to step in and fix things. I told you that before." Anger swelling within Tamson's eyes, she began to gather her clothing, tearing the paper gown off and crying out as she forgot about her arm. "No!" she shoved helping hands away.

Erin took a step back, deciding to give Tamson her space. She tried not to notice the naked body before her. Though far too thin, Tamson's body was the model of feminine perfection. She tore her gaze away and focused on the situation at hand, even if she did gather Tamson's clothing setting them on the bed. "No, Tamson, you're right. I'm not your mother and I can't fix your life. But I *am* your friend, and I can at least offer you a safe place to heal."

Tamson looked at the women who stood her ground, arms defiantly crossed over her chest. Tamson was quiet for a long moment, reaching for her jeans and tugging them on, wincing at the pain that radiated through her body at the move. Finally, she glanced over at Erin and nodded. She then turned away as she finished getting dressed.

The pain medication Dr. Gonzales had given Tamson had already set in. She was out cold, head swaying against the headrest with the movement of the car. Her face was aglow with the green instrumentation of the dash.

Erin tried to clear her head, knowing that right now she just needed to get them home and get Tamson safely tucked away for the night.

She had seen the extent of Tamson's injuries after Tamson had ripped off the paper gown. Her skin was a virtual roadmap of bruises and cuts, old and new. The one that got her the most was the purple handprint, all five fingers very visible across her back. She wondered if actual fingerprints could be ascertained.

Knowing that Alex, and probably Kyle – Erin's brother and Alex's husband – deserved an explanation, Erin flipped open her phone and hit Speed Deal 3 for the second time in as many hours. She was *not* looking forward to that conversation. She'd not told anyone in her family about her new acquaintance, and certainly not the fact that she'd helped her a couple times. The lectures would be unending, no doubt. With a final sigh of dread, she put the phone to her ear and listened to it ring on the other line.

The call had gone better than Erin had expected with the support and understanding, yet kind words of concern from her favorite sister-in-law and the expected disapproval from her oldest brother. Erin turned into the parking lot of her complex. She got the car parked and the engine turned off before she glanced over at Tamson, who was still asleep.

"Oh boy," she blew out, unbuckling both her and Tamson's seatbelt before Erin climbed out of the car. She hurried around to the passenger side of the car and looked down at Tamson. Though she had an extremely petit build, Erin wasn't all that much bigger, and wasn't entirely sure if she'd be able to get Tamson inside on her own.

Leaning slightly over the woman, Erin brought her hand up and gently nudged Tamson's shoulder. "Tamson? Tamson, can you stand?" she whispered, lightly shaking the dancer. Tamson groaned, a loud snore blowing out her nose. "Okay," Erin muttered, trying to think.

Leaving the door open, she ran up the flight of stairs to her second floor apartment door, unlocked it, and pushed it open. Running back down, she took a deep breath. She could do this. She *had* to do this.

Grunting, Erin pulled the small woman from the car, holding Tamson's thin body against her own as she tried to get a grip on her. She leaned Tamson against her, bending down until Tamson's waist was at shoulder-level. Pushing up with her thighs, Erin got to her feet, hefting Tamson off her feet.

"God, you're heavier than you look," she grunted, steadying her rise up the stairs with a hand on the rail. Finally bursting through her apartment door, she managed to get Tamson to her own bedroom, doing her best not to drop her on the bed.

"I'm sorry," she whispered, Tamson landing a bit harder than she'd intended. Tamson groaned softly, but never woke up.

Adjusting her shoulders and knowing full well her back was going to chew her a new one, she hurried back out, closing and locking up her car and apartment for the night.

Exhausted, Erin checked on Tamson once more, tucking her into her own bed. She left the door open just enough to hear if anything was wrong before gathering the same sheets and blankets Tamson had used the night before. Erin made herself a bed on the couch and fell fast asleep.

※ ※ ※ ※

2008 – San Diego, CA

Tamson draped her arms up around Josh's neck, grinning up at him as the dance continued. She was feeling wonderful and could do this all night. She and Josh had just returned from the bathroom after having a little fun and a few poppers. Oh yeah. She was feeling *no* pain, and the drugs gave her the stomach to be with her boyfriend.

Warmth moved up behind her and Tamson knew exactly who it was. Enjoying the attention, she reached behind her, grabbing Tanner's belt loops and drawing him closer until it was a Tamson sandwich. She felt large hands on her hips and another set wrap around to cup her ass.

Josh leaned down, taking her lips in a hard kiss. She responded best she could, but the kiss was brutal and possessive. She pulled away, glaring up at her boyfriend and hoping he'd get the idea to chill out with the jealousy. If he didn't know by now Tanner did nothing for her, he never would.

The body heat was rising, tension in the room thick. Tamson pushed Tanner away, reaching up to leave a quick kiss on Josh's lips. She wandered off through the crowded party. Making her way back to the bathroom, she leaned over the sink, looking closely at her reflection in the mirror. Fingering the bruise around her eye, she blindly reached into her pocket, bringing out the stick of concealer she'd brought.

"Shit," she muttered, the makeup not doing

such a great job. The bruise still stung, but it had been an accident, after all.

With a sigh, she put the tube of makeup away and grabbed another tube instead. Looking around the small confines of the unfamiliar bathroom, she saw a hand mirror hanging near the toilet. Making a little mirror table atop the closed toilet lid, Tamson sprinkled some of the beloved white powder to the smooth, reflective surface. Using a razor she'd found tucked into the medicine cabinet, she chopped up the clumps, spreading out the coke into two, neat lines.

Digging through her pocket, she found a five-dollar bill. Within seconds, she had it rolled, and ready to go.

As Tamson rejoined the party, she realized it had grown louder, more vivacious. It took her a minute to realize it was because there was a fight. Pushing through the gathered crowd, she was stunned to realize it was Josh and Tanner.

"What the fuck, man?" Josh boomed, long dark hair disheveled as he picked himself up off the floor. Two of the other partygoers held Tanner back, his chest heaving and sweat beading his features.

"Wait!" Tamson fumed, finding herself in the circle that had been made around the two men. Putting a hand on Josh's chest, she looked at Tanner. "What's going on?"

"Look, guys. I don't need no trouble here. You guys need to go."

The three turned to see a small, bald guy entering into the circle. Tamson thought she remembered hearing he was the owner of the house.

"Fuck, no!" Tanner exclaimed, walking over to the guy that was nearly a foot shorter than he was.

"Tanner, let's go." Tamson grabbed his hand, tugging gently. Eyes still boring into the mini Mr. Clean, Tanner allowed himself to be dragged away.

Once outside into the warm, July night, everyone was quiet as they headed toward Josh's truck. Tamson squeezed in between the two men, Josh throwing the truck into gear, and screeching out into the night.

Looking from one man to the other, Tamson settled on Tanner. She knew between the two, he had the worst temper and was most likely responsible for whatever had happened.

"What was that all about, Tan?" she asked, auburn brows drawn in disapproval. She also wasn't thrilled that all the bullshit was killing her newly-acquired high.

He looked down at her. "Why you asking me? Ask the asshole over there." He glared over at Josh.

"Fuck you, man. You *know* what happened, so don't push this shit off on me."

"Come on, fucker! Let's go! Right now!"

"Stop it!" Tamson pushed at Tanner with her shoulder. "What are you on?" Looking into the tall man's face, she could see his eyes were dangerously dilated, his face pale.

"Stop the truck," Tanner growled.

Tires screeched to a halt at the side of the road, throwing up a wave of dirt and rocks. Tanner slammed out of the cab, a spider web crack inching its way across the passenger door window.

"Jesus! Look what he did to my window!" Josh yelled, voice booming in the small cab, bouncing around Tamson's head.

"Let's go," she muttered, scooting across the bench seat to where Tanner had just been sitting.

She glanced out into the night. Tanner had already disappeared.

※ ※ ※ ※

Josh was upstairs pouring them a tequila. Tamson dug around in her messenger bag until she found the tiny envelope she'd bought the previous day.

"Bingo." She grinned. Reaching inside, she brought out the tiny square of paper. Slipping it into her mouth, she tucked the rest away.

Flopping down on the red chair that looked like a giant hand, she allowed herself to be engulfed in its palm, leaning back into the fingers. One leg hanging over the thumb, she arched her head back and closed her eyes. The feel of the acid beginning to merge with her system was a wonderful rush, the world becoming a swirl of color and movement.

Unable to keep the grin off her face, she tried to stand up but fell back into the chair, which grabbed her in its fist, locking her in bars of fingers and thumbs and tight grip. Somewhere she heard the front door open. She opened her mouth to say hello, but it came out as a warbled, thick soup.

Somewhere she heard raised voices, yelling, screaming, and purring. She giggled. Finally managing to pull herself up, Tamson ran her hands all along the walls, making her way toward the stairs. Halfway up, she fell to her knees, face hitting the carpeted step. She cringed at the burn. Raising her head, she reached for the next step, only for her hand to slip through the wall, stuck in the plaster.

"Le'go!" she whined, tugging weakly. Finally managing to get to her feet and pull her hand from the wall–the force nearly knocking her back down the stairs–she continued on.

At the top of the stairs, she yelped, startled as someone was running at her. She felt hands on her shoulders and a voice in her ear.

"I don't unnerstand," she slurred, head lulling back and eyes trying to focus on the face before her. The features looked more like a Picasso painting than a man. She grinned. The nose looked kinda funny on the side of the face. She was led down the hall then all went black.

Chapter Ten

Tamson hit reality as a sledgehammer of pain hit her. Unable to open her eyes, she lay still, taking mental inventory. Everything was still attached, but she wanted to cut it all off. Her arm ached near to the point of making her nauseous. Her face hurt, her eye hurt, and her entire middle felt like a street cleaner had rolled on over her.

"God, kill me now," she whispered, attempting to sit up. "Uh, no. Not happening," she murmured.

Taking a deep breath, she decided to try opening her eyes again. Her left eye wasn't having it but right eye managed to creak open. It wasn't the first time she'd awoken in an unfamiliar room. She took in what she could without moving too much: brass headboard with window with trees outside behind it. She noted a tall, cherry wood dresser with an alarm clock on it and a lamp. There were framed pictures – black and white – on the wall and there was a huge framed poster from Lord of the Rings on the wall across from her that seemed completely out of place.

"Hey."

Tamson's eye found Erin standing at the partially opened bedroom door. She looked wrinkled and tired, dressed in clothes that it looked like she'd slept in. Tamson said nothing. Walking further into the room, Erin brought up a brown prescription bottle and glass of juice.

"How are you feeling?" she asked, sitting on the side of the bed, eyes narrowing in concentration as she took in Tamson's injuries. They almost looked worse today than they had the night before.

"Got a gun?" Tamson asked, closing her eyes. She heard a soft chuckle.

"No. But I do have pain pills." Erin gently helped Tamson to raise her head, whispering an apology at Tamson's wince and soft groan. "I know it hurts."

Tamson placed one of the foul tasting pills on her tongue, gladly washing it down with the juice.

"Are you hungry?" Erin asked, taking the glass from her and setting it aside on the bedside table. Faded pink hair shook as Tamson shook her head. "You know, what is your natural hair color, anyway?"

"What is it with you people?" Tamson asked, eyes still closed. "No one likes my hair. My boss, Tanner, you ..." She didn't see Erin's smile. "It's red."

"You should go back to it. I'm sure it's gorgeous with your eyes."

Tamson opened her one cooperating eye and glanced at Erin, brow raised in surprise before shutting her eye again. "I guess."

"Can I get you anything? Need to go to the bathroom or anything?"

Tamson consulted with her bladder then nodded with a heavy sigh. "Got a bed pan?"

"Nope. Sorry. Come on."

Tamson gasped as fresh tendrils of pain tickled her insides, almost making her fall back to the bed as Erin helped her to sit up. Once on her feet – an arm around Erin's shoulders – she took a deep, steadying breath then made the short, painful trek to the bathroom.

Erin waited outside the door, head leaning back against the wall. It had been an early morning for her already. She had gone out before eight to get Tamson's prescription filled at Walgreens on the corner. The night before, she had fallen into a deep sleep right away, but had been awakened throughout the night with Tamson's cries of pain, felt in her sleep. She'd spent a good portion of the night running back and forth between her bedroom and the couch.

Hearing the toilet flush, Erin prepared herself for another trip to the bedroom. The water ran and Tamson moaned, long and loud. Finally, the door opened and Tamson allowed herself to be helped back into the bed.

"We need to check your bandages, Tamson," Erin said, her voice soft. She went into the living room where she had all the supplies Nurse Shay had given her. Bringing them all into the bedroom, she set it all up on the dresser. Tamson sat on the edge of the bed, shoulders slumped and head hanging. Her hair hung like a curtain of Pepto, completely hiding her face.

Erin glanced at her. "I've got to get you into something that doesn't have to go over your head," she said, walking over to her closet. "Something that can be buttoned up."

Erin opened the closet door and saw a couple button-up shirts and decided that would be their best bet. Grabbing one off the hanger, she walked back over to the bed and set it down before reaching for the hem of the sweatshirt Tamson wore.

"Are you ready?" Erin asked, tugging lightly at the material of the sweatshirt. Tamson nodded. Together they slowly got the sleeve of the sweatshirt over the bulky cast then eased it over Tamson's bruised face. Tossing it aside, Erin looked at her but wasn't able to fully hide her thoughts and feelings.

"I know I look like shit," Tamson said, looking away.

"Who did this to you?" Erin asked, carefully peeling the bandages away from the more severe cuts. "Do you have a boyfriend or husband or something?"

"Something like that," Tamson muttered, hissing as the air hit her newly-uncovered injuries.

"Honey, you have *got* to press charges. He almost killed you."

Tamson smirked. "Trust me, he's not worth the trouble."

"He keeps doing this. It is always him, isn't it?" Erin asked, watching as she received a small nod. She grabbed some of the cleanser Shay provided her with, explaining that it would be cool to the skin, but wouldn't burn. She used soft, easy touches as she cleaned out all of the cuts, tugging down the bandage on Tamson's side to get a particularly ugly bruise/cut combo.

"He's a bastard," Tamson agreed, closing her eyes to try and not think of her pain and humiliation at Erin having to see her this way.

"So why stay with him, Tamson?" Erin asked, glancing up into her face.

"You wouldn't understand," Tamson said through gritted teeth, a fresh wave of pain soaring through her ribs at the slight touch.

"No. You're right," Erin muttered with a sheepish grin. "Are you a Denver native?" she asked, changing the subject.

"No." Tamson opened her eye, watching as Erin spread some antibiotic goo on her wounds then patched them back up. "I'm from Texas."

"Yeah?" Erin glanced up at her. "I've never been there. Have any brothers or sisters? Are your parents still there? This is probably going to hurt, Tamson. I'm sorry."

Tamson gasped loudly as Erin slowly pulled off the bandaging on some of the more heinous injuries on Tamson's ribs, the skin mottled with deep cuts and ugly bruises. One such bruise was in the shape of a full shoe print. She heard the soft intake of air as Erin saw the extensive injuries. She was surprised when she looked at Erin and saw tears in her eyes as she continued to tend to her.

"No," she grunted, looking away. "My dad's dead. Died when I was two. Just me and my mom." She tried to take in a lungful of air to counteract the pain, but it only made it worse. Her breathing became light, shallow.

"Are you and your mom close?" Erin asked, trying desperately to keep Tamson talking to get her through the pain.

"Where do *you* come from?" Tamson asked, a bit more harsh than she'd intended. She said nothing, offered no apology. That's what Erin gets for being so damned nosey.

"I come from Pueblo," Erin said softly, leaning in to examine the deep purple skin around Tamson's ribs, trying her best to ignore the fact that Tamson's breast was mere inches from her face. "It's a town about two and a half hours from here. I have four older brothers, all sweet and ridiculously protective." She smiled.

"That's cool. Are you close?" Tamson grunted, eyes closed as she bit down on her lower lip, praying

Erin would be done soon.

"Yes. Very. My parents, too." Erin set aside the rag she'd been gently wiping down Tamson's skin with.

"Why are you here?"

Erin sighed, sitting back to think about the question and her answer. "When things didn't work out with my ex." She shrugged. "I don't know. I needed a change, something new. My family is great, but they smothered me to the point I was starting to lean on them so much I had nothing that was mine. You know?" At Tamson's nod, she continued. "Denver seemed like a good idea. Bigger city, more opportunities, yet not far enough away that I couldn't go see my family for the weekend if I wanted to." She grabbed fresh bandages, glancing up into Tamson's eyes. "Are you ready?" At Tamson's nod, she began to process of re-bandaging Tamson's torso wounds.

Tamson felt lightheaded from the pain as the bandages went on. She truly thought she'd pass out. It was all she could do to nod at Erin's question if she was okay.

"Hopefully that pain pill will set in soon," Erin said, apology in her tone.

After getting the button-up shirt on Tamson's small frame, she pulled the blankets down, helping Tamson to slide down in the bed. "Lay back and I'll work on your face."

"Shouldn't you be at work or something?" Tamson asked, starting to feel the calming effects of the pain pill. Her body was beginning to relax, her head feeling heavy.

Erin smiled. "I don't start quite yet."

"Where do you work?" Tamson's voice was

getting more slurred, her tongue feeling thicker.

"I'll be starting Monday, working for a lawyer."

"Aw, fuck." With that, she was out.

⁂

Erin awoke with a gasp, her dreams haunting her into reality, visions of blood and the cries of a woman lingering.

Looking around, she saw her living room, TV quietly humming and the clock ticking away the sands of time. Her laptop still lay on her thighs, her hands resting on the cushion beside her. Erin shook the sleepies from her eyes and ran her hands through her hair to brush it away from her face.

Glancing at the clock above the entertainment center, she was surprised to see that it was after noon. Her screensaver weaved across the darkened screen of her computer, coming to life in the jolt of Erin setting it aside. A half-finished sentence waited to be completed.

Getting to her feet, she headed into the kitchen, knowing she had to eat. She was starving, but exhausted, both physically and mentally. Her emotions had taken a huge toll over the past couple days. Grabbing the leftover pizza from the fridge, she plopped four slices onto a plate and popped it into the microwave, letting it heat up as she went in to check on Tamson.

The bedroom was dark, blinds still pulled tightly shut. The room was still, warm, and only the even, deep breaths of Tamson could be heard.

Leaning over her, Erin checked her face, noting that once in a great while a muscle in her cheek or at the corner of her mouth would jump with what seemed to be a grimace of pain. Deciding she was okay, Erin headed back to her warming lunch.

A green eye popped open at the sound of three sharp beeps of a microwave. Looking around the room, she found herself alone and very groggy. She was surprised to feel hunger pangs edging into her consciousness. Then again, it could be because of the smell of something cooking. She couldn't remember the last time she'd eaten.

Using her good arm, she pushed herself up then swung her legs over the side of the bed. She had to sit there for a moment to get her orientation.

Ripping a paper towel from the roll, Erin glanced up when she saw Tamson enter the small kitchen.

"Hey. What are you doing up? Hungry?" she asked. Tamson looked like a small child, shyly nodding. "Want pizza? I don't have a lot else. Um." She headed to the fridge, but Tamson's voice stopped her.

"No. Pizza is fine."

Opening the microwave, Erin bounced the plate from hand to hand, accidentally letting it get a wee bit too hot. "Come on. Sit down and eat," Erin said, placing the hot plate on the counter and grabbing a second plate, where she transferred two of the slices. Together, they moved into the living room and sat on the couch to eat after Erin had snagged a bottle of water for both.

They were quiet, both absorbed in lunch and their own thoughts. Putting her plate aside, Tamson glanced over at the laptop that sat on the end table.

"Is that a story you're working on?"

Erin nodded, sucking some pizza sauce off her thumb. "Ironically enough, you helped to inspire it."

She gave her a sheepish grin. "I haven't written this much in one shot in a long time."

"Really?" Tamson smirked. "Well, I guess it's good that the shithole that is my life can be of some service to someone." She sipped from her water. "When can I read it?"

"Oh." Erin looked away, suddenly feeling very shy. "I don't know. It's not done yet."

"What made you decide to start writing?" Tamson leaned her head back against the couch, eyes hooded. She was fighting the urge to fall back to sleep. Erin smiled full out. Tamson thought she had a wonderful smile.

"Well," Erin began, "I was in fourth grade. Our teacher, Miss Moore, assigned this ridiculously long assignment. I was nine years old and was told I had to write a story that was at least thirty-five pages." She glanced at Tamson and saw the widening of her eyes in surprise. "So," she sighed. "I went home, complained and moaned and groaned, but eventually did it."

"Masterpiece in the making?"

"Yeah." Erin chuckled. "Something like that."

"What was the story about? Did you make your thirty-five pages?" Tamson watched Erin's face as she spoke. Her eyes lit up, the obvious passion for creating pouring from her in waves.

"And then some. I think it turned out to be close to sixty pages, or something crazy like that. Well, certainly you've heard the old adage write what you know?" At Tamson's nod, she continued. "I wrote about a little boy who hated to do homework. A little leprechaun-type guy, Keebeeweetzee came out from the little boy's closet, and whisked him away to another world."

"Keebeeweetzee?" Tamson could barely slur her mouth around the word.

"Hey, I was nine! I plead the insanity of youth. Anyway, the boy entered a land of his own making. Anything was possible. If he wanted a sky of chocolate, the sky would turn into chocolate. Unicorns, dragons, fairies, whatever. Anyway, he had to fight the mighty dragon king of the land to stay alive. Eventually, he realized that maybe homework wasn't such a bad thing." She looked at her again, Tamson's eyes becoming heavier. "Hey, want me to help get you back to bed?"

"No," Tamson shook her head. "I like your story. Think I can find my own fantasy land like that?"

Erin smiled, nodding. "Life is what you make of it. Or so I'm told."

Tamson struggled to keep Erin in focus. She looked into troubled blue eyes. "You don't take many risks in life, do you, Erin?"

Erin met her gaze for a long moment before finally shaking her head. "No. Not really." She looked down at her hands, which rested in her lap.

"Safe car, safe apartment, safe Monday through Friday job." Tamson grinned, her voice growing thicker and thicker, almost incomprehensible. "Workin' for a lawyer." With that, her eyes finally fell closed, unable to fight it anymore.

Erin took a deep breath, her gaze once again dropped to her hands. "Yeah," she said with a sigh.

Standing, she piled the toss pillows on the end of the couch and gently positioned Tamson's head to land on them, stretching her legs across the length of the couch. There was no way she was going to carry her again.

Hands on her hips, she looked down at her. "If this is what taking risks is like, I want no part of it," she whispered.

With a heavy sigh, she cleared up their lunch dishes then grabbed her keys, phone, and purse and headed out.

2008 – San Diego, CA

Tamson tried to fight the hand that tugged on her, her arm feeling like it was about to be pulled from its socket.

"Come on," he growled.

She thought it was Tanner, but wasn't entirely sure. Fear was beginning to override her trip, but the world was still swimming.

"Look! Look what you did!" he demanded.

Tamson fell to the floor when she was released on all fours in what she thought was the bedroom she shared with Josh. A hand grabbed her face in a cruel, vice-like grip, ensuring she was looking where he wanted her to look.

On the floor, near the dresser, was the sprawled body of Josh. From the doorway, she could only see from mid-chest down to his cowboy boots. Her head began to clear as a feeling of panic and dread gnawed at her brain.

Crawling forward, she cried out. Lying on the floor next to Josh was the wooden baseball bat that Tamson's mother had given her years before. It had belonged to her grandfather. Blood covered the bat and a long crack ran the centerline of the wood.

"How could you do this?" Tanner asked, his voice shaky and filled with emotion. "I tried to stop you."

Tamson shook her head. No. There was no way she could do something like this. Her gaze left the bat, coming to rest on Josh's face. His eyes stared at the ceiling, wide and shocked. And sightless.

A sob ripped from her throat and she felt her stomach rebelling. Gaining her feet, she ran to the bathroom, barely making it to the toilet before she lost everything she'd drank, the regurgitated alcohol burning and make her heave.

"Come on, Tam. We gotta go. The cops will be here soon."

She felt Tanner pulling on her. Always pulling on her.

"We gotta tell them it was an accident," she whispered, trying frantically to bring back every memory she had. How could she have done this? She shook her head. No way. No.

"No! There're drugs all over this fucking house, Tam! Let's go. Now!"

Tamson screamed Josh's name as she was rushed from the place, nearly tripping down the stairs and out the door.

Present Day

Tamson gasped, eyes wide open. Her heart was pounding, the fear of that day returning with a vengeance. She felt wetness on her cheeks and reached up to find trails of tears mingling with bandages and lumpy, bruised skin.

Taking as deep a breath as she dared with her bruised midsection, she tried to push all of it from her mind. It was a long time ago. It was ancient history. It had to be.

Deciding to try to take her mind from it, she pulled herself from her sleepy haze and looked around the living room. She was alone, that much was clear. There was an uneasy silence that she found unnerving.

She slowly sat up and moved her legs off the couch, her feet hitting the floor. Sitting for a moment to catch her breath, she slowly stood from the couch, chewing her bottom lip to keep in the hiss of pain. Finally on her feet, she took it slow as she made her way to the bathroom. Looking in the mirror over the vanity, she wanted to cry. She almost didn't recognize herself. Her left eye was nearly swollen shut. The shiner was immense. Man, he swung a mean right hook. She was amazed that her nose wasn't broken, but instead just a small cut across the bridge.

Looking at her hair, she could see that – she wasn't willing to admit Hank was right, but it wasn't exactly ready for the cover of Cosmopolitan Magazine – her roots were coming in. It pissed her off to prove Hank right, but she couldn't ignore it anymore, either.

Shuffling back to the living room after using the bathroom, Hank on the brain, she decided to check in and see if Tanner had come round looking for her, or if he had sent anyone else to do it.

Finding Erin's cordless phone, she grabbed it and dialed the familiar number. The call was picked up after four rings.

"Freddie, is Hank there?" she asked, making her way back to the couch and carefully sitting down. "Hank? It's Tamson."

"Hey. What's up? You coming back to work tonight or what?" he asked with his usual aplomb.

"I don't think I'll be back for awhile. Hank,

Tanner went nuts last night. Look, has he been in looking for me?"

"Ah, hell. I told you to get rid of him, kid. Great. Just great! No, he ain't been in here."

"Has anyone else?"

"No. Why? Should there be?"

"No. Thanks, Hank. Listen, I'll try and be back as soon as I can, okay?"

"Yeah, take care of yourself, kid. Oh, wait. Hang on a sec. Kelly wants to talk to ya."

Tamson waited for the club's accountant to come to the phone, wondering what she wanted. Tapping her fingers on the arm of the couch, finally the line was picked up.

"Tam? Hey. Listen, there's some guy who's been calling for you. I hadn't seen you in awhile so forgot to tell you," Kelly said, her soft voice hard to hear over the music in the background.

"What? Who?"

"Um, lemme grab the sticky I wrote the info on," Kelly said. Tamson could hear papers shuffling in the background. "His name is Cal Franklin. He's a detective."

Tamson felt her blood go cold. She swallowed, squeezing her eyes tightly closed. "When did he call? What does he want?" She barely recognized her own voice. If a voice could turn pale, hers just had.

"He called the last time on Monday. He says it's about Connie Young. Do you know her?"

Tamson's eyes popped open, the blood in her veins replaced with the fire of fear.

"Does any of this make sense to you?" Kelly asked when she didn't get a response.

"Uh, yeah. Did he leave a number or anything?"

Tamson looked around, trying to find paper of any kind. Only seeing the laptop next to her, she stood, hurrying as best she could to a desk tucked into the corner of the dining area. She found an envelope and a red Bic. "Go ahead."

As Tamson ended her call with Kelly, she absently tapped the phone against her knee, looking down at the number she'd written down. It was a Texas area code. Her mind flew back, frantically trying to figure out what this detective could want with her. Was her mother looking for her? Her gut told her that wasn't it.

Sitting back on the couch, she curled her legs up under her, setting the envelope onto the arm of the couch, unable to take her eyes from it.

Chapter Eleven

Humming to herself, Erin pushed her buggy down another aisle, trying to decide what sorts of things Tamson would eat. The woman was entirely too skinny. No doubt she didn't have much of an appetite when she was high. Erin knew nothing about drugs nor those who used them, so she was trying to wrack her brain to think of any and all movies she'd seen with addicts, looking for clues on how to handle the situation with Tamson.

Taking a chance, she grabbed a little bit of everything, which she herself would eat, too. She grabbed some more supplies to clean up Tamson's wounds, as well as a package of underwear and socks for her.

"Thank god for decent prices at Super Wal-Mart," she muttered, looking down at all that was in her buggy and trying to do a quick mental cost tally.

Watching the cashier run her purchases over the table scanner, she waited patiently for her to finish. Buggy loaded with bagged groceries and supplies, Erin headed out into the mild, sunny afternoon. The breeze gently blew her hair back and the sun shone down on her face.

Today was going to be a good day, she felt.

Hanging plastic bags on every finger, both arms, and clutched in one fist, Erin managed to push her way into the apartment. The door was locked, just as she'd left it. Setting everything on the kitchen counters and table, she looked around.

Tamson was no longer on the couch, nor in the bedroom or bathroom.

"Tamson?" Walking toward the living room, she felt a cold breeze. The sliding glass door was open, the vertical blinds blowing softly in the breeze. "Tamson?"

Tamson had pulled a kitchen chair out to the balcony, her small frame pulled up, good arm wrapped round her knees.

"Hey," Erin said, walking out to stand beside her.

Tamson didn't respond, nor did she acknowledge Erin's presence. She stared straight ahead, rocking slightly. Erin sensed something wrong, something was *terribly* wrong.

"Tamson? Honey, are you okay?" She knelt down beside her friend, looking up into her face and trying to find any sign of what might be wrong. "Are you in pain? Do you want to talk?" Something white snagged her gaze. A ripped piece of paper floated lazily to the balcony floor, fallen from pale fingers. Erin picked it up and glanced at it before looking back to Tamson. "Who's Cal Franklin?"

"A detective."

Tamson's monotone answer almost startled Erin. "For what? What does he want?" She stood, holding the slip of paper in her hand. The area code wasn't a Colorado one.

"He's looking for my mother." Tamson's voice was so soft, Erin almost didn't hear it. Erin felt her heart drop. Tamson said no more and she had no idea what to say.

Sighing, she ran a hand through her hair, looking

out over the day. "Well, um, I got something for you." She disappeared into the apartment, returning moments later. "Listen, I don't condone this, but I have a father who smokes and I know how hard it is to deal with a smoker going through nicotine withdrawal." She handed the pack of smokes to a grateful Tamson, along with a book of matches. "Just please don't do it in the house, okay?"

Left alone, Tamson nearly let out a groan in relief. She had never been so excited to see a cigarette in her entire life. She quickly lit up, eyes hooded as she exhaled. The relaxation was immediate.

"This is Detective Franklin."

"Uh. Hi. Um, this is Tamson Robard."

"Tamson, yes, hello. Nice to hear from you."

Tamson sighed, squeezing her eyes shut. "What's this about my mother, Detective?"

"What do you know about Dale Young, Miss Robard?" the detective asked, voice deep, calm.

That was easy. "I know he's a no good son of a bitch. What has he done?" Tamson lowered herself to the couch, wincing as she got settled.

"Why do you think he's done anything?" Cal Franklin asked.

"Because he's a bastard, that's why. He's a bully and not worth my spit."

"Well, your mom is missing, Tamson. She has been for more than two months. A friend of hers called us a few weeks ago." Tamson's hand trembled as it covered her mouth. "Now, I'd really like to talk to you, Tamson. When's the last time you spoke with your mother?"

2004 – Dallas, TX

"Isn't it great?" Connie gushed, taking her daughter's hands in her own, nearly giddy.

Tamson looked at her mother, slowly shaking her head. "Mom, this guy—"

"What? What about this guy?" Connie leaned toward her daughter, voice falling to a hiss. "Don't do this to me, Tamson. Don't you dare."

"Mom, I don't trust him," the teenager hissed back.

"You've been out of my house for two years, now. I don't have nobody else, Tamson. Dale keeps a roof over my head, and clothes on my back." Connie looked away for a moment, briefly glancing back to her daughter, but never looking her in the eye. "Sometimes that's all you get. Remember that when you want to judge me."

"Mom, I'm sorry, but I think it's a mistake to marry him."

"Yeah?" Connie looked her daughter full in the eye, her face all hard lines. "Well I don't care what you think. Dale is my life now. If you don't like it, you can just leave."

Tamson looked at her mother, studied her. Connie meant what she said, and it was written plain as day on her features.

"It's not the first time some man came before me." Tamson was stunned, hand rising to her cheek, which stung, the echo of the slap hovering between them.

Connie showed no emotion. "Get out."

Grabbing her jacket, Tamson glanced back at her mother one more time then shoved out through the back door.

Present Day

"Tamson?"

"Sorry," Tamson said and brought her hand up, swiping at a runaway tear. "Uh, the last time I talked to her was years ago. I was seventeen or eighteen."

"You haven't seen nor heard from her since?" the detective asked, his voice growing soft, compassionate.

"No."

"Okay. Well, uh, the house your mother and Dale were renting was cleared out. Your grandmother, uh," Tamson could hear him flipping through some papers, "Charlotte Robard, has your mother's personal effects."

"I don't know her." Tamson was surprised to hear the words come out of her mouth. She took a heavy breath, looking out the sliding glass doors.

"You don't know your grandmother?"

"No."

"Oh. Well, here's her number. I'm sure you'll want to go through your mother's things. You know, hold them for her until hopefully we can bring her home."

"Look, Detective. If Dale Young was involved, she's not coming back."

Cal Franklin was quiet for a moment. "Why do you say that?"

"Let's just put it this way: I saw Dale's mean streak first hand. He had a dark side to him. I begged her not to marry the bastard."

"Is that why the two of you stopped talking?"

"Yeah. Something like that." Tamson pushed up to her feet, slowly pacing around Erin's living room.

"Well, listen, I'd really like to sit down with you and talk face to face, Miss Robard."

"Yeah, we'll see. I have no desire to go back to that shithole, Texas."

"I see. Well, we'll need to set up a good time for a full phone interview, then. Here's that number."

Erin glanced up from time to time as she put away the groceries. She could smell cigarette smoke vaguely, and wondered how many smokes Tamson had had.

Shoving the empty bags together, Erin put the medical supplies and Tamson's new underwear and socks in her bedroom then headed to the sliding glass door. Tamson still sat where she had been before, cigarette dangling between her fingers, slowly burning itself down.

"Do you miss your momma?"

Erin was surprised at the soft question. She walked out onto the balcony, leaning on the rail. "Sometimes." Turning, she leaned her back against the rail and studied her friend. "Where is your mom, Tamson?"

Tamson shrugged her shoulders. "Dead, I'd say."

"Why do you say that?"

Tamson smashed another cigarette against the balcony rail. In lieu of answering Erin's question, she asked, "When can I have another pain pill?" She stood, looking back out over the day.

"Oh, uh," Erin looked at her watch. "You can have one now. Do you need one?"

"Yeah." Tamson walked back into the apartment, heading toward the bedroom.

Erin sighed, gathering all of Tamson's used cigarette butts in her hand and heading inside, dragging the kitchen chair behind her.

Pain pill and bottle of water in hand, Erin headed to her bedroom where she heard Tamson getting settled on the somewhat squeaky bed. "Hey," she said, stepping inside the room.

Tamson looked up from where she sat on the bed. "Hey." Her eyes followed Erin as she sat next to her on the bed. Erin held out her hand, the small, white pill in her palm. Tamson took it, rolling it between her fingers. "I haven't spoken to her in eight years," she said, watching the pill's movement. Erin said nothing, just listened. "She had been dating this asshole, Dale Young. I didn't like him from the start." Her chuckle was bitter, eyes narrowed at very dark memories. "The first time I ever met him I was sixteen. He looked me up and down and licked his lips. Bastard. When I left the room he laughed, hard and cruel, you know? Like he was playing with me, or something."

"Did he ever touch you?" Erin asked, still holding the cold bottle of water in her hand.

"Nah." She shook her head with a sigh. "And looking back on it, I don't think he would've. I think he figured that if he creeped me out enough, I'd stay away. He always tried to isolate her." She chuckled ruefully. "But I saw him touch Momma, though. Saw him make her bleed."

"Did you do anything?"

"No." Tamson's head fell, her voice a whisper.

"It's not your fault, Tamson, whatever happened to your mom." Erin placed a comforting hand on Tamson's back, rubbing in a small, comforting circle. "Your mom was a grown woman, honey. Only she could make her own decisions."

Tamson nodded. She smiled weakly at Erin then reached for the bottle of water in Erin's hand. Pill taken, she lay down. "Just hope this shit kicks in soon," she said with a sigh. "Seriously not looking forward to tomorrow."

"Why?" Erin asked, standing from the bed and helping Tamson to get underneath the covers and settled.

"Because it's the third day," Tamson said, her voice getting softer and her eyes heavier. "It's always worse on the third day."

≈≈≈≈

"I don't know, Alex. I want to help her, but I just don't know how." Erin nodded at a guy she recognized who lived in her building as she sat on the curb to the parking lot, her cell phone tucked to her ear.

"Be careful, Erin. This woman sounds like she has some serious problems. Don't get in over your head," Alex warned. "Shay told me this Tamson woman has several old injuries. Sounds like this isn't her first rodeo."

"She has no one, Al. How can I walk away from her? Just drop her off on the curb and tell her good luck. I can't." Erin shook her head, bringing her knees up to hug them to her chest.

"I know, and I do understand that. But you're just getting your own life back together. Do you really think you have what it'll take to help this girl? Illegal stuff, Erin. You could be brought in, too, if she gets arrested with drugs."

"I know. And I'd be lying if I said the drugs

didn't scare me. I hate that she does them, but again, I can't turn my back on her," Erin sighed, moving slightly aside as a UPS man was heading towards her with an armload of packages.

"You're a good person, Erin. Just promise me you'll be careful."

"I will."

"And call if you need *any*thing. Okay? Promise?" Alex chuckled. "Regardless of how seriously unhappy Kyle is about this situation."

Erin smiled, nodding. "Yeah, shocking." They both laughed. "And I will, I promise."

The two ending their call, Erin snapped her phone shut and stood, wiping the backs of her jeans with her hand. She'd been thinking about Tamson's situation all afternoon. It seemed as though Tamson's world was unraveling before her very eyes, and Erin wanted so badly to help her. She wasn't sure what she could do or what Tamson needed, but she had made the decision to do whatever it took to be there for her. It certainly didn't seem like Tamson had *any*one else in her corner.

Erin had the distinct feeing that her new friend was at a critical turning point in her life. It seemed that Tamson was fairly unstable right now, so Erin made it her new mission to keep her from falling further into a dark life than she already had.

Nodding to herself – resolve firmly in place – she trotted back up the stairs to her apartment.

༄ ༄ ༄ ༄

Lights. Lots and lots of lights. Scary lights. Talking and yelling. Loud voices. Held safe, held tight.

That smell. The sweet, flowery smell. Inhale, feel better. Warm rain falling, hot on top of the head. Crying? Momma crying?

"Penny!" Green eyes snapped opened, frantically looking around the room in disoriented desperation. Her heart was pounding and breaths came in quick, painful gasps.

She was alone, sadly, painfully, alone. She remembered nothing of her nightmare, but did remember the name of her guardian angel on her lips. Closing her eyes, she took as deep a breath as she could, knowing without doubt that Penny was with her. She felt her presence, filling that hollowness inside.

As her surroundings came into focus, Tamson heard the comforting sounds from the TV in the living room. Pulling herself from the bed, Tamson held onto the dresser to steady herself for a moment before continuing on out of the room.

Erin was tugging on her bottom lip with the fingers of one hand as the other tapped the backspace key until the sentence was gone. Poising her fingers above the keys again, she glanced up, looking startled to see Tamson standing just outside the ring of lamplight.

"Hey," Erin said, setting her laptop aside. She stood and stretched her back with an amusing little squeak.

"Hi," Tamson greeted a bit shyly. She nodded toward the kitchen. "Mind if I get something to drink?"

"No! Please, help yourself. I bought food, so whatever you want." Erin followed her into the kitchen. "Listen, I figured you might want a bath tonight. May help to kind of relax you. I got some small trash bags to tie around your cast. I know you're not supposed to get it wet, or anything."

"Uh, okay. Thanks."

"Did you sleep?"

"Yeah," Tamson lied. Truth be told, nightmares and strange images riddled her sleep. She saw her mother's face, eyes wide, lips moving though no sound came out. She had been reaching for her daughter before she'd vanished into darkness, heartbreakingly final.

Turning to the fridge before her, she scanned the contents, deciding on a can of Pepsi and a pudding cup. Peeling the foil top from the snack, Tamson let her thoughts run rampant. Decision made, she glanced up at Erin, who leaned against the counter, sipping from a bottle of water.

"Erin?" Tamson met Erin's incredibly kind and patient gaze. "Can I get a lift to the bus station downtown?"

"Sure. Where are you going?" Erin asked, sipping from her water.

"The cops gave my mother's things to my father's mother."

"Are you and your grandmother close?" Erin asked, confused by Tamson's choice of term for the woman.

Tamson shook her head. "No," she spat. "That woman made my mother's life hell. We had nothing to do with her. She was evil."

"Oh. Wow. I'm sorry. What did she do?" Erin asked, eyes wide with interest.

Tamson stood there, stumped. What indeed? Her mother had never told her. Sipping from her Pepsi, she changed the subject. "I want to go tomorrow. Get this over with."

Erin studied her friend for a moment, very obviously the wheels in her head turning from the look in her eyes. "How about this," she said at length, "I've got the weekend free. I'll drive you."

"Erin, you're going to drive me to Fort Worth, Texas? That's nearly a twelve hour drive," Tamson said, crossing her arms as best she could over her chest.

"Okay, okay. How about I get you through Colorado, then we get you a bus on into Fort Worth?"

Tamson snorted. "Or how about I just catch a Greyhound down on Curtis Street and save us both some grief."

"No way," Erin insisted, shaking her head. "I know you don't have money for a ticket, and you're hurt. Not a chance in hell I'm going to let you do that, Tamson." Erin was firm, chin set in a stubborn hold.

"Let me? What am I, three?" Tamson challenged, hands moving to her hips.

"No. But you *are* hurt," Erin retorted.

It was a battle of wills, and Tamson knew she couldn't win. She had absolutely no leverage, no cards left to play. Eyes falling, she acquiesced.

Chapter Twelve

"Thanks, Mike. Yeah, it's early for me, too," Tamson said, eyeing the front door. "I'll see you then, and thanks again. I owe you one." She flipped the cell phone shut as the front door opened and Erin stepped through with a smile.

"Ready?"

"Uh, yeah," Tamson said, tossing the cell back to Erin, who caught it easily.

"Hank okay with everything?" Erin asked, holding the apartment door open for Tamson, who nodded.

"Yep. All set."

"Okay. Come on. The car's all packed."

Getting Tamson belted in was an adventure. They eventually had to settle on unhooking the belt that would go across her chest, just leaving the lap belt in place.

"Okay?" Erin asked from where she stood outside the opened passenger-side door.

Tamson nodded, letting out a deep, pain-filled breath. "As okay as it's gonna get, I think." As Erin got herself settled in and the car moving, Tamson glanced over at her. It was nearly six o'clock Saturday morning. The morning was cold and the streets bare.

Erin spared a glance at her as she was turning onto 120th Avenue. "What?" she asked with a small, confused smile.

Tamson shook her head with a small smile of her own. What she didn't tell Erin was she honestly had not one clue why this stranger was going completely out of her way for her. It baffled her, made her feel uncomfortable and comforted all at once; a strange dynamic of feelings. Finally, she allowed her head to rest back against the seat and her eyes to close.

The city passed by in a blur of golden rays and orange clouds. The occasional car looked gray and insignificant in the morning hue.

The early hours had always been Erin's favorite time of day. It was a chance at a new start, and brought peace and hope with each passing minute – a dawn of a new day filled with new possibilities.

She glanced over at Tamson, who had fallen asleep. She couldn't help but wonder what the end of this day would bring. Tamson would be on a bus, headed to Fort Worth, Texas to face an unknown ending to what Erin could only assume was a painful past, just from the tidbits Tamson had given her. Erin absolutely hated the fact that she couldn't be there for her, if even as a silent supporter.

Tamson's wounds looked worse today than they had the past two days. The third day was absolutely the worst, just as Tamson had predicted. Tamson's pain pills had been one of the first things to be packed.

Erin let out a heavy sigh as she hit the turn signal, getting the little car turned on I-25 and headed south.

ﾐﾐﾐﾐ

"You have *got* to be kidding me," Erin said, brows drawn as she glanced at her grinning passenger.

"Something brown?" Her eyes scanned the car and the surroundings outside it. "We're surrounded by brown, Tamson."

Tamson grinned wider, nodding. "Yeah, so figure out what brown I'm talking about." She brought her cigarette to her lips, inhaling before raising the smoke up next to the cracked window.

Erin rolled her eyes at Tamson's suggestion, sighing and continuing to scan the surrounding area. She had already guessed almost all there was that was brown in the car, all to no avail.

Noticing a dark brown, weathered barn far off in the distance of the lonely stretch of road, Erin was about to point it out when the mid-morning still exploded. She grabbed the wheel with both hands, desperately trying to keep the car on the road. Her heart was pounding as the car finally screeched to a halt on the shoulder of I-25 in a cloud of dust.

"Shit!" Tamson muttered, having dropped her cigarette on herself in the chaos. Patting her burning jeans, she chuckled, tossing the cigarette butt out the window. She looked over at the frazzled driver, grin sliding off her face. "Are you okay?"

Erin nodded numbly, still trying to recover. She pulled one hand then the other off the steering wheel, surprised there wasn't a sucking sound accompanying each. She was pale and shaky. "Whoa."

"Yeah. Blown tire, I guess." Tamson opened her door, stepping out into the calm, mild day. It was December in southern Colorado, and a gorgeous day. If she had to guess, she'd say it was fifty degrees with pure sun. "Beautiful day."

"Beautiful day?" Erin repeated, incredulous. "Tamson, the tire exploded! I don't have a spare. We're stranded out here!" Her voice was flat in the open fields around them. She raised her arms in exasperation, turning in a circle to see what was around them. All she saw, ironically, was the barn. "I guess if need be, we could get shelter there," she muttered.

Tamson followed her line of sight. "I Spy." She grinned, meeting Erin's glare. "Oh, come on, Erin. This isn't the end of the world." She walked over to her, who was obviously upset. "We'll be fine. Really. Just relax." She snorted. "Been in much worse than this, trust me."

"What are we going to do?" Erin asked, walking around to the trunk. Opening it and looking inside, she prayed that maybe, just *maybe* she was wrong about the no spare tire thing.

"Well," Tamson muttered from just behind her, "we can either try and drive on what's left of the tire to the next town, we can walk, or hitch." They both walked around to the front of the car. The right tire was in shreds, down to the rim. Tamson looked over at Erin, who was chewing on her bottom lip. "Walking or hitching it is."

Erin was quiet. She was angry and riddled with worry. What were they going to do? What if they didn't find a town? She had already found that they were truly in the middle of nowhere; her phone had absolutely no service. She glanced up at the sky, expecting to see hungry, pregnant clouds swarm in.

"Erin." Tamson chuckled, glancing over at the other woman who sulked next to her. "You really need to get that stick out from up your ass." A fiery gaze met her comment. "We're going to be fine. Shit, I've been here before." Tamson waved off the fear she saw in those blue eyes.

"But I haven't."

"Well, good thing you're with a pro then, isn't it?"

Erin looked at her, at first stunned by Tamson's cavalier attitude with it all, but seeing the twinkle in those beautiful eyes, surrounded by bruises and healing cuts, she knew it could be worse.

Heaving the bag she grabbed from the car – some food, water, keys and her cell phone tucked inside – she walked on, trying her best to let go of some of her fear.

As they walked on in a somewhat comfortable silence, Tamson glanced over at Erin, studying her profile: straight nose, pleasing lips, and a strong jaw. She hadn't noticed before, but Erin was actually a beautiful woman.

Erin looked over to find Tamson staring at her. "What?"

Tamson shook her head, but didn't look away until a few moments later.

Tamson felt a wave of guilt wash over her. Why was it that she always managed to drag other people into her shit? Here Erin was trying to do something nice for her, and yet again someone got fucked for trying to help her. Maybe she was cursed.

Tamson shook these thoughts from her head. Erin was a big girl. She made her own decisions, and she had decided to drive Tamson's sorry ass to some little town called Alamosa.

"Do you believe in fate, Tamson?" Erin asked, her voice soft and somewhat distant.

Tamson thought about that for a moment, never giving it any real thought before. "I don't know. But if there is such a thing, you know, like the Fates from

Greek mythology, they sure are bitches." Erin burst into laughter. Tamson's first reaction was to get angry. "What? Why are you laughing at me?"

Erin sobered, clearing her throat, though a smile still teased her lips. "I'm not laughing at you, Tamson. Really. I don't know. That just struck me as funny. And you're right." Hearing something, Erin looked back over her shoulder at the long, lonely road behind them. Her car was just a shimmering spot in the distance, and another was coming up the road. "A car," she said, fear clenching her gut. "Maybe we should walk a bit in the brush."

"What? Why?" Tamson saw the car swimming in distant haze. She traded Erin places, walking along the outer shoulder. As the car got closer, she raised her good hand, waving at the sedan. The car gained speed as it neared them. Tamson began to wave more frantically, shouting a curse that the roar of the car's engine swallowed. "Fucker," she muttered, watching it go with a single-finger salute.

"What were you doing?" Erin asked, incredulous.

"What do you mean? Do you seriously want to walk all fucking day? I'm trying to get us a ride." Tamson continued on.

"Do you have any idea how dangerous that is?" Erin sputtered, jogging the couple steps to catch up with her again.

Tamson grinned at her. "And this isn't?" She indicated the barren landscape around them, the weather not as snow-heavy in the southern part of the state, leaving it cold and barren. "Sure, it's nice now, but come nightfall," Tamson imitated a shiver, "Ain't gonna be so fun come nightfall when all we've got is each other and the frozen ground."

With a heavy sigh, Erin begrudgingly conceded.

Twenty minutes later, they heard the approach of another car. Tamson stopped, looking at the car, nothing more than a shiny dot. Turning to Erin, she grinned.

"Maybe there's something good about this after all," she said, raising her cast-encased arm. It made a perfect hailing arm, and they burst out laughing, giggling like little girls. "Okay, okay, here he comes."

Tamson raised the arm, wiggling her fingers just above the rough cast. The truck blew by.

"God, what am I, a leper?" she asked, turning stunned eyes to her still giggling friend. She'd never had a problem getting a ride before.

"Maybe they're afraid that thing is a registered weapon." Erin lightly flicked the cast. Tamson snorted. "Come on, let's keep walking. At least it'll help to keep us warm."

"Let's see you do better next time," Tamson challenged. She caught a raised eyebrow.

"But I thought you were the pro, oh Obi-Wan of the hitchhikers."

Tamson chuckled. "Off day."

Smiling, Erin swung her bag around so she could unzip it. "Want some water?" she asked, rifling through the contents. When Tamson shook her head, Erin grabbed her own bottle, shoving the bag back around to her side. She twisted the cap off the Aquafina brand water, and took a long gulp.

"So why did you ask about fate?" Tamson asked, looking down at the skeletal remains of some poor animal, toeing the skull before stepping over the death site.

Erin shrugged, tucking the bottle into a side

pocket of her bag. "Well, I've always been of the mindset that everything happens for a reason. So, as I walk along I-25, I'm just trying to figure out what the hell the reason could be behind it."

Tamson chuckled. "Maybe the reason is something's trying to tell you to check your tires before you go on a road trip."

"Smart ass," Erin grumbled.

"Hey, better than being a dumbass." Tamson chuckled. After a moment she said, "I don't believe in that. I think we're in charge of our own destiny." She took her pack of smokes out from where they were tucked in her cast's sling. Sliding one between her lips, she lit it. As she inhaled, she moved to the other side of Erin to keep her smoke away.

"Can I ask you something, then?" Erin asked. She saw the wary glance of her companion, but Tamson eventually nodded. "If you believe we make our own way, then how did you end up here?"

"You *brought* me here," Tamson muttered. She knew exactly what Erin was saying, but her hackles had been raised, along with her defenses.

"But you could have made better choices for yourself—" The look on Tamson's face when she whirled on her struck Erin mute.

"Don't you dare fucking judge me, Erin, miss play everything so fucking safe you squeak when you walk. I've been judged all my life. When you can make your life perfect, then we'll talk. Until then, fuck off!" With that, she stormed away as much as her ruined body would let her.

Erin stood in place, stunned and thoroughly chastised and humbled. Taking a deep breath, she continued walking as well, like the slave walking behind a very upset master. She watched Tamson, seeing a faded pink head dip before it was raised high, long strands of hair falling down Tamson's back. Tamson angrily tossed her half-smoked cigarette out into the field around them.

"Please don't let that thing start a fire," Erin muttered. "That would so be our luck today." With a heavy sigh, she kept going.

2000 – Oklahoma City, OK

The girls giggled again, covering their mouths as old man Higgins glared.

"Come on." Rebecca giggled, grabbing Tamson's hand and pulling her further down the street.

Tamson went happily, almost skipping with giddiness at her new friend. "I didn't think his dog would actually run after the stick," she said, trying to catch her breath.

"Oh I know!" Rebecca crowed. The girls fell into silence, walking down the tree-lined street.

Tamson couldn't help but glance over at the pretty girl from time to time. She was almost beside herself with Rebecca sometimes. They had been best friends for three whole months!

"Come on, Tam!" Rebecca grabbed her hand again, tugging her across a carpet of thick, green grass. The house was small, but beautiful. It was painted white with light blue trim and had colorful flower boxes dotting the windows. Tall, trimmed shrubs lined the front of the house, creating a gate to enter through before reaching the three steps up to the painted cement stoop.

The little blonde dug out her key from her

pocket, unlocking the blue front door. Tamson noticed a brass knocker as she passed through into the inner sanctum. The living room was cool, a relief from the hot, summer sun. Floral print furniture was scattered with new and crisp doilies placed on the coffee table and top of the large television. A tall vase of flowers adorned the sofa table

"Your house is pretty," Tamson said, her wide eyes taking everything in. Even the carpet, with its fresh vacuum tracks, was nice. So different from the worn, green carpet in the trailer she shared with her mom. Connect-the-dots could almost be played with the cigarette burns in it.

"Thanks." Rebecca smiled, leading her friend into the spacious kitchen. The cabinet doors were painted white, more flowers stenciled onto their fronts.

"Does your mom like flowers?" Tamson asked, seeing yet another vase filled with sunflowers on the round, oak table.

Rebecca rolled her eyes. "I know, right? They're everywhere. Do you like Sunny D?" she asked, leaning her head into the coolness of the fridge.

"Uh, sure." Tamson had no idea, but figured it would be rude to say so. Soon she had a tall glass filled with cold, yellow liquid. Sipping, the sugary citrus rush was instantaneous. It wasn't like orange juice, and it wasn't exactly like Kool-Aid. She liked it.

"Come on. Let's go to my room."

The girls walked down a hall with walls littered with family pictures, framed and smiling faces. Tamson recognized Rebecca's mother instantly – mother and daughter looked almost exactly alike. Both had light blonde hair, twinkling blue eyes, and deep dimples.

Rebecca's room was all girl: pink walls, pink carpet with gray swirls in it. There was a white canopy bed with a lace canopy and a matching white vanity, with attached mirror. Dozens of pictures were tucked into the sides of it, friends, boys, and Rebecca's cheerleading camp picture from the summer before.

"Come on," Rebecca chirped, throwing herself on the bouncy bed. She patted the spot next to her, which Tamson took, careful not to spill her drink.

It wasn't long before the girls were giggling again, getting high on the enormous amounts of sugar in their drink, and finding common ground.

Just about every day of the first month of summer, Tamson would be with Rebecca at the flowery house. They talked incessantly and Rebecca even gave her new friend clothes that she didn't wear anymore. Soon Tamson wore her hair just like her best friend, high up in a ponytail, and was even beginning to learn some of Rebecca's cheers. Tamson felt even better about herself as Rebecca told her often that she was impressed and just a little bit jealous at how high Tamson could kick and how flexible she was.

"You should try out for cheerleading next year, Tam," Rebecca commented one day as the girls hung out on her trampoline, where they'd spent the afternoon jumping and practicing their jumps. "You'd make the squad, no doubt."

"Oh." Tamson grinned shyly, picking at her sock. "I doubt it."

"No, seriously!" Rebecca exclaimed, the enthusiasm of youth sparkling in her eyes. "Miss Wayne would l.u.v. you!"

"Really?" Tamson asked, her brows raising in hope. She grinned at her friend's vigorous nod. She flopped to her back on the heated tarp, looking up into the cloudless sky. Visions of football games and short skirts marched across her thoughts. "I don't know, Rebecca." She knew she'd never fit in that world. And not only that, but her mother would *never* go for it. Besides, she thought with profound sadness, they may not even be there come fall.

"Rebecca? Honey, where are you?" a light, pleasant voice called from inside the house.

"We're out here, Mom!" Rebecca called back. It wasn't long before her older look-alike stepped out into the afternoon sunlight. Her hair shone like spun gold, just like her daughter's.

Mrs. Deacons walked across the flawless lawn to the girls, smiling at Tamson. "Who's this?"

"Mom, this is Tamson. Tamson, this is my mom."

"Hello, Mrs. Deacons," Tamson said shyly.

Rebecca's mom's smile widened. "So polite. Hi, Tamson. Nice to meet you finally, honey. Lord knows I've heard your name enough."

"Mom!"

Ignoring her daughter's whine, Virginia Deacons started back toward the house. "Come on in and get some lunch, girls."

Tamson watched her go then turned to her friend, stunned. "Wow. Your mom is really cool."

Rebecca only rolled her eyes as she scooted off the trampoline.

❧ ❧ ❧ ❧

"You should see her clothes!" Tamson gushed, putting the bowl of heated Spaghetti-Os on the table.

"She's got skirts and shorts and pants and—"

"Well, Tamson, that's easy to do when you've got two incomes coming in. It's just me, sweetheart," Connie Robard reminded, placing a plate with a couple pieces of bread on it.

"I know." Tamson took her seat, snagging one of the pieces from the plate at the center of the two-person table.

Her mother sat across from her, dipping a couple large spoonfuls of the canned pasta onto her plate. "So what did you do today?" Connie asked, sipping from her cold can of Bud.

"I was at Rebecca's."

"Oh. Right." She brought her hand up to her forehead as though a headache were on the way.

Tamson chewed slowly, studying her mother for a moment before taking a drink of her milk to clear her throat. "Momma?"

"Hmm?" Connie said, sounding bored.

"Rebecca's family invited us to a barbeque on Saturday."

"I think I'm working Saturday, Tamson."

"You said you were off this weekend. Remember? You said we might be able to do something." Tamson looked at her mother with pleading eyes. "Please, Momma?"

Connie sighed, draining her second can of beer of the night and looked at her daughter. Finally, with a nod and a sigh, she turned back to her dinner.

"Yes!" Tamson exclaimed, clapping her hands. She ran around the table to her mother, taking her in an enthusiastic hug. Connie smiled, kissing her little girl on her forehead.

"Go sit down and finish your dinner."

The sky was blue with clouds puffy white and the birds were singing their song. Tamson had walked over to Rebecca's house in the early afternoon to help set up. It also gave Connie a chance to sleep off Friday night fun undisturbed.

Rebecca's older brother, Adam, had come home from college in Louisiana to enjoy the weekend with his family. His girlfriend, Lydia, had also joined him.

"Tamson, honey, would you take out the bowl of rolls?" Virginia Deacons asked, not bothering to look at the girl as she was busy pouring the homemade baked beans in a bowl from the crockpot.

Without a word, Tamson happily carried out her task, happy to be back out in the sunshine. She watched as Adam and his father wrestled out in the grass, the family dog barking as she ran around the duo.

Tamson was so amazed. Looking at her friend, who was coming out with a bowl of salad, she couldn't help but wonder what it would be like to grow up in such a house.

Feeling disloyal, Tamson shook the idea from her head, and went back inside to help.

The afternoon wore on, the family and Tamson all seated around the large patio table, passing around plates filled with freshly grilled burgers and hot dogs. Potato salad was heaped onto Tamson's plate, as well as corn on the cob and coleslaw. She'd never had such a bountiful feast in her life! And the watermelon for dessert was almost too much.

The sun moved, chasing shadows around the

backyard. Tamson tried to ignore the looks of pity that were passed her way. She didn't want it.

"Do you want us to give you a ride home, Tam?" Rebecca asked, her voice quiet and discreet.

Tamson shook her head and smiled bravely, tucking a strand of hair behind her ear. "No, that's okay."

"Well, honey, I'm sorry your mom couldn't make it," Virginia said, walking up to the girls, putting an arm around Tamson's narrow shoulders.

"Oh." She smiled. "I'm sure she got called into work. It happens sometimes."

"Well, we'll try again." Virginia smiled. "Listen, I'm going to drive you home, Tamson. I'd like to talk to your mom about cheerleading tryouts."

For a moment, Tamson felt her stomach roil and all the food she'd just eaten wanting an encore appearance. Swallowing, she shook her head. "No, that's okay, Mrs. Deacons. I really can't."

"Well, I want to give it a try." With a small squeeze to Tamson's shoulder, the older woman walked away. "Get ready to go, girls!" she called over her shoulder.

Idle chatter between mother and daughter filled the drive to the Mount Carmon Trailer Park. Tamson rested her forehead against the backseat passenger window, watching the scenery fly by, seeming to go from lush and green to stark and brown the closer they got to her house.

Pulling up to the white and green trailer, Tamson saw her mother's olive green VW Bus parked next to the sagging steps and porch. She glanced at the other two occupants in the car, doing her best to swallow down her shame. She led the way up the creaky stairs, trying the knob. Locked. For a moment she thought about lying, telling them that her mom had taken the other car – that they didn't have – and wasn't actually home. Finally, with a heavy sigh she unlocked the wobbly knob and opened the door.

Eyes closing, Tamson wanted to cry as she smelled absinthe and the sweet smell of marijuana. A man laughed from deep in the trailer, followed by the high-pitched screech of a woman.

"Damn it, Dale! Stop that."

"Come on, baby." The rest of his words were muffled. Tamson didn't even want to guess why.

Tamson turned to her visitors, head slightly hanging. "Um, maybe you could come back. Later." She spared a glance to Rebecca, eyes squeezing closed again when she saw the girl's eyes on something behind her.

"Who's this?"

Tamson turned to see her mother standing in the entrance to the living room, a sheet loosely wrapped around her body. When Connie saw her daughter's face, her eyes dropped, finding the heating vent.

"I'm sorry, baby. Dale came by to pick up those magazines of his, and—"

"Momma, this is my friend Rebecca and her mom, Virginia Deacons. This is my momma," she finished lamely.

"We're so sorry we missed you today," Virginia said, her smile pasted in place, and it didn't reach anywhere near her eyes.

"Yeah, well, something came up," Connie said, chin raised, defiant.

"Well, um," Virginia cleared her throat, "I wanted to talk to you about the cheerleading tryouts.

Tamson has been working with Rebecca this summer, and she's quite good—"

"Tamson's not trying out for no damn cheerleading squad," Connie said, a hand finding her hip.

"Well, uh." Caught off guard, Virginia tried to recover. "I wish you'd reconsider, Miss Robard. I think Tamson could really benefit—"

"You come into my house with your religious name and try'n tell me what to do with my kid? What she will and will *not* like? You got some pair on you, lady."

"Momma," Tamson whispered, pleading.

"No. This bitch comes in here, thinking I can afford that kind of shit. I don't appreciate that too much." The slur in Connie's voice was a dead giveaway to what other activities she'd been engaging in all afternoon.

"You can't afford an activity for your daughter, yet you can afford alcohol and marijuana cigarettes?" Virginia asked, pointing to three empty bottles lying on the floor and an ashtray filled with smoked roaches.

"Get out of my house, lady," Connie growled, taking a menacing step toward her. "You get out, and take your high horse bullshit somewhere else."

"Rebecca, let's go," Virginia said. She shoved the girl out the door, then turned back to look at Tamson. "Come on, Tamson. You girls can have a slumber party."

"My kid ain't going *no*where!" Connie hurried to them, the sheet flowing behind her.

"There is no way I'm leaving this child in a house filled with drugs." Mrs. Deacons met Connie toe to toe, her eyes ablaze. To Tamson's utter shock, her mother backed down, taking a step back. Virginia turned her attention to her. "Do you need anything, Tamson?" she asked, eyes returning to Connie's. At the shake of Tamson's head, she too was pushed out onto the stoop.

The next morning, not even eight a.m., the Deacons' doorbell chimed. Adam opened the door, surprised to see the disheveled woman standing on the stoop.

"I've come to take Tamson home," Connie said, her voice firm.

"Oh, uh, sure. She's still asleep. Let me go wake her."

Tamson dressed quickly, looking out the window into the street. She saw the VW Bus, the back loaded. Her eyes began to sting with the swell of tears she tried to hold down.

Walking downstairs, followed by Rebecca, she turned to her friend. A long hug later, she was ushered out into the warm summer morning. Settled into the front seat, Tamson glanced out at the family who stood in the open doorway of the small, peaceful house. She raised her hand, Rebecca doing the same.

Chapter Thirteen

Present Day

"Tamson? Tamson?"

"What?" Tamson was shaken from her walk down memory lane. Looking around, she saw what Erin was looking at. A minivan was on its way up the road and looked to be slowing. Raising her arm again, Tamson acknowledged them.

The dark green van pulled to a careful halt and Erin felt her heart stop. Everything her mother ever told her about strangers and getting into a car with them flew into her mind. She was profoundly relieved when the passenger window rolled down to show a woman with a sweet smile and a harmless-looking man looking over at them from behind the wheel.

"Got some problems, girls?" the woman asked.

"Was that your car way back?" the man asked, hitching his thumb in the direction they'd just come.

"Yeah. Sure was." Tamson smiled disarmingly. "Lost a tire. You folks got a little extra room?"

"Absolutely!" The woman nodded. "Just squeeze in behind the kids."

Erin let out relieved breath. "Thank god," she muttered. "I don't think the Mansons would hurt us with kids." She met Tamson's glare. "What?"

"Shush," Tamson warned under her breath.

Erin stayed quiet as the side door was slid open. Inside, three identical pairs of curious eyes looked out at them.

"Do you gals need to go back to your car and pick anything else up?" the man asked.

Erin and Tamson exchanged a look before Erin met the man's friendly gaze and shrugged. "Well, uh, if that's not too much trouble. I have some things in the trunk I'd really rather not leave."

"Sure thing." The man smiled at her through the rearview mirror.

The triplet that had been sitting in the very back bench seat moved to join her sisters in the seat behind their parents, making room for Tamson and Erin to squeeze back into. A moment later, the minivan made a u-turn and headed back north.

Tamson stayed in the van while Erin and father of six, Sam Malone, helped her at the car.

"Well." He chuckled as they walked across the two-lane highway to Erin's Civic. "We have two teenagers and a twenty-two year old daughter back home. The three little ones in the van were a bit of a surprise."

Erin laughed. "I can imagine. I bet it's not easy to run after triplets all day. How old are they?" She dug out her keys, unlocking and opening the trunk. She gathered an expensive tool kit her father had given her for Christmas her first year out of the house, as well as a flashlight.

Sam took the First-Aid kit, closing the trunk as Erin moved out of the way. He stopped her with a hand to her shoulder.

"Is your friend okay?" he asked, dark brows furrowed in fatherly concern. "She's awful beat up."

Erin nodded. "Yeah. She's had it rough, but I'm hoping once she gets where she's going, things will get better for her."

"Well," Sam said, heading back across the highway, waiting while a big rig roared past, "let's get going, then."

"Where you gals headed?" Zea, Sam's wife, asked, turning in her seat.

"Tying to get to the bus station in Alamosa," Erin said, buckling her seatbelt in the darkness of the back of the minivan. The group of three nine-year-olds were all turned around, staring.

"Kristen, Karen, Kylee, stop staring," Sam barked, looking at his daughters in the rearview mirror. The triplets quickly turned around.

"Well, ladies, I can't get you there, but we can get you as far as Walsenburg. How'd that be?" Sam asked, once again looking at the two through the rearview mirror.

"That'd be great, Sam. Thank you." Erin smiled, then allowed herself to relax and sit back, attempting to enjoy the ride.

Looking over at Tamson, she saw just how exhausted she looked. Her eyes were half-hooded, head resting against the back of the bench seat. Erin knew that she'd managed to hurt her again, or at least say the very wrong things again, and though she felt bad about it, she couldn't understand Tamson. So much of her was enigmatic and seemingly untouchable. She wished Tamson would open up to her, talk to her. Help her to understand so she wouldn't say things that hurt her.

"Tamson?" she whispered, feeling guilty for bugging her, but needed to talk to her. Tamson rolled her head along the back of the seat to look at her. "I'm sorry for hurting you. Again. I truly wasn't trying to judge you."

Tamson rolled her head back, her gaze on the blank screen of the television screen mounted to the ceiling of the minivan. "It's okay."

"People judge you a lot, don't they?" She watched her friend nod. "Do you have any friends? Anyone in your life other than your boyfriend?"

"No. Not really. And, he's not really my boyfriend." After a moment, Tamson's brows drew in thought. She glanced over at Erin again. "Do you have a life at all, Erin?"

An unintentional jab, Erin felt walls of her own rise. "I like my life." She fingered the strap of her bag, which sat in her lap.

"Every time I've called you or been at your place, nothing changes, nothing out of place. You're always there," Tamson said softly, sounding almost as though she were thinking aloud more than asking a true question.

A small smile appeared on Erin's lips as something occurred to her. "I'll answer your question, Tamson, but you do realize this isn't going to work forever, right?" She glanced up at Tamson's confused expression. "You always turn my own questions back on me."

Tamson looked down, sheepish. "Habit."

"I *will* figure you out, you know."

"You think so?"

Erin nodded, fully confident in her claim. "I don't make friends easily. I tend to sit in the corner of life and watch everyone else."

"Why?"

Erin shrugged. "Just have always been that way, I guess," she murmured, suddenly overcome by the day. She rested her head back against the seat. With a soft breath, Erin gave in, leaving their conversation unfinished as she allowed her body to relax fully. She hadn't slept well since Tamson had stumbled into her life nearly a week ago.

Tamson looked at Erin for a moment, watching as her head gently fell to the side as she lost her battle with sleep.

She leaned her own head back, thinking over the past week. Her life had been turned upside down yet again, but why did it feel so different? Thinking of Erin, she was amazed that she somehow saw the quiet, elusive writer as a friend. The only friend she'd had that did not belong to her world, since she'd been thirteen, that is. How had Erin chosen this path? Could it have been Tamson, living a quiet, safe life?

She sighed heavily as she felt so world-weary. Her body ached almost as much as her spirit. She longed for a place to finally feel safe, free, maybe even grounded. Sighing heavily, she just didn't know if she'd find that place before life killed her. Or, as Erin had so succinctly pointed out, her own choices.

Opening her eyes, she saw a pair of brown looking at her. One of the girls had turned around, hiding behind the seat so that she could only be seen from the bridge of her nose up. She was contemplating Tamson as though she were trying to unlock the universe. Tamson had to stop herself from growling at the girl, hating nothing more than to be stared at. She managed a smile, though could feel it was somewhat twisted and warped.

"Why is your hair pink?" the girl asked, words

muffled into the material of the back of the seat.

"Why are your eyes brown?" Tamson countered.

"'Cuz God made them that way."

Good point kid. "I accidentally dunked my head into a cotton candy making machine," Tamson said nonchalantly. Brown eyes grew wide in shock, eyebrows nearly shooting off the girl's forehead. Tamson chuckled. "Bad dye job, kid." With that, her eyes slid shut.

※ ※ ※ ※

Christmas, 2000 – Salt Lake City, UT

"Tamson? Bring me the box with a 'c' written on it," Connie called out, stepping back from the snowman clock, head slightly tilted. When she realized Frosty was looking at her eye-to-eye, she knew he was crooked. Straightening the plastic clock out, she stepped back again. Satisfied that it was straight, she turned to see a sour faced Tamson dumping the box she had asked for on the living room floor. "Be careful. There's breakable stuff in there."

"So," Tamson muttered with a shrug, stomping back toward her room.

"Tamson Renee Robard! You get your little smart ass back here."

With a heavy sigh, the teenager glared at her mother. She saw that her mother was pointing at the spot in the floor right in front of her. Sighing dramatically with rolled eyes, Tamson stepped to the spot. To her shock, Connie bent down and grabbed something from the box she'd just brought in. Lifting her arm, her mother grinned, holding up a piece of plastic, and slightly dusty, mistletoe. Tamson's eyes and face wrinkled up as she was given a big, wet kiss to her cheek.

"Ew, Mom!"

"Ew, Mom!" Connie mocked, tossing the mistletoe onto the end table, which was nothing more than a plastic lawn table. "Ew, Mom!" she sang, grabbing her daughter's hands, and making the stunned girl move around the small room with her, dancing to the tune she hummed, which broke up every couple seconds with an unstoppable grin.

The mirth in her mother's eyes and features was contagious. Despite her urge to pout and be alone, Tamson couldn't help but giggle as they danced, nearly knocking over the coat tree by the door, her mother squealing as she whirled her daughter around, away from the danger.

"Frosty, the snowman," Connie began to sing, at the top of her lungs. Tamson joined in, the duet sounding more like dying cats than the next mother/daughter group.

As Tamson played with her mom, she let loose one of the first genuine smiles she had in a very long time. They'd been in Salt Lake for nearly six months, the longest they'd been anywhere. Connie had left Dale behind in Oklahoma City and had found a decent job as a night stocker at Wal-Mart, bringing home a steady paycheck and making a stable, yet humble, home for the two of them.

It had taken a long time for Tamson to forgive her mother for yanking her away from the only real friend she'd ever known. Actually, it wasn't accurate to say she'd forgiven her mother. She'd just put the memory away, tucked neatly into an elaborate filing system, a sturdy lock on the door.

Tired and giddy, both fell to the floor, panting from their impromptu concert. Connie looked over at her daughter, Tamson's cheeks rosy with laughter and the health of youth.

"Want to get a tree?"

Tamson met her mother's gaze. "Mom, it's Christmas Eve."

"So? Come on." Getting to her feet with a small grunt, she reached down, yanking her daughter to her feet. "God, you're getting tall!" she exclaimed, noting that they were close to the same height.

"I still don't understand why we didn't do this weeks ago," Tamson muttered, following her mother toward the front door.

"Yeah, well we couldn't afford this weeks ago." She smirked. "Still can't, but what's Christmas without one?"

"This is all we got, lady," the Christmas tree lot clerk muttered, chewing on the stick of a long gone Dum Dum. He looked extremely tired and impatient.

"Hmm." Connie walked around the few trees that they'd been shown. "And how much did you say they were again?"

"Thirty-five fifty."

Connie chewed on her bottom lip, mentally tallying the money she had in her pocket. "Um, do you have any cheaper ones?"

"Nope." Visions of making one last sell began to fade fast. Looking at the girl, the man saw disappointment flash, plain as day. The Christmas spirit inching into his gold-lined heart, he sighed. "Hang on. Might have something over here."

Connie and Tamson followed the burly man

dressed in black and yellow plaid toward the back of the lot, near where his truck was parked. There, leaning against the rickety chain-link fence stood a tree, about four and a half feet tall, branches missing and filled with holes.

"This here was cut off the top of a tree that was too big for some guy's van. I'll give it to ya."

"Really?" Connie asked, excitement beginning to surge. She looked to Tamson, who looked at her with doubt. "We'll take it!"

"Mom, this tree is pathetic!" Tamson said, standing back from the thing, which barely stood straight in the green, plastic tree holder.

"Oh, come on, Tam. I know it's a Charlie Brown tree, but at least it has a home, right?"

"I guess." Still doubtful, she helped her mother bring out the smattering of decorations they had.

An hour later, Connie hit the lights and mother and daughter sat huddled on the loveseat, which was their only piece of furniture in the small living room. They watched the bright lights that winked at them from the scattered branches of their new tree. Tamson took a sip from her glass of eggnog. It was a rare treat during the holidays, as it was an expenditure they usually couldn't afford.

Connie put an arm around her daughter's shoulders. Hope filled her for the first time in far too long. She felt good about herself, and about where they were. Maybe things could work out this time. Placing a soft kiss to Tamson's temple, she sighed.

"Things are going to work out for us, baby. They really are."

Present Day

Green eyes blinked open, looking around. Tamson realized near complete darkness surrounded her, save for Sam's dash lights. There were voices all around her, loud and joyous. As sleep dissipated, she realized that the triplets and their parents were singing. Christmas songs? 'Frosty the Snowman'. She realized there was singing coming from beside her, too.

Erin's eyes glittered in the darkness as they met Tamson's horrified eyes.

"What?" she asked, joining in the chorus.

Shaking her head, Tamson stretched as best she could in the confines of the back seat of the van.

"Come on, Tam. Join us." Erin didn't wait for Tamson's reply, but went right into 'Silent Night, Holy Night'.

"You people are crazy," Tamson muttered, reaching into the bag Erin had been carrying and snagging a bottle of water.

"Tamson, honey, we got this while you were sleeping," Zea said. "Karen, hand this back to Tamson."

A bag of Wendy's drive-thru was handed to her. Near ravenous, Tamson smiled with profound gratitude and began to dig into the cheeseburger and fries. Erin handed her a biggie drink, the paper cup covered in condensation from sitting for the past thirty minutes. She muttered a "thanks" before taking a huge gulp.

As she ate, she listened to the joyous voices of those around her, unable to help the grin that kissed her lips from time to time as she chewed, even if she thought they were all awful singers. She chuckled to herself, sighing in contentment of a full belly. She threw her trash into the paper bag and scrunched it up and tucked it between her thigh and the side of the van.

Foot tapping with the beat of 'Deck the Halls', she began to hum along, looking out the tinted windows at the nearly midnight black scenery with only an occasional streetlight or random building breaking through the ink. Soon she began to whisper along, slowly getting louder, not even realizing it. Suddenly she was singing all by herself. Realization dawning, she whimpered off, looking around her. Zea and the girls were all looking back at her from the front of the minivan, Erin from her right.

"What?" she asked, feeling shy and small, literally trying to press herself into the corner of the seat.

"Honey, you've got talent!" Zea grinned.

"Yeah!" one of the girls added, "you're better than Mrs. Worth at school!"

Face turning pinker than her hair, she turned her full attention back to the outside.

༄༄༄༄

"Take care, honey." Zea hugged Tamson close, trying to be mindful of her many injuries. She didn't see the wince on Tamson's face as her ribs were pressed. Pulling back, she looked into what looked like was actually a lovely face without the bruising and cuts, and smiled, cupping her cheek. Tamson smiled back, though it was weak.

Erin allowed herself to be taken in a tight, motherly hug, and in fact, welcomed it.

"You take care of that girl, Erin," Zea said

into her ear. Looking into Erin's eyes, Zea looked so concerned. "She needs a friend right now."

"I'm trying." Erin smiled. She watched as Sam, Zea, and the girls climbed back into their van, headed to Zea's mother's house for an early Christmas celebration. She stood with Tamson, their stuff at their feet, in the lit parking lot of the truck stop just outside of Walsenburg. They waved as the van pulled back out onto the highway, disappearing from sight.

Chapter Fourteen

Erin gasped at the cold water, bringing up another handful. Blinking it out of her eyes, she looked into the spotted mirror above the sink. Running her wet fingers through her hair, she looked at her reflection. She looked tired, her face pale and worn out.

Grabbing a few paper towels from the dispenser, she dried her face and hands. There was a knock on the bathroom door.

"Someone's in here," she called out, tugging her brush from the bag she'd been lugging around all day.

"Come on, Erin. I got us a ride," Tamson called from the other side.

"Okay. Be there in a sec." One last look at herself as she brushed out tangles from the day then Erin gathered her stuff together and headed out.

Tamson waited next to a large, king-cab truck, whose engine was idling. The driver's bright blue baseball cap in the cab was the only thing Erin could make out of their savior, but she didn't care. At this point, she just wanted to get to the bus station in Alamosa and get back on the road, headed home.

Tamson climbed into the bed of the truck, taking the bag from Erin to stow up by the driver's massive toolbox, along with the stuff Erin had taken from her trunk. Erin grasped the top of the tailgate, hitching her foot to the bumper. Without warning, the truck lurched forward, nearly sending her back to the pavement on her backside.

Tamson lunged at Erin, grabbing her wrist with her good hand. Erin's eyes were huge as she struggled to climb into the bed, Tamson using her body weight to help pull her in.

They stumbled into the bed, Erin knocking her elbow against the wheel well. Giggling as they got situated, Erin grinned at Tamson who grinned back at her, both resting their backs against the toolbox. Erin was shocked to see Tamson lean towards her, pressing soft lips against hers for just a moment then the touch was gone. Their grins returned, Erin understood what Tamson was trying to say with that kiss: *thank you*.

With a small nod, her grin turned into a full out smile. She grabbed the blanket that had been pulled from her trunk and spread it out over them. The night was cold, and they had an hour and a half to go.

As Tamson settled in, shoulder to shoulder with Erin – trying to share their body heat – she felt a twinge of guilt gnaw at her stomach.

As Erin had been in the bathroom trying to clean herself up, she had called and met with Dave, Mike's contact in the area. She had hurried to the back of the diner with him, glancing over her shoulder, hoping to finish up the deal before Erin got back. She'd owe Mike money when she got back to town.

After her hit, she felt her body tingling, relief and guilt all mixed into one nice little bundle of energy. As the wind whipped her hair in every which direction, she turned to Erin, who was watching the road behind them, more and more ground covered. She knew Erin had called her closest brother, Joel, at the truck stop. She made arrangements with him to get her car and take it back to her apartment where she'd meet him after she took a bus back to Northglenn.

Turning her focus to the night sky above them, she smiled. "Look at that moon," Tamson murmured, staring up at the huge, full eye of Luna looking down at them.

"It's beautiful," Erin whispered, quiet for a moment then she turned to her friend. "What's your plan once you hit Fort Worth?"

Tamson shrugged. "I'm not sure. Call the cop, I guess."

"And not your grandmother?"

Tamson shook her head. "Why would I do that?"

"What did your mother tell you about her, Tam?" Erin pulled the blanket up a little tighter. The air was definitely getting colder and the smell of moisture was in the air.

"She said that she was a busy body, wanting nothing more than to tear my mom and me apart," she answered, shrugging her portion of the blanket away. She could feel sweat gathering under her armpits in her jacket, waves of heat flowing through her with affects of the drug zinging through her veins.

"Why would she want to split you two up?"

Tamson shrugged. "I guess 'cuz her son was dead, so she had this weird obsession with getting to me, you know, like the last little bit of him, or something. Weird, if you ask me."

"Hmm." Erin looked back out into the night, brows furrowing when she felt something land on her nose. Crossing her eyes, she saw the white flake fly off. Looking up into the sky, she felt more chilled brushes against her cheeks and forehead. *Oh boy.* "When did you see her last?"

"I think I was about five, maybe six. We met her at a McDonald's. She tried to make me get into her car when my mom went to the bathroom."

"She tried to kidnap you?!" Erin nearly barked. Tamson nodded. "Wow." Bringing up the blanket even more, Erin watched the flakes fall. She couldn't help the smile that slowly appeared. She loved snow.

"Kinda reminds me of *Star Wars*, you know where they go light speed, or whatever? The way the stars would fly at them."

"Yeah, you're right." Erin grinned at Tamson then stuck her tongue out, trying to catch any of the flakes that whirled around them, misplaced by the truck's speed and momentum.

"My mom was so pissed," Tamson continued. "She ran out of the restaurant, screaming, tugging on my arm through the car window as my grandmother pulled on my legs from the open door. It was out of hand."

"What's your mom like?"

Tamson sighed, trying to figure out how to answer. She wasn't sure which side of Connie Erin wanted to know about. "She could be fun. We had some good times. But then she could be irresponsible, impulsive." Tamson couldn't help but chuckle at the irony in that statement. "Guess you could say she was a lot like me."

"What does she look like?"

"Me with blonde hair. And big, fake boobs." Tamson looked down at herself, thinking of her much smaller bust. "Yeah, definitely not like me." She snickered and Erin smiled.

"I'll give you some of mine, if you want." Erin smiled at Tamson's chuckle. "Do you miss her?"

"Sometimes."

Not wanting to push her luck, Erin left it at that.

※ ※ ※ ※

"Take care, ladies," the driver of the truck said then tipped his cap and drove the big truck back out into the night.

Erin and Tamson made their way into the small, quiet bus station. Walking up to the service desk, a tired-looking clerk waited for them to decide what they wanted.

"The bus to Fort Worth leaves in two hours," Erin said, squinting to read the tiny writing on the board above the clerk's head. "And mine leaves in six hours."

"There's a Best Western just over that way," the clerk offered, hiking her thumb toward the back of the depot.

"Oh, okay. Uh, I guess a one way ticket to Fort Worth, and one for Denver." Erin slid her credit card across the counter as the clerk typed into her computer.

Tickets in hand, they headed over to the tiny lunch counter, surprised to see the ticket clerk wrapping an apron around her waist.

"Do you want anything?" Erin asked Tamson, who was looking around the depot, chewing on her bottom lip. "Who are you looking for?"

"Huh? Oh. Nobody. No. Not hungry." Tamson walked over to a magazine rack, absently flipping through the pages as her eyes continually scanned the terminal. She saw Erin walk over to a table with a cup of coffee and Danish in her hands. Tamson slid into the seat across from her.

"So what'cha going to do for six hours?" Tamson asked, picking a small piece of icing from the plate the Danish sat on.

"Sit here and be bored out of my mind," Erin said, sitting back in her chair, chewing the sticky snack. Sipping from her black coffee, she sighed, loving the bitter taste that swept through her sugar-coated mouth.

"Fun for the whole family!"

Erin smirked, nodding. "Yeah, but at least I only have a six hour bus ride."

"Yeah, yeah. But by time you get on your bus, I'll only have twelve hours left."

"This is true." Erin ate more of the Danish.

"So what's the craziest thing you've ever done, Erin?"

"Hmm." Erin thought about it, trying to send her mind back through the years to hit on something, *any*thing. "Oh! I remember." She chuckled lightly at the memory. "When I was in seventh grade, I spent the night at this girl's house; she lived down the road from me. It was her birthday and there were a lot of us there. One girl got the idea to go out and egg and teepee houses." She giggled like the little girl she once was. "Anyway, so we all go out there, rolls of toilet paper tucked into sweatshirts, jackets, whatever. My friend, whose house we were at, didn't even know. She was still sound asleep. Me and another girl stood out front on the lawn to make sure she or her mom didn't wake up. God, I was so *scared*."

Tamson looked at her, blinking. "*That's* the craziest thing you've ever done? Like, *ever*?"

"Hey, I got my ass busted for that. I had to go

to each and every house they hit, tell the owners that *I* had done it and ask if there was anything I could do. Plus I was grounded for two months on top of that. It was so humiliating." Erin turned back to her food.

"Jesus," Tamson muttered, stealing another glob of icing. "I knew you were a nun, but didn't know you were a saint, too."

Erin glared up at her. "I'm no saint, or a nun. I'm just," she searched for the word, "careful."

"Tomato, tamato."

"Cute. Here." Finished with the Danish, which was way too sweet, she shoved the plate across the small table to Tamson, who immediately tucked into it. Sitting back in the chair, Erin sipped from her coffee, watching her friend eat and lick icing from sticky fingers. "Were you and your mom close?"

Tamson met Erin's gaze through pink bangs. She shrugged. "When I was little. As I got older, I got sick of—" Tamson looked down at the food, which was almost gone.

"Sick of what?"

"Nothing." Tamson stuffed her mouth full of a bite of Danish she didn't really want, but it kept her from having to answer. Somehow, she felt like she wasn't being loyal.

"Tam," Erin said softly, reaching over to touch her friend's hand lightly. Tamson's eyes met her own briefly.

Sitting back in her chair, Tamson pushed the plate away, suddenly losing her desire for the icing chunks that had fallen to the plate. "I got sick of picking up the pieces."

Erin studied her closely. Though Tamson tried to hide it, she could see the turmoil swirling in her eyes – a tempest of emotion and memory.

"I'm so sorry, Tamson."

Tamson pulled her hand away, pushing back from her chair and walking over to a window, hugging herself.

Pushing her own chair back, Erin walked over to her, standing slightly behind. Placing a tentative hand on a hunched shoulder, Erin sighed. "She really hurt you, didn't she?"

Tamson shrugged. "That's life, Erin. The real world, not your sheltered, Beaver Cleaver house. Welcome," she snapped, turning away from Erin.

Erin tried not to take the remark to heart. She knew a woman, possibly dead, and at the very least, gone, hurt Tamson. There was so much about this woman that Erin didn't understand, and probably never would. Her heart broke for Tamson. Underneath the hard life and exterior, Erin could see there was a beautiful soul, a little girl crying for her mother, who just couldn't be there.

"Tamson, I didn't do this to you. Please don't take it out on me," she said, her voice soft.

Tamson's face was the epitome of a woman warring with her thoughts. She had so much anger inside, like a layer of lava just under the surface; one tiny cut and she would erupt. Erin hadn't even seen the tip of the iceberg. She had no idea what kind of anger Tamson was capable of. She'd been taking it out on herself her entire life.

They watched in silence as a bus pulled into the terminal, unloading a dozen weary passengers who hit the lunch counter and bathrooms, a few heading to the payphones or smoking a cigarette outside.

"I'm going to go sit down," Erin said quietly,

hurrying back to their table where all her current-worldly goods sat.

Tamson stayed at the window, watching as two more disembarked from the Greyhound. A young woman – maybe early twenties – held the hand of a tiny girl, three years old at the most. The child looked tired, her eyes big in a small, round face, red-rimmed and lined with too many worries for such a young one. The woman holding her hand had telltale signs in her gaunt cheeks and tracks that chugged up her arms.

Tamson suddenly felt angry, *really* angry. *How can you do that to that child? Don't you see you're ruining her life!?* She met the little girl's gaze, sad eyes of the young looking into those of the wise. The girl raised a tiny hand, matched by Tamson's palm on the glass.

As the bus pulled out, Tamson and Erin were alone once more. Erin had bought a notepad in the gift store and was contentedly writing away, ideas flowing from her pen almost too quickly for her to capture them legibly.

"Writing your last will and testament?" Tamson snickered, leaning against the table. Erin didn't even bother to look up at her.

"Uh, yeah, no."

Tamson grinned, watching the pen fly across the lined paper, trying to follow along but it was almost making her dizzy so she gave up. "Bus will be here soon."

Erin glanced at her watch, shocked to see that indeed, Tamson's bus should be arriving within twenty minutes. Finishing the paragraph she was working on, she set her pen down and looked up at her friend.

"How do you feel about that?"

Tamson shrugged as she sat down again, taking the discarded pen between her fingers and rolling it around. "Gotta do it."

"Is there anything you need me to do once I get back to Denver? Anyone I need to call, or grab anything from your place?"

"Nah. I'm sure Tanner has destroyed everything already."

"Is Tanner your boyfriend?"

"Kind of," Tamson hedged.

"But, he *is* the one who did this to you," she clarified, pointing to Tamson's injuries. "How are you feeling, by the way?"

"They'll heal, and yes."

"How about while you're in Texas I go over there and kick his ass for you?" Erin growled, followed by a sweet, disarming smile.

Tamson chuckled. "Yeah, you do that. I'll glue you back together again."

They sat in silence, both realizing this was it, the end of their journey together and just the beginning of Tamson's. The roar of a huge engine and flash of headlights drew their attention across the room, followed by the loud *whoosh* of air brakes.

"Guess this is it," Tamson murmured. She was surprised at the sadness she felt, new sadness, not laced with time. Standing, she stretched her back, wincing as her torso disagreed with the move.

Erin swallowed and took a deep breath. She walked over to her friend, smiling bravely. "Yeah. Guess it is." The shimmer of unshed emotion was in the corners of her eyes.

A voice began to boom from the public address system, announcing the arrival of Tamson's bus.

"Well, um, it's been fun." Tamson smiled, though it was weak. Before she knew what was happening, she found herself tucked into a warm embrace. Her first instinct was to pull away, but instead allowed herself to sink into it, the warmth enveloping her and helping to melt away some of her fears for what lie ahead.

Erin released her, giving her a smile. Putting something into Tamson's hand, Erin closed cool, pale fingers around the slip of paper. "If you need anything, you call me. Okay?"

Tamson nodded. "Okay."

"Please take care of yourself, Tam," Erin begged, her stomach roiling with dread. Tamson nodded again. "Okay. Let me know what happens."

"I will." With a final smile, Tamson tucked Erin's number into her pocket then headed for her gate.

Erin watched, stuffing her hands into the back pockets of her jeans so they'd stop shaking. She was afraid for Tamson and felt on some level like she was abandoning her, which was ridiculous. Tamson was a grown woman, and had known more life than Erin could even imagine or create in one of her stories.

As Tamson disappeared through the silver door of the bus, Erin turned away, headed back to her table. Standing there, looking down at her messenger bag, folded blanket, tool and First Aid kits, her mind began to wander, then race, then scream.

1995 – Pueblo, CO

The six-year-old Erin tore up the stairs, a door slamming in the distance. Erin's mother stood at the open front door, the new neighbor girl looking up at her with big, shocked eyes.

"I'm sorry, honey. I guess Erinbeth doesn't want to play today and make new friends. Why don't you come back tomorrow?"

1995 - Pueblo, CO

"Honey, you've got the highest grade in your class," Bill Riggs said, trying to convince his daughter. "You should be so proud that you were invited to participate."

"Yeah, Erin. You'll kick butt in the spelling bee," Charlie agreed, glancing at his sister across the dinner table from him. The girl remained quiet, pushing her food around her plate.

"Listen, honey," Janice, Erin's mother said, voice soft. She covered her youngest child's hand with hers. "You'll do wonderfully. We'll all come to watch, and win or lose, which I know you'll win, we'll all cheer you on, and then we can go out for dinner at the Dew Drop for some good pizza. What do you say?" She smiled, big and bright.

Erin chewed on her lower lip, watching the pretty pattern the mashed potatoes made in the gravy. She wasn't sure. "I'll look stupid." She pouted.

"No you won't!" the entire table said at once. She grinned her great big, missing tooth grin.

"It'll be cool!" Joel gushed, getting enthusiastic nods from his brothers and family.

⁂

Erin looked at herself in the mirror attached to her closet door. The new white dress was pretty with lots of ribbons and new shoes. Her mom had surprised her with it for the spelling bee. She was nervous, her stomach hurt, and she felt sick. She didn't want to do this. She'd fail, she just knew it.

"Erinbeth, honey, are you ready?" her mother called from the other side of her bedroom door.

Erin looked at her reflection, her hair brushed to a shine, framing what some called a pretty face, though she didn't buy it. Her big, blue eyes looked herself over, doubt creeping in around the edges, taunting her with laughter if she messed up during the spelling bee. Her confidence shattered, she ran to her bed, flopping on her stomach and hiding her face with her arms.

A moment later, there was a knock on her bedroom door. "Erin! Come on, honey," her mother's muffled voice said from the other side.

Erin lifted her head just long enough to yell, "I'm not going!"

The door opened and her mother stepped into the room. "Erin, now you get downstairs –" She cut herself off when she saw Erin on the bed. "Honey? What is it?" Hurrying over to Erin's bed, she sat on the edge, rubbing the crying girl's back.

"I don't wanna do this, Mommy," she sobbed.

Taken aback, Janice looked over at her husband, who stood in the opened doorway, brows drawn. He shrugged.

"Erinbeth, honey, why not? You can do this. You're so good at spelling. You always get the highest grades on all your spelling tests. Mrs. Reynolds believes in you, sweetie. And Daddy got the night off from work just so he could go watch you."

Swiping at red, swollen eyes, Erin rolled over and looked up into her mother's concerned eyes. "Do you really think I can do it?"

"Of course I do." Janice wiped some tear-wet strands of hair from her daughter's red face.

❦❦❦❦

"Erin Riggs, please step forward."

The fourth grader took her place at the microphone. Somewhere in the darkened auditorium, she could hear her family cheering her on.

"Your word, Erin, is restaurant, restaurant."

Erin could feel her palms sweating, her fingers closing into a slimy fist. She hated that word. Clearing her throat, she tried to think, tried to clear her mind of everything except that one word. She always had a hard time with it.

"Restaurant." She cleared her throat. "R, E, S, T."

Janice sat in the audience, mouthing each letter as Erin spoke it, holding her hands together. She knew how badly her little girl needed this. It was the first round. *Please Lord, let her get this.*

"Um, rest," Erin muttered to herself, trying to focus, "A," she wiped her palms on her dress, then remembered it was new so clasped them in front of her. "R, A, N, T. Restaurant."

Janice's eyes slid closed, her heart breaking for her youngest child and only daughter.

"That is incorrect."

Erin sat in the window seat in her room, legs drawn up with arms wrapped around them. She refused to eat the pizza she so loved, ashamed and angry at herself. How could she miss such a stupid word? And in the first round?! The next day at school, she'd have to watch Kirsten Hentch walk around all proud and snotty with her first place ribbon.

The tears fell.

1982 – Pueblo, CO

Erin felt stiff and exposed. Standing by the back wall of the gym, she and her best friend, Robin, watched their fellow Pleasant View Middle School students talk and laugh, and a few of the braver souls, dance.

Catching movement out of the corner of her eye, Erin looked, breath catching when she saw Kiern Radford walking toward them. He looked *so* cute in gray slacks, white button up shirt and black tie. He was an eighth grader and cutest boy in the entire world.

"Hey, Erin," he said, the metal of his braces glinting of the swarm of lights dancing off the gym walls.

"Uh, hi." She wanted to die where she stood!

"Would you like to dance?"

Erin's eyes grew as wide as her dad's beloved fifty-cent pieces. Her mouth went dry, palms sweaty and feet fidgeting. He looked at her expectantly. She felt a soft nudge from beside her. Turning to Robin, she saw the girl nodding toward the dance floor with insistent eyes.

"It's okay if you don't want to." Kiern smiled, then turned and walked away.

"Wait," Erin whispered. Too late, he had disappeared into the throng of kids.

2004 – Pueblo, CO

Erin looked at the form in her hands, leaning against her car in the parking lot of Pueblo County High School. Her English teacher, Mr. Romero had given it to her. A competition. A *writing* competition.

Mr. Romero's words came back to her.

"Erin, I really think you can do this. You've got a wonderful imagination and seem to grasp the human emotion wonderfully. I really think you've got a heck of a shot at this. Here's the entrance form. Fill it out and bring it back to me Monday. The worst that can happen is they say no. The best that can happen is you win yourself a full scholarship."

Reading the form for the sixth time, Erin sighed, crushing it up in her fist and tossing it into the backseat of her car.

Present Day

Erin glanced over her shoulder, hearing the idling rumble of the Greyhound bus.

Tamson found herself a seat at the back of the bus, her favorite place. Placing her jacket in the aisle seat next to her to stop unwanted guests, she rested her head against the cool, tinted glass, waiting for the last leg of her trip to begin. She could feel the vibration of the bus' massive engine under her feet, the cool, fake air circulating through the coach and the smell of sterilizing cleaners mixed with human inhabitation.

The bus was about three-fourths full, Alamosa just another stop on a continuous route. People were getting themselves settled, talking quietly amongst themselves or getting in as comfortable a sleeping position as the claustrophobic seats would allow.

Fellow riders' feet shuffled along the narrow, ribbed walkway of the bus, someone plopping down in the seat in front of her, their sudden weight bouncing the back of the seat back into Tamson's personal space. Her irritation was interrupted when she felt a presence, someone standing near her.

"Is this seat taken?"

Glancing up, Tamson's eyes widened in shock as she saw Erin grinning down at her.

Chapter Fifteen

"What are you doing?" Tamson asked as Erin slid her bag into the overhead compartment.

Erin sat next to her, a goofy grin on her face. "I realized I was going to be getting on the wrong bus."

"Um, I'm thinking you're on the wrong bus, now."

Erin's grin turned into a peaceful smile as she rested her head against the back of the seat, nothing more forthcoming.

Tamson settled back in, a smile of her own brushing her lips. She figured, let the crazy chick do what she wanted – it was her dime. Though she'd never admit it to Erin, she was more than glad to see her.

Erin could feel fingers of doubt and fear walk their way up her spine. This was crazy, nuts, and completely irresponsible. *What about your job? You start it in less than twenty-four hours! What about meeting Joel and Charlie at the apartment with your car? What about—*

Erin shut her eyes, blocking out the voices of reason. She had to do this. There was no way she'd ever forgive herself for not seeing it through to the end for Tamson. Tamson needed someone in her corner, her own personal cheering squad. How can something so damn crazy feel so good? So right?

As good as it felt, she was exhausted. Within

moments, she was sound asleep.

Tamson noticed her friend nod off and she also noticed the notepad Erin had been feverishly writing in, resting on her lap. Watching Erin's face to make sure she didn't wake, she slowly slid the pad out from under limp hands. Giving her one more look, Tamson turned to the pad, her curiosity getting the best of her.

It was strange to read, and didn't make a whole lot of sense. This was obviously something that Erin had continued on paper. Probably what she'd been working on at home before they left. Even so, the writing was good, more than good. Erin made it possible to disappear into her written world, lose all sense of time and reality.

All too soon, the story had come to an end, Erin only having time to scribble out less than ten pages. Sighing happily – and yearning to know more – Tamson laid the pad in her lap, staring out the window, knowing that the scenery was racing by, though the thick, inky blackness cloaked their progress.

Sighing as she rested her head against the backrest, she noted a few scattered overhead lights that blazed down on passengers, allowing them to read. She also heard the tap, tap, tapping of fingers on laptop keys. Such a strange sound when disembodied.

In the lonely darkness of the bus, Tamson allowed her mind to wander to places she'd been avoiding for years. She thought back to the nine months she and her mother had spent in Utah. It had been the happiest of her childhood. They had gotten so close, forming a bond that Tamson had truly thought was unbreakable. How wrong she'd been.

Spring 2001 - Salt Lake City, UT

Tamson jumped up, whacking the newly green leaves on the cotton tree as she whistled her way down the sidewalk, backpack bouncing on her back as she landed. Satisfied that she'd gotten a good, solid hit, she continued on.

It had been a good day. Her choir teacher had given her a huge compliment and she had gotten an A on her history assignment. First time that had happened since the second grade. She'd never been very good in history. Too much to remember.

Tamson's steps faltered as she got closer to the tiny house they were renting. A car was in the driveway and it looked familiar. The house was quiet for the most part, only the soft murmurings of conversation from the kitchen.

Setting her backpack on the couch, she slowly made her way to the small room, the smell of fresh coffee in the air.

"Listen, Connie, I'm talking like three weeks. That's it."

"I can't, Dale. Please don't ask that of me. I'm making a life for me and Tamson. I don't need this shit anymore."

"I've gotten away from all that, Con. You gotta believe me," he pleaded.

Tamson peeked around the corner. She could see the back off Dale's dark head, partially covered by his usual dirty, straw cowboy hat. A pack of Camels was tucked into the old, leather band.

"Baby," he was saying, "you an' me is so good together." He reached for her hand, but Connie pulled it away, standing. It was then that she saw her daughter.

"Hey, baby. How was school?"

Figuring that was her cue, Tamson entered the small room, ignoring Dale, whose eyes she felt on her, and headed to the fridge. Shrugging, she didn't respond. All her good news didn't seem to matter anymore.

"Don't fill up, Tam. I've got dinner started," Connie warned, eyeing Dale at her hint to him.

"Aw, baby. I was thinking we could go out an' eat. The kid can stay home and eat her dinner like a big girl," he said, glaring over at Tamson who glared back.

"Dale!" Connie warned, turning on him. "You barged in on our life. Stay out."

Without a word, Dale pushed up from the table and went out to the living room, the sound of the TV blaring a moment later.

Once Dale was gone, Tamson turned to her mother. "What is he doing here?" she hissed.

"He just showed up this afternoon." Connie sighed, a hand running through her hair.

"Mom!"

"I know, Tam. I'm working on it." Connie glanced up to make sure Dale wasn't listening. "He needs a place to stay for the night then he'll be on his way in the morning."

"Promise?"

"Promise." Connie smiled, giving her daughter a quick hug, then, "Come on. Help me finish dinner."

Present Day

Tamson sighed heavily, looking down at the page torn from Erin's pad. She had begun to write, just randomly, whatever was on her brain. It was almost as though she were under a spell. She began to write of her disappointment of getting home the next day, and not only finding Dale's car still parked in the driveway, but also to hear raucous laughter bursting from the open front window. She'd sat on the front porch for almost two hours, crying tears of dread.

It had been the beginning of the end. Connie hadn't been able to stay strong, and Dale had convinced her that he knew of a great job for her and that they should pack up and move with him to Dallas.

Tucking the end of the pen between her teeth, Tamson thought about the profound disappointment she'd felt as they'd packed up the U-Haul. She could tell her mother knew it was wrong, and was riddled with guilt. She refused to look into her daughter's accusing eyes. Everything she said was lilting, light, and fluffy. No room for explanation or self-recrimination. The moment they'd gotten to Dallas, Tamson had decided she was going to make her mother pay for every single mistake she'd ever made, and for ruining her daughter's life. Sadly, the logic of a hurt teenager had ruined everything.

2001 – Dallas, TX

Everyone laughed even harder as Mitchell snorted. The normally shy teen was too buzzed to be embarrassed. Tamson was handed the bottle of tequila, and with a flourish, she downed the liquid fire, her entire body shivering violently for a moment as it burned down her throat and landed in a roaring lump in her stomach.

Ande finished off the bottle then threw it, the

glass shattering against the garbage bin on the side of the building. This sent another wave of laughter through the otherwise still, summer afternoon.

The sight of Mr. Stanley looming in the mouth of the alleyway behind his small grocery store suddenly cut off the laughter. His dark, beady eyes landed on a very inebriated Tamson.

"Tamson," he growled.

Tamson managed to get to her feet, her fear warring with the good times rolling inside her. She stumbled over her friend, Mitchell's, leg. She tried to keep her snicker in but it fell out with all reason and common sense. Once in the privacy of the storeroom, where Tamson had been stacking incoming boxes of oranges, Mr. Stanley pinned the girl with a hard look.

"Real sorry, Mr. Stanley," she slurred, wavering on her feet.

His round face was red, the ends of his mustache actually twitching. "Me, too. I did you a favor, kid, gave you a job. Knew there was a reason I don't hire no kids. You fucked up and you fucked up bad." His voice rose with every word. "Now get out!" His pudgy finger pointed to the loading dock and beyond.

"What the fuck were you thinking?" SLAP. "You got that job to help out." SLAP, SLAP, SLAP.

"Dale! Stop it! Stop it!" Connie cried.

Panting, the man turned away, jaw muscles bulging in rhythm with his heartbeat. Tamson cowered in the corner, suddenly very sober. Her eyes were huge, the coppery taste of blood swirling around in her mouth. She spit it on the floor, glaring at her mother.

Connie was stunned by the events of the past hour- her fourteen year old daughter stumbling in, drunker than a skunk, muttering something about being fired, then Dale's whirlwind reaction and temper that followed. Now, her daughter, just picking herself off the kitchen floor, had spat a mouthful of saliva-pinkened blood on the floor and was now making her way toward her bedroom.

Shaking herself from her stupor, she stormed into the living room where Dale was watching the game, can of Budweiser in hand. She dreaded this, as he had become... difficult... when he was drinking a little too much beer.

"What did you think you were doing?" she asked, standing next to the recliner, faux leather and covered in the smell of stale cigarettes. Dale didn't bother to look up at his live-in.

"She did something stupid. She needs to be punished," he said simply, as though that explained it all.

"Isn't that my job to do?" Connie tried to keep her voice quiet, unexcitable. Best to keep his temper in check. Leaving him be, she went to her daughter's room, the door closed with finality.

"I hate her, Penny," Tamson whispered, rocking back and forth, arms wrapped around drawn knees. "I fucking hate her. *And* him." The girl felt a strange sort of comfort as she spoke to her guardian angel. "We gotta get out of here, Penny." Her voice broke as tears sprang to her words. "I gotta get out." There was a knock on the door. "Leave me alone!"

"Tam—"

"Fuck off!"

Connie stood there, stunned, hand frozen halfway to the doorknob. Where had she gone so wrong? Over the last few months, Tamson had been lashing out at her like she never had before. Her beautiful, sweet-mannered daughter had turned hard, was getting into more and more trouble, and more than once since Easter she had been missing money, and Dale had said the same thing.

Worry mixed with anger, Connie pushed open the cheap door. She was glad there weren't any locks. Her daughter, a petit redhead who was growing up so fast and was maturing into a beautiful young woman, was curled up on the floor, slowly rocking back and forth.

"Get out!" Tamson screamed. "Go fuck your boyfriend or let him beat *you* up while I catch my breath."

Connie was struck dumb, Tamson's words striking a resonating cord deep within her. Years of guilt and doubt erupted in anger. "Don't you dare talk to me that way," she hissed, taking a threatening step toward the girl who was getting to her feet.

"Why not?" Tamson wiped her mouth with her fingers, a trail of blood staining the skin red. She raised it like a badge. "Don't like to see the truth? Who are *you* to tell me *any*thing?"

Connie couldn't say anything, her head beginning to pound, feeling as though it were ready to explode. Her lips trembled with unbridled rage, hands curling into fists at her side. Breathing hard through her nose, she stormed out of the room.

Present Day

Two months later, Tamson stopped coming home after school, when she went. She stayed with friends, her soon-to-be first boyfriend, Mitchell, or in the park. From the time she moved out, she didn't see her mother for months at a time, flat refusing to go anywhere where Dale was.

Tamson looked down at the paper she'd filled with tiny handwriting, trying to cram as much as she could on the single page, front and back.

Glancing at a still-sleeping Erin's watch, she was surprised to see that the sun would be making its entrance soon. She looked out the window that her left shoulder rested against and could just barely see a line of gold easing up from the dark horizon, a few sparkles reflecting in the heavy clouds. She looked up into the sky, marveling at the colors that were quickly spreading, fingers of orange and pink reaching into the new day. It was truly a wonder.

❧❧❧❧

"God, I'm ravenous," Erin mumbled as she bit into her egg McMuffin with sausage. Her hash brown had been gobbled down seconds ago, her large coke a third gone.

Tamson sat across from her friend, amused. Erin had slept right through their first stop early in the morning, and now in Vernon – just about three hours outside Fort Worth – she was finally up and raring to go.

"So when's the last time you were in Texas?" she asked, wiping her hands on one of the small, thin napkins the joint offered.

Tamson pretended to look at a non-existent wristwatch. "About twelve hours ago."

Erin chuckled, sipping from her drink. "Are you glad to be home?"

Tamson sighed, sitting back in her chair. She played with the paper cup that had held her Orange Crush, but now was just filled with orange-tinted ice cubes. She grabbed one, tossing it into her mouth. One thing she hated about candy was that she was always dehydrated. She suddenly remembered that there was a question on the table. Biting down onto the cube, she shook her head. "Not really."

"Tam?"

Tamson looked up at her friend, a little nervous by Erin's very serious tone. "Yes?"

"Can I ask you something?"

Sighing, Tamson popped another piece of ice into her mouth, nodding as she sucked any remaining orange sweetness out of it. She knew she wasn't going to like the question.

"What kind of hold does Tanner have on you? Why won't you go to the police about what he's done to you?"

Oh boy. Tamson hadn't been expecting that. She figured the Tanner topic had been effectively dropped. Looking into her cup, as though it held all the answers to life, she sighed heavily. Maybe it was time.

"A few years ago, he saw me do something... bad."

"And he's holding it over your head?" At Tamson's nod, Erin began to understand. "What did you do?"

Tamson's first instinct was to tell Erin to mind her own business and to fuck off. But, looking into blue eyes filled with nothing but compassion and genuine interest, she couldn't do it. Though at the same time, she couldn't afford to be completely forthcoming, either. "I... hurt someone, I guess."

"You guess?"

Tamson nodded, poking her straw in between the melting cubes. She looked like a twelve-year-old girl, slumped in her seat, her expression decidedly petulant. Her eyes were sight unseen, staring back three years ago to a different time and place. Confusion, blackness, and chaos, the soundtrack of her life. Blinking rapidly to moisten them, she saw Erin's concerned face for the first time in a few moments.

"I was pretty messed up. I don't remember doing it. I just." She shook her head again, seeing herself being pulled up from the floor. "Don't remember," she whispered. She spared a glance at Erin to see that she was staring at her, brows knit in thought. "What?"

"I'm looking at you right now, and you look so confused about this. Are you sure you were there? Are you sure *you* did it?" she asked gently.

Tamson's gaze fell back to her cup. "I think so." But even to Tamson's ears, it didn't sound right. She hadn't given that night a great deal of thought, hadn't wanted to. As messed up as she'd been, she'd never forget the sight of Josh's body laying there, a bloody mess where his face had once been. She still had nightmares about it on occasion.

"Hey, the bus is reloading," someone said from near the bathrooms.

Tamson glanced up, and sure enough, people were beginning to re-embark. "Come on." Standing, she helped to gather their trash, tossing it in a nearby trashcan.

As Erin climbed into the seat after Tamson, she couldn't help but wonder just exactly what had happened. What had she done? Or at least, perhaps witnessed? She had no idea, but couldn't help but think of the worst case scenario. Was that why Tamson hadn't allowed herself to be taken to a hospital? What or who was she afraid of?

Chapter Sixteen

Erin's brows knit. Lifting the page again, she saw that, yes indeed, there was the remnants of a page that had been ripped out. Glancing at Tamson, she saw a sheepish grin.

"Sorry. I needed a piece of paper."

Erin chuckled. "Need any more?"

At the shake of Tamson's pink head, she turned back to her writing. It was tough to write on the bumpy bus, so eventually she gave up. Tucking the pad back into her messenger bag, she turned to Tamson again, who was looking out at the new day.

"Would you let me dye your hair?"

Tamson's head whipped around, eyes huge. "What?"

Chuckling, Erin raised a hand, fingers touching the frazzled ends of pink. "You need a trim, too. I think you've abused your hair a little too much."

"Thanks, Obi-Wan of the shears," she muttered.

"Seriously! I bet you're a real knockout with your natural color of hair. You've got great features, and some of the most beautiful eyes I've ever seen."

Ego efficiently soothed, Tamson looked away, a bit embarrassed. She hadn't heard that kind of praise in… ever.

"Would you? Let me?"

Knowing damn well she would, Tamson shrugged. "Maybe."

The last three-hour leg of the trip went far too quick, as far as Tamson was concerned. She still had no plan, no idea how she was going to handle this business of her mother's disappearance, or what to do with her stuff. And then there was her grandmother.

The bus pulled into the large terminal, coming to a squeaky stop. Passengers gathered all of their belongings, those in the back of the bus waiting patiently for those further ahead to get a move on. At the tail end of the processions, Erin and Tamson joined in.

Stepping out into the bright, warm Texas sun, they looked at each other, not sure where to go from here.

"I guess I should call that cop," Tamson finally said. Erin followed obediently behind as they headed inside the bus station. There was a bank of payphones along the back wall. Tamson was going to use Erin's cell phone, but sans charger, Erin didn't want to chance the battery dying on her while so far from home. Besides, she needed to call her brother.

"Hey, Tam, I need to make a call of my own. I'll meet you back outside, front of the building, okay?"

With a nod, Tamson headed across the busy lobby to the phones and Erin headed out into the sunlight.

Setting her bag on a planter, she dug her phone out, turning it on. Thrilled to have signal again, the bile in her throat that was quickly rising quickly overpowered her joy. She found Nancy Pierce's business card, where she remembered her perhaps ex-future boss had scribbled a cell number.

The phone rang twice then was answered. "Nancy Pierce."

"Hi, Nancy. This is Erin Riggs," Erin said nervously.

"Yes, Erin. How are you on this crappy day? Can you believe the snow we got last night?"

"Oh, uh, well, I hadn't realized we had."

"What? Look out your damn window!"

Erin chuckled. "I'm in Texas, Nancy." Her stomach flipped at the sudden silence.

"What on God's green earth could make you go there?"

"Listen, Nancy, I understand if you let me go. I have a friend who needed me. Her mother has disappeared, been gone for several months, I guess. She really needs a friend through this. It was very late notice; we just got here on the bus, actually. I'm standing outside the bus station as we speak," Erin said, looking up at the sign on the building, as though Nancy would see through her eyes and believe her.

"I see," Nancy said, her voice quiet and unreadable. "Tell me what's going on."

"Well, Tamson got a call from a detective down here. All of her mother's stuff is with a relative and Tam needs to pick it up, sort through it, help out in any way she can."

"Oh, dear," the lawyer said, concern clearly in her voice.

Erin waited, her heart pounding in her chest and throat. She wanted to throw up.

"How long do you think you'll be gone?" Nancy asked at length.

"I don't know. I'm going to make a wild guesstimate of a few days."

"Well, I'll tell you what. My gut tells me you're good people, so I'll keep the temp on for another week, even if she is completely inept at everything except how to spell her name. You've got until Monday, a week from tomorrow. Your butt best be here at eight in the morning or not at all. Got me?"

"Oh, Nancy!" Erin gushed, hand to her chest. She truly had expected to be told nicely to go fly a kite. "Thank you! Oh my gosh, yes. Okay. I'll be there."

"Okay. The best of luck to your friend. If she needs any legal help, you let me know."

"Yes, I will. Thank you, thank you."

"Have a good one, Erin," Nancy said, a smile heard in her voice.

Erin was almost giddy as she replaced her phone, certainly filled with gratitude. She still had a job! Sitting on the planter, she waited for Tamson to finish. Her heel tapped a staccato beat on the cement as she leaned back on her hands. Throwing her head back, she could feel the soft wisps of her hair brushing against her arms. What she wouldn't do for a nice, long hot shower.

"Hey."

Erin turned to see Tamson walking up to her, hands buried in the pockets of the jeans that she swam in. Erin tugged on the oversized waistband. "We need to fatten you up." She chuckled at the rolled eyes she got. "So what's up?"

"That detective guy is going to send a car for us then take us to the police station."

"Jeesh. You're in town for five whole minutes and already in trouble," Erin joked. The look on Tamson's face told her she didn't think it was very funny.

The Fort Worth Police Department was the same as any other PD Tamson had ever seen. And she'd seen a lot of them. Officer Billings, who had picked them up from the bus station, led them to a small waiting room, offering coffee, soda, or anything else they may want.

Sitting at the heavily scarred wooden table, Erin tapped her fingernails on it, looking around. The walls were painted a boring beige color, only broken by the large two-way mirror planted in the far wall. She tried to see through it to the other side, barely able to make out the light coming in from an open door. Turning to Tamson, she saw she was nervous, arms crossed tightly over her chest and pacing the short length of the room.

Before long, the door was opened and a tall, solidly built man stepped into the room. His white dress shirt was wrinkled, black and gray striped tie loosened.

"Welcome, ladies," he said with a smile. "Which one of y'all is Tamson Robard?"

Tamson took her seat next to Erin. "That would be me."

The man also sat down. "Nice to meet you. I'm Detective Franklin, and I thank you for coming." He set a notebook and pen – as well as recorder – on the table and got settled across from them. "Now, just so you know, your grandma knows you're here."

Tamson felt her stomach flip flop at that bit of information, but said nothing.

"Now," he continued, about to hit the record button on the recorder. "Mind if I record this, Mizz Robard?" he asked, Texas accent coming through. At her consent, he hit the button and clicked his pen into life. "Would you mind answering some questions for me, Mizz Robard?"

"No. I don't mind at all."

"Okay. Great." He turned to Erin. "Would you mind leavin' us, darlin'?"

"Yeah, I do. I'm not going anywhere." Erin looked the detective in the eye, determined to hold her ground. She hadn't come all this way, risking her job, to leave now.

Cal Franklin looked at the equally determined face of Tamson Robard, and nodded, conceding. "All right then, ladies. Shall we get down to it?"

Erin sat back in her chair, watching the detective do much the same, his tape recorder spinning silently at the center of the table. Tamson spoke in a quiet, monotone voice, the basic facts, spelled out in easy to follow memories. She spoke of violence, drinking to the extreme, introduction of a swinger lifestyle that Connie never agreed with, and the threats. Many, many threats.

"So you're sayin' Dale threatened your mom?" Franklin asked, pen poised above the page, which was already half-filled with notes.

"All the time," she said with a nod.

"What types of threats?"

"He used to tell her he'd hack her up and make great barbeque, then laugh it off."

"And how would your mother react to this?"

Tamson shrugged. "At first she'd laugh it off, too. But later on," she shrugged again. "Not so much."

Erin listened as the questions went on and on, Tamson's voice never changing pitch, never faltering. She sat rigid, arms still hugging herself tightly. The cup of coffee the detective eventually sent for was still sitting, cold and untouched. Much like Tamson, herself.

"Well," Detective Franklin said, slapping his hands on his thighs. "We're done, ladies." Standing, he turned his attention back to Tamson. "I'll keep in touch with you. If we find your momma, we'll let y'all know."

Left alone in the small room, Erin watched Tamson, unsure what to say. A curtain of faded pink hair covered her face, shoulders slumped.

"Are you okay?" Erin asked softly, reaching out to rest her hand on Tamson's arm. The curtain of hair bobbed as Tamson nodded.

"Tamson?" Both women looked up to see a female officer poke her head in. "Your grandmother is here."

Tamson nodded again, swallowing visibly. She felt the butterflies batting around her ribcage, and wanted to throw up. Finally pushing to her feet, she felt Erin close behind, which helped to dissipate some of the stress.

About to step out of the interrogation room, she stopped, Erin nearly plowing into her. Glancing briefly over her shoulder, she mumbled, "I'm glad you're here." She didn't wait for a response as she hurried out into the hall.

The lights overhead made strategic dim patches on the neatly cropped carpet for a more dramatic effect. The walls were dotted with doors, some closed and others open, phones ringing and voices, some distant while others were loud blurs of sound as they were passed. Finally, the hall broke out into a heavy door that opened up to the lobby of the police station.

A row of chairs lined one wall, a few occupied.

An older woman who was slowly rising to her feet caught Erin's gaze. Grey streaked her deep red hair. Though the skin of her face and hands may have been wrinkled and freckled with age spots, her green eyes told a very different story.

Charlotte Robard walked slowly toward them, her hands rising as she reached Tamson, who stood still, unsure what to think or say. She had no memories of this woman, other than those planted inside her heart by her mother. By rights of loyalty, she should feel hatred for her grandmother. Curiously, she felt nothing. All she could be was numb, overridden by the story she'd just shared with the detective, and unsure of where she was headed.

Erin stood back, feeling like she was intruding upon something sacred and private. It was all she could do to concentrate on the brochure she found sitting on one of the abandoned chairs. She had no idea what it was about as she flipped through the stiff, glossy pages. Her heart pounded in her ears, nervous for her friend

Tamson looked down at the short, slightly plump woman standing before her. She saw her own eyes reflected back at her, eyes that were becoming moist, tears welling. She felt soft fingertips brush against her cheeks, over her hair and finally settling on narrow shoulders.

"Dear, dear child," Charlotte whispered, her red-tinted lips stretching into a shaky smile. "My Tamson."

Tamson felt herself lulled into a gentle embrace. She heard a sob escape her grandmother, which brought her to reality. Pulling away, she saw only gentle understanding in eyes made verdant from the tears that trailed down rounded cheeks.

Charlotte beckoned Erin over. "Who is this?" she asked Tamson.

"Hello, ma'am," Erin said softly. "My name is Erin. I'm a friend of Tamson's."

"Good, good. I'm so glad my granddaughter has a good friend to stay with her." She smiled, head slightly tilting to the side as her eyes sparkled. Looking back at Tamson, Charlotte sighed. "My granddaughter. You have no idea, child, how very much I've wanted to say that. Nearly twenty-two years is far too long, my dear Tamson. Far too long."

Tamson's brows drew. Twenty-two years? She'd seen her grandmother less than twenty years ago. Hadn't she?

"Come along, you two," Charlotte said, leading the way towards the door.

Erin sat in the back of Mrs. Robard's town car, eyes darting back and forth between Charlotte, who kept looking over at her granddaughter, almost to make sure she was actually there, and Tamson, who looked out the passenger side window. The Texas scenery passing by the speeding car seemed to enthrall Tamson, but Erin had to wonder if she were actually even seeing any of it. What was going through her head? What was in her heart?

Charlotte began to point out various things along the way, places Tamson's father liked to go when he was a boy and things he used to do. The older woman's voice trailed off when she realized her granddaughter wasn't even listening. Feeling bad for Charlotte, Erin began to ask questions of her own, what things were, certain buildings, what it was like in Fort Worth, how long she'd lived there. Charlotte answered and was kind, though a note of sadness was easily discernible in her voice.

"So did Tamson's dad live here until he died?"

Charlotte looked at Erin through the rearview mirror. "Died?" she asked, brows knitting. She glanced over at Tamson, who had finally looked over at her with mild curiosity. "I see," Charlotte said quietly. "Well look, you gals need some rest. It's been a long trip. We'll talk later."

༄༅༄༅

The town car pulled up to a beautiful, two-story farmhouse situated on what seemed to be endless acres of land.

Tamson climbed out of the car, feeling as though her head were about to roll right off her shoulders. She was crashing, and was crashing hard. A hand suddenly appeared on her arm. She saw Erin's concerned eyes.

"Are you okay?" she whispered as they made their slow, unsteady way up to the wrap-around porch.

Tamson nodded. "Tired."

"Okay. Almost there."

The house wasn't huge, but was spacious, filled with large windows allowing the afternoon sunlight to reflect off highly polished wood floors. The furniture was antique Queen Anne, taken care of and beautiful. They were led up the stairs where a bedroom was all ready for Tamson. The room was simple, but definitely comfortable.

"Come on, a few more steps, Tam," Erin encouraged, one of Tamson's arms around her waist.

She got her to the bed, gently pushing her down onto it. She unlaced Tamson's shoes and tossed them to the floor before helping her lie down. She covered her with the light blanket that had been folded at the end of the bed.

Tamson safely tucked away and her breathing deep and even, Erin left her. Creeping down the stairs – not sure where she should be or what she should be doing – she found Charlotte in the kitchen by simply following the wonderful smells emanating from there.

"Do you like bread?" the older woman asked, her back still to her guest.

"Yes. Very much so."

"Good, good. You're in the right house, then." Charlotte turned and gave Erin a warm, welcoming smile. "Sit, please." She carried a plate of sliced cinnamon bread over to the table. "Fresh from the oven."

Erin's mouth was nearly watering at the prize laid before her. When asked what she wanted to drink, she asked for milk. Her fingers itched to partake in the offering, but good manners dictated she wait for her hostess.

"Eat up while it's still warm!" Charlotte exclaimed, sitting across from Erin, cup of coffee in hand.

No need to be asked again, Erin grabbed one of the soft, warm slices and brought it to her mouth, closing her eyes as she savored the slight sweet taste.

"Tamson is so thin," Charlotte said, her voice soft, almost as though she were speaking to herself.

Erin nodded, sipping from her milk. *Suppose that's what happens when you eat drugs instead of food.* She kept her thoughts to herself. It wasn't her place to reveal Tamson's secrets.

"Why did you think Vincent was dead?" Charlotte asked.

"Vincent?"

"Tamson's father." Charlotte sipped her coffee, the single gold ring worn on her left ring finger clinking against the porcelain.

"That's what she told me." Erin sat back in her chair, wiping her fingers on the napkin taken from the holder at the center of the table.

"So my granddaughter thinks her daddy is dead." Charlotte sighed, shaking her head sadly. "Wonder what else she was told. Or," she amended, "*not* told."

"He's alive?" Erin grabbed another slice of the wonderful cinnamon bread.

Charlotte nodded. "Oh, yes he is," Charlotte said with a nod, grabbing her own slice of the bread to nibble on.

"Where is he? Does he still live in Texas?"

Charlotte sighed, the wrinkles around her eyes deepening. "In a way. He's been in a prison in Dallas since 1992."

Erin was stunned, her mouth hanging open.

"I always wished he'd get out before Wayne died, but," she sighed, "sadly, that didn't happen. My husband died three years ago."

"When does Vincent get out?"

"He's up for parole again in eighteen months."

"Wow. Tamson sure got the short end, didn't she?" Erin breathed, sitting back in her chair.

"That she did. We tried for years to find her." Charlotte pushed back from the table, refilling her coffee cup and refilling Erin's milk glass. "We just wanted to make sure she was okay. I knew how badly Connie had taken the accident. What mother wouldn't?" She shook her head and clicked her tongue. "She wouldn't allow it."

Erin had no idea what Charlotte was talking about. What accident? Why on earth did Tamson think her father was dead? Is that what her mother told her, or was he dead in Tamson's mind?

"How old was Tamson when her father was put in prison?"

"She was four years old."

Erin was stunned to see tears gathering in Charlotte's eyes. Charlotte was obviously becoming upset, so Erin decided perhaps they should continue this another time. Most likely when Tamson was around to hear the details, too.

"Listen, um, can I please maybe take a quick shower?" she asked, pushing her plate away, as she'd had her fill.

Charlotte gave her a blinding smile, even as she wiped at her eyes. "Of course!" She led Erin up the stairs and into the bathroom, showing her where towels were and anything else she'd need. "Why don't you give me your clothes, honey, and I'll wash them for you. I don't have anything that would fit you."

"Are you sure?" Erin felt bad for this woman to have to wait on her.

"Certainly!"

"Okay."

Once left alone with nothing but an oversized robe to wear, Erin turned the water on full blast. She was told to take her time and take as long a shower as she wanted, which she intended to take Charlotte up on her generosity.

As she enjoyed the feel of the warm water

streaming over her naked body, her mind began to wander. How on earth could Connie tell Tamson that her grandmother was such an evil, awful person? It was very obvious that Charlotte loved her granddaughter deeply, and was thrilled to have found her again.

What secrets was this family hiding? Why was Connie running from the Robards?

Erin's creative mind began to spin, ideas filling every nook and cranny of her imagination, no matter how she tried to shut it all out. Images and words formed, characters spoke to her, and scenes developed. Finally, as she began to wash herself, she knew it was pointless to try and stop it and allowed it to come full force, reveling in the story that was quickly unfolding. She couldn't wait to get out and begin to write it all down. Oh, what she wouldn't do to have her laptop with her.

Chapter Seventeen

The door. It's open. Light coming out. Bright light. Bright, icky light. Loud voices. Daddy? Is Daddy mad? Something crashed real bad. Looking up and up, angry face. Don't like Daddy's angry face. He isn't nice when he has the angry face.

Something holding, fingers pressing. Looks just like me. So much like me! See Daddy looking, looking down, face more angry, Momma standing in the way, voice loud, begging. No! Put that away! Momma moves, angry Daddy. What is that? Black, shiny. What is it? Pointing at me, at my face.

BOOM!!

Gasping loudly as terror roared through Tamson's body, she scurried up until her back hit the headboard. Her heart was pounding painfully in her chest, taking her breath with each pulse. Gaunt green eyes looked around the room, rippled in shadow from the gently swaying lacy curtains; the heating vent directly beneath them sent them dancing.

"Jesus," she breathed, hands shaking as she ran them through her hair. "What the fuck was that?"

Crawling out of the bed, Tamson hurried over to the jacket she'd been wearing, which had been tossed over the back of a wingback chair in the corner. Rifling through the pockets, she pulled out the small, jewelry bag. One precious bundle of candy left.

"Tam? Are you okay?" Erin asked from the open doorway, stopping short as her gaze immediately rested on the small bundle in Tamson's hand. She met wide, surprised eyes. Shaking her head, Erin pleaded. "Please don't do that, Tamson." She looked into Tamson's eyes, which were still huge and deeply troubled from her dream. "Listen," Erin said softly, stepping over to her. "I can see that something is really bothering you, but," she brought a hand up, fingers gently cupping Tamson's cheek. "Please." The stubborn set of Tamson's jaw was easy to see, so Erin slowly began to back out of the room. "You're an adult, obviously. Do what you will."

With those soft words, Tamson watched the door slide shut with a click. Indecision made her feel angry. Looking down at the candy in her hand, the bitter taste already in her mouth, making it water, she was caught and completely torn.

"Did you enjoy your shower?" Charlotte asked from her place by the roaring fire. A decorated Christmas tree shimmered in the corner of the room.

"Yes. Thank you very much." Erin pulled the robe closer to her body to ward off the December chill. It may be Texas, but it was still December.

"Your clothes should be done in about an hour, honey."

"Thank you so much, Mrs. Robard." Erin sat on the couch, tucking her bare feet under her.

"Call me Charlotte," the older woman said with a smile as warm as the fire, wrinkles around her eyes crinkling. "So, how did you meet my granddaughter?" The look on Charlotte's face showed Erin what she must have looked like as a young, spry woman. "Can't seem to stop saying that: granddaughter." Charlotte smiled at her, looking so proud. "Such a lovely word."

Erin smiled, happy for Charlotte, though her smile quickly faded, as she wished she had a better story to tell of her meeting Tamson. Quickly her mind spun, trying to think of a way she could tell a waiting Charlotte, without completely smearing Tamson's character.

"Well," she began, "one night Tamson had some car trouble and needed to call a cab. My place happened to be nearby, so she used my phone." She shrugged it off as though it hadn't been the crazy, frightening experience it was.

Charlotte studied Erin for a long moment before she returned her gaze to the fire. "You know, Erin, I look at you and I see a lovely young woman who seems to be intelligent and loyal. I look at my granddaughter – whom I'd give my life for – but I can see that she followed the same path as her father." She let out a heavy sigh. "I just hope she doesn't do anything as irreversible as him." She looked at Erin again, a fond smile on her lips. "You're a good person, Erin," she finally said, patting Erin's arm and squeezing it lightly before returning her hand to her own lap. "It's a cold night tonight, isn't it?"

"It sure is."

"What do you do in Denver, Erin?"

"I'm actually about to start a job working for a lawyer next week."

"Oh, wonderful!" Charlotte exclaimed. "Do—" She was cut off when they heard feet racing down the stairs. Tamson appeared briefly before the front door slammed shut. Charlotte rose, but stopped at the hand on her shoulder.

"Let me, Charlotte. It's cold out there."

It was dark out but Erin could see the flicker of light as the end of a cigarette was brought to life, the smell of smoke beckoning.

"Hey," she said, her voice soft so as not to interrupt the peace of night. She barely saw Tamson nod in greeting.

"Had a pretty ugly nightmare," Tamson said, just as soft.

Erin couldn't tell if Tamson had given into her craving or not, but her voice sounded clear and sober, if not sad. Though she had no clue what she was looking for whether someone was high or not. Her silent question had been answered when the security light flickered on as a dog ran across the driveway. Looking deeply into Tamson's eyes, she saw all of Tamson in there – tired and tortured – but *there*. She was so happy, she wanted to grab Tamson and squeeze her tight in a hug.

Instead, she simply said, "I'm sorry." Standing in companionable silence for a moment, Erin continued. "What do you dream about, Tamson?"

Tamson was quiet for so long that Erin didn't think she was going to answer. Finally, "I don't remember them. As soon as I wake up, they're gone," She snapped her fingers, "just like that. But every time I wake up, I feel …" Tamson chewed on the thought for a moment as she took a long drag from her cigarette, "Really afraid."

Erin watched her and could see how profoundly the nightmare she'd just had touched her. "Was that why you went directly for your … drugs?"

Tamson didn't answer, but she didn't have to. It was written all over her body language: arms crossed tightly over her chest, completely closed off.

Erin decided to give her a much-needed reprieve. "Your grandma is a real great lady."

Tamson was quiet for a very long time. She took a long pull from her cigarette, the smoke lazily curling up from her lips a moment later. "She's not what my mother said she was, is she?" she asked, not looking at Erin.

"Why don't you go in and get to know her?" Erin suggested, placing a gentle hand on her shoulder.

Tamson nodded. "I'll be there in a minute. I just need some time."

"Okay," Erin said quietly, giving Tamson's shoulder a quick squeeze before she let her be.

༄༅༄༅

Dinner was served and would be the best meal Tamson and Erin had had in days, and perhaps in all of Tamson's life. The formal dining room was set up, all of Charlotte's best china set out and gleaming under the twinkling lights of the chandelier.

"You two sit on down here," Charlotte insisted as she made her way back through the swinging door to the kitchen.

Erin's appetite was making itself known as she sat down. She gave Tamson a sheepish grin as it spoke again with a grumble. Tamson, for her part, was looking around, trying to figure out what on earth all the fuss was about. It was just dinner.

"Alright, girls, here we are," Charlotte sang as she pushed through the swinging door again, a tray of sliced, steaming pork roast, garnished with baby potatoes, carrots, and onions. The smells wafted through the room, even making Tamson feel dizzy with hunger. Charlotte had gone all out and was more than solicitous to both Tamson and Erin. Tamson's grandmother had been seated for no more than three minutes before she was up again, getting any and everything that the women needed, or what she worried they *might* need.

Tamson watched with mild curiosity as Erin begged Charlotte to please sit and eat before it got cold. Finally the older woman did. Tamson steeled herself, as she knew she had to face her nerves – and her grandmother - sometime.

"More meat, honey?" Charlotte asked Tamson, brows raised in hope.

"Oh, uh, sure." Tamson felt her stomach become more and more heavy with each helping Charlotte put on her plate.

Silence reigned again as the trio ate, the scraping of forks or knives on the china or the swallowing of a throat taking down iced tea.

"This is really wonderful, Charlotte," Erin said with a grateful smile.

Tamson nodded in agreement. "Yeah. It's good."

"Thank you. It's not often that I get to cook like this anymore. Not since your grandpa died, Tamson."

Tamson glanced up through her bangs. "When did he die?" She had no memories of him, but assumed that the old man in the pictures that lined the staircase were of him.

"It's been a few years, now. Lung cancer." She was quiet a moment then continued. "You know, honey, you've got lots of family that has been looking for you as long as your grandfather and I had. Aunts, uncles, all sorts of cousins." Charlotte couldn't keep the smile from her face. "They're all so excited to meet you, Tamson. They're glad to get you back into the family, where you should have been all this time."

"I'm here for my mother," Tamson said, her voice low in warning.

"Honey," Charlotte said softly, reaching across the table to cover Tamson's hand with her own. "Your mom must have had her reasons for keeping you from us, though for the life of me I don't know what they were. But, you're an adult now, and can make your own choices. You have an entire family who loves you and wants desperately for you to accept us."

"I guess that's what you guys get for trying to take me away from her. After my dad died, she told me what you did," Tamson said; her words were biting.

"Take you away? Honey, we did no such thing. Tamson, your daddy isn't dead. I hate to say it, honey, but your momma filled you with all sorts of bull."

Tamson stared at the older woman, stunned and filled with confusion. "Where is he?"

Charlotte sighed softly. "I think we're in for a very long conversation." She pushed her plate away and clasped her fingers on the table in front of her as she gave her full focus to Tamson. "Honey, what do you remember of your daddy?"

Tamson thought about it for a long moment. She shook her head. "I don't."

"Do you remember anything from your time here, honey? In Fort Worth?" Again, Tamson shook her head. Getting to her feet with a soft grunt of effort, Charlotte led her granddaughter out of the dining room.

Tamson stopped just before leaving and turned to look at Erin, who still sat at the table. "You coming?"

"No, Tam. This is personal – Whoa!"

Erin was almost pulled off her feet, barely getting her balance before she did a face plant in the bowl of green beans.

They were led through the house to a door at the back of the kitchen that led down a long, narrow case of stairs. The basement was cool and dark, the walls cement with a washer and dryer sitting against the far wall.

Charlotte flicked on the light switch in an adjacent room, seemingly the only finished room in the basement. Once the room came to life by the single, naked bulb at the center of the room, racks of clothing, hung in neat, straight rows was revealed, along with stacks of boxes, some taped shut and others with flaps flopped down like a four-petaled flower.

"All of this is your momma's, honey. You go through it if you like, or do with it whatever you want. After your momma's landlord demanded all her things be removed so as to re-rent the house," she shrugged, "I was the one they managed to find."

As Charlotte explained, Tamson looked around, unsure what to think or where to start. Hands on hips, she felt like she was in a maze of stuff.

"I think I need to tell you something, honey," Charlotte said, walking up to Tamson and placing a gentle hand on her cast-covered forearm. "Something very important."

Tamson looked at Charlotte, feeling a bit nervous at the serious look in Charlotte's eyes. "Alright."

Erin stood off a bit to the side, arms hugging herself as she took in everything around them. She returned her attention to Charlotte and Tamson, studying her friend for a moment to make sure she was okay.

"Sit down with me, honey." Charlotte grunted as she lowered her bulk to a metal, fold-up chair.

Tamson took a seat on a wooden trunk. She remembered that trunk well. She used to hide in it as a child. She glanced over at Erin, making sure she was still there. They exchanged a quick smile before Tamson's attention returned to Charlotte. "Alright. Let's get this over with."

"Honey, your dad is in a prison in Dallas, where he's been since you were four years old."

"What? Why is he there?" Tamson asked, suspicion in her voice. She began to feel her stomach roil and wish she hadn't eaten all that food for dinner.

Charlotte sighed then began her tale. "Honey, when you were four years old, your parents got into a horrible fight. Your daddy had himself an addiction to just about anything he could get his hands on. He was mean, and didn't think too clear when he was on the drugs." Charlotte swallowed before she continued. "Tamson, you had a sister, her name was Jenny."

Tamson felt a spear slice through her heart, the strangest feeling passing through her. Like an echo, the news was so familiar yet so distant.

"She was your twin sister, honey. That night your momma and daddy fought, there was an accident. Little Jenny was killed."

The door. It's open. Light coming out. Bright light. Bright, icky light. Loud voices. Daddy? Is Daddy mad? Something crashed real bad. Looking up and up, angry face. Don't like Daddy's angry face. He isn't nice when he has the angry face.

Something holding, fingers pressing. Looks just like me. So much like me! See Daddy looking, looking

down, face more angry, Momma standing in the way, voice loud, begging. No! Put that away! Momma moves, angry Daddy. What is that? Black, shiny. What is it? Pointing at me, at my face.
BOOM!!

Tamson started as the roar echoed through her skull. Her head fell, air driven from her lungs and hand to her heart.

Erin nearly flew up from where she'd seated herself on another fold-up chair, but a hand to her arm stopped her. She met Charlotte's gaze, the older woman shaking her head.

Tamson gasped for breath, trying to gather enough air to speak. "Was," she took another breath and cleared her throat. "Was she shot?"

"Yes. Do you remember, Tamson?" Charlotte asked, touching Tamson's shoulder. She started as Tamson pulled away.

"This can't be," Tamson whispered. She felt the blood drain from her face, her life crumbling before her eyes. "Why didn't she tell me?" She looked up at Charlotte, eyes brimming with unshed emotion. She looked like a lost little girl. "Why didn't she tell me?" Her voice was gaining force as she slowly got to her feet, looking around at what was left of her mother's miserable life. "Why?!" She kicked the trunk, listening with a satisfying smirk as it skidded across the floor, smacking into a rack of clothing.

"I don't know, honey," Charlotte whispered, tears streaming down her cheeks. It was easy to see how much pain Tamson was in at the news. There was nothing Charlotte – or anyone – could do to spare her or help her. Tamson deserved to know the truth.

"Why? Why, mother? Why!" Tamson's devastation erupted into rage as she grabbed the first thing she got hold of, a lamp, slamming it into a stack of boxes, sending books scattering to the floor and the lamp shattering in her hands. "Damn you!"

Again, Erin made a move to go to her friend and again a hand on her arm stopped her. Charlotte shook her head.

"My god," Erin whispered, tears brimming in her own eyes.

Out of breath and energy, Tamson fell to the floor in a heap, kicking out at one last box, knocking it off another pile. She froze, eyes settling on a box that the violence revealed. The faux-wood exterior was cracked from time, one of the handles ripped through. The lid was pulled down tight, hiding the forbidden contents.

Heart stopped, breathing stopped, the world seemingly stopped, she crawled over to it, gently pulling it out from the corner it was tucked in. It was heavy. Tugging it over to where she sat, Tamson took a deep breath as she eased the lid off, gently setting it aside.

Closing her eyes, Tamson tried to get herself under control. She was trembling and there was no stopping it. Opening her eyes again, she reached inside. Softness, fabric, then something hard. Wrapping her fingers around the material, she pulled it out. It was a light pink blanket. A child's blanket. As it cleared the box for the first time in she had no idea how long, Tamson saw it: a hard, dark brown, crusty substance clinging to the soft material. It kept the blanket from fully falling open.

Erin brought her hands to her mouth, the scene

before her dancing through tear-filled eyes. She could hear Charlotte softly crying next to her. She watched as Tamson brought the blanket up to her face, rubbing her cheek against the softness before her face fell. Hugging the blanket, she began to rock gently back and forth, her shoulders shaking.

Taking a deep breath – swearing she could catch a scent that was as familiar to her as her own name – Tamson set the blanket in her lap, needing to hold it close. Reaching inside the box again, she brought out a shoe, a tiny Mary Jane, the brown leather still supple. A teddy bear followed another shoe. The left eye was missing, leaving an asymmetrical face and smile.

Tamson thought of her own teddy bear she'd had as a child; the right eye had been missing since she could remember. Setting the bear aside, she reached in once more, feeling something hard. Bringing out a framed five by seven photo, she felt her breath catch. It was color, though turned slightly yellowish over time. Two little girls, identical in every way, save for one wore a red dress, the other blue. They sat on Santa's lap, smiles plastered to their faces. Across the jolly man's big, padded tummy, they held hands.

She felt her entire being crumble, her spirit broken and the missing piece of the puzzle finally filled.

"My Penny," she whispered, a finger reaching out to wipe away a teardrop that landed on the dusty glass covering the picture. She closed her eyes and brought the picture up to her face and left a soft kiss where that tear had been. "My Jenny."

Chapter Eighteen

"Tamson!" Erin ran out of the room, following a very upset Tamson. They burst out into the night, Tamson's sobs leading the way. "Wait!" Erin panted, finally catching up with her friend, the security light blazing to life.

Tamson fell to her knees, caught in two strong arms, her head guided to rest against a shoulder. "Let it all out, Tam. Let it go, honey," Erin said, her voice shaky with her own reaction to what she'd just witnessed.

Tamson clung to her, fingers digging almost painfully into Erin's shoulder. She cried for the first time in more than ten years. She cried for her twin that she never really got to know. She cried for her father. She cried for her mother, and finally, she cried for herself.

"Why, Erin?" she sobbed.

"I don't know, sweetheart. I just don't know." Erin held her close, placing a soft kiss atop tussled hair then resting her cheek where her lips had just been.

Eventually Tamson's body grew limp, all her upset turning her body to jelly. Allowing herself to be held, Tamson stared up into the night sky, stars twinkling above their heads as the security light, sensing no more movement, flickered off. Her mind was filled with the images of the sister she now realized she had always felt, but never really knew. *I had a twin.*

"Erin?" she said softly.

"Yeah?" Erin responded, fingers running through Tamson's hair.

"Why do you think Connie did this?"

Erin was quiet for a moment before finally responding. "Maybe your mom just couldn't deal with what happened, you know? Maybe telling you or talking about it, made it too real for her."

Tamson contemplated Erin's theory. Finally, she nodded. That could be it. "Erin?"

"Hmm?"

"My grandmother isn't a monster, is she?"

"No, Tam. She's not."

Tamson sighed, trying to find a single star. She was surprised when she saw one falling. Closing her eyes, she made a wish: *Don't ever leave me, Jenny. I love you.*

"What are you going to do with your mom's stuff?" Erin asked, gently massaging Tamson's scalp.

Tamson closed her eyes at the feel. She felt so safe. "I don't know. I don't really want it. There's this part of me that doesn't want to get rid of it in case …" She suddenly moved out of Erin's embrace, sitting forward with her face buried in her hands. "God, I'm so confused," she said from between her fingers. She felt a welcoming touch to her back, Erin's hand rubbing circles over the expanse as fresh tears chilled her cheeks in the cool night. "There's this part of me that hopes that she's dead, Erin. After she could do this, turn my entire life into a lie. Is that bad?" She looked at her friend over her shoulder, pleading eyes glistening in the moonlight.

Erin shook her head. "No, honey, that's not wrong. I can totally understand that." She gave

Tamson an understanding smile.

Nodding, Tamson turned away once again. "Then there's this other part of me, that little girl inside, who just wants her momma." These words were whispered

Erin said nothing, letting Tamson get out anything she needed to.

Tamson let out a heavy sigh. "I've been so angry with her for so long, Erin."

"Why?"

Tamson's voice trembled. "I always came last. There was always something, some *man*, who came first. I was never a priority to her, Erin. God, that hurt. Still does." She reached up, wiping away twin tears. "How could she let her daughter be killed? Why wasn't it me instead?"

"Oh, Tamson. Don't say that," Erin said, voice thick with rising emotion.

"Why not?" Tamson turned so she was facing Erin, eyes so filled with unresolved pain. "Why not me? Why not Jenny sitting here? Why not Jenny going on and living a good life." Her head fell. "Then again, I wouldn't wish this – *my* life – on anyone."

"You know something, though?" Erin asked, using two fingers to urge Tamson to look at her, their faces no more than six inches apart. "Though all of this is awful, so, so awful, you're obviously loved, Tam. You've got a grandmother in there who has been searching for you for twenty years, and who just wants to love you. She said you've got more family out there that wants to meet you. You've got support now, Tamson. I'm so sorry you had to go through all that, but doesn't that mean something? That you've got people who love you now? Hell, I consider you a close friend. You've definitely got me in your corner, too."

Tamson looked at her friend, deeply touched by just how hard Erin was trying to be there for her. She wasn't sure if Erin would ever truly understand what it meant to her. What *Erin* meant to her. Rising up on her knees, she wrapped her arms around Erin's neck, resting her cheek on a strong shoulder.

"Thank you, Erin. It's meant so much to me what you've done for me. You're the first friend I've had in a really long time, and the best friend I've *ever* had," she whispered, pulling away just enough to look into Erin's eyes.

Erin smiled. "Any time."

Tamson could feel the heat of Erin's body against her own, and could feel a connection between them that - with a fairly sober mind - she felt acutely. Erin was gorgeous, no question about it, but it was more than that. Suddenly she felt her heart begin to pound in her chest and a need to bridge the slightest gap between them.

"Thank you," she whispered again, moments before she pressed her lips to Erin's, feeling their softness as she lingered, fingers gently caressing the side of Erin's face.

She pulled away, once again looking at Erin, noting her cheeks were slightly flushed. She wasn't sure if it was from the cooler temperatures or something else. This kiss had been different than that given in the back of the truck in Alamosa. Tamson felt it, and from the look on Erin's face, she did, too.

Tamson's gaze flicked to the front door as it opened, Charlotte stepping out into the cold, December night. She watched as Charlotte tugged her jacket a little closer around her body as she made her way over to them. Tamson moved away from Erin, both getting to their feet.

"Honey?" Charlotte said, uncertainty in her voice. She met Tamson's gaze then opened her arms.

Tamson saw the invite and glanced at Erin for a moment, looking for guidance. Erin smiled, giving her the briefest nod of encouragement. Tamson took a deep breath and walked the few steps to her grandmother, feeling a warm, soft body against her own, as she stepped into the hug, arms wrapping around her back.

"We're going to get through this, Tamson," Charlotte promised. "That's what family is for."

※ ※ ※ ※

Sighing in her sleep, Erin turned over, absently licking a bit of drool from the corner of her mouth. She started to make herself comfortable in her new position when she was suddenly startled awake. A small gasp escaped her lips when she saw the curled up figure sitting in the wingback chair by the window. Tamson's face and hair were painted with the blue hue of the moon.

"Tamson?" she whispered. Tamson looked at her. "Are you okay?"

Tamson nodded, looking sheepish. "Couldn't sleep." She turned away.

Erin pushed herself up in the bed, trying to blink the Sandman away. Though exhausted, she wanted to help. "Do you want to talk?"

Tamson shook her head. "No." Unfolding herself, she got to her feet. "I'm sorry I woke you. I guess for a minute I didn't want to be alone. I'm okay.

I'll go." Heading toward the door, she stopped when she heard Erin call out her name.

"Come on," Erin said, folding the covers back and patting the mattress in invitation.

Tamson looked at Erin, at the bed, then back to Erin. Finally, she gave in, climbing onto the bed and sliding between the sheets, warmed from Erin's body heat. As she laid her head on the pillow, she glanced over and saw that Erin was studying her.

Erin could sense that Tamson needed some comforting, so she opened her arms. Tamson slid over to her, both women giggling as they fumbled with the position until Tamson's head finally ended up on Erin's shoulder, her arm draped loosely across Erin's stomach.

"Not used to being the one who holds," Erin murmured, trying to give some sort of explanation of why she had no idea how to cuddle with someone in this position.

Tamson chuckled. "Yeah, me neither. Well, actually, I'm not used to cuddling at all."

"Is this okay, then?" Erin asked, hoping she hadn't misinterpreted what Tamson had wanted.

"Yeah. It's good," Tamson whispered, cuddling in a bit closer. "This is really nice, actually." She adjusted her head a bit so her nose was closer to the warmth of Erin's neck. A moment later, she inhaled. "Your skin smells really good."

Erin shivered a bit at the soft words almost spoken into her skin. She felt her heart skip a beat and her chest seize, and she wasn't entirely sure why. "Thank you," she managed. "Your grandma has some really great toiletry products." She squeezed her eyes shut, feeling like a dork for saying that. "You don't cuddle?" she asked, hoping a change in topic would make her body behave, but it made it worse, as it brought back the very real situation that Tamson, wearing nothing more than an oversized t-shirt and panties was pressed against her side, with Erin, herself, only in an over-sized t-shirt and panties.

"No, not really," Tamson said, readjusting her head again as her fingers began to play absently with the material of Erin's shirt at her side. "Used to with my mom when I was little, but that stopped. And, I don't exactly tend to get into the kind of relationships where cuddling is part of the dynamic."

"Oh. Mark didn't like to cuddle."

"Who's Mark?"

"My ex."

"Ah. What about any other exes?" Tamson asked, her gaze stealing to the window, watching as the branches of the tree outside blew against the wind.

Erin was quiet for a moment, not wanting to look foolish. But, finally, she did. "I ... I don't have any other exes."

"Just the one dude?" Tamson asked, raising her head and looking down into Erin's face.

Erin looked away, feeling ashamed by the shock in Tamson's voice. "Yeah," she said softly. "Just the one."

"Oh hey," Tamson said, her voice filled with apology. "I'm sorry. I didn't mean to imply anything Erin, really. To be honest, I'm just pretty damn shocked because you're hot as shit and have a body to die for."

Erin's blush hit her hard and fast, making her heart skip another beat. She cleared her throat before responding. "I don't agree, but thank you."

"What's not to agree with?" Tamson challenged,

her gaze scanning over Erin's face and down to her t-shirt-clad upper chest and shoulders, which the blankets didn't cover.

"Certainly not the body to die for," Erin said, forcing herself to look into Tamson's gaze. She couldn't believe how unnerving it was for her having Tamson's body pressed against her own and that intense, beautiful green gaze studying her. "My hips are huge."

Tamson laughed, shaking her head. Her hand drifted down Erin's side to the body part in question. "No. Don't you know that men love a body like yours? You're fit but have womanly curves in *all* the right places."

Erin gasped slightly when that hand went on the move again, back up to its starting point at her side, and beyond.

"I really hope you don't slap me for this," Tamson said, her voice taking on a lower, somewhat huskier tone as her hand moved up to gently cup the underside of Erin's right breast. "With gorgeous breasts like these, you would make some serious cash at The Swagger."

For a moment Erin couldn't speak, could barely breathe, with Tamson's hand still on her. Part of her wanted to ask Tamson to remove it and be angry, but she couldn't quite get her brain to catch up to that or to make her mouth do her bidding.

"You know," Tamson said softly, her voice not losing the tone that was making Erin's blood run a bit warmer. "A few months back at the club, there used to be this woman who was a dancer named Joy. She had this serious thing about women's breasts: big, little, black, white, didn't matter," she began, her hand beginning to massage the fullness of Erin's breast, though she had yet to come into contact with the hardening nipple. "See, before a girl goes out to do her set, it's mandatory for her nipples to be hard, which trust me, as cold as Hank keeps that place, is not hard to do." She grinned at Erin, who shyly returned it. "So anyway, Joy, before either she went out for her set or you went out on yours, she'd find you and tug the top from your costume down and tug hers down and rub her nipples against yours, telling you it was time to 'nippy up'." She chuckled. "Used to unnerve some of the girls – the ones who were straight, that is – but for the rest of us, it was amusing and hey, gives you a little jolt before the show."

Erin tried to focus on Tamson's story, even as her body begged her to arch her back, just that tiniest little bit. "That had to feel strange," she managed, her words a bit breathier than she would have liked.

"No," Tamson whispered, her gaze locked on the movements of her hand and fingers. "It feels wonderful."

"Does she still do that to you?" Erin asked, shocked – and confused – when she felt a slight bolt of jealousy rush through her at the thought and image that popped into her mind.

Tamson shook her head. "Nah. Joy died of an overdose last month."

"Oh, Tamson," Erin breathed, sad for the news but almost relieved from the reprieve of the absolutely confusing sensations and emotions running through her mind and body. "I'm so sorry."

"Don't be," Tamson said absently, her gaze seemingly riveted to what her hand was doing to Erin's breast. "We warned her so many times. Wasn't a huge surprise."

Erin watched Tamson's face, her eyes adjusting to the dim light in the room enough to see Tamson's features clearly. Not for the first time, she realized just how absolutely stunning Tamson actually was. Even with bruises and cuts marring the perfection of her face, the potential was plain to see. She could see Tamson on a movie screen somewhere or gracing the glossy pages of a magazine doing an ad for some product.

"I think breasts are so amazing," Tamson said, the words not much louder than a whisper. "So feminine, you know? So soft." She lifted her hand and allowed her fingertips to just barely graze Erin's nipple, causing a gasp to slip from Erin's lips. Tamson met her gaze, hers hungry. "It's amazing to me how they can be the ultimate symbol of maternal love or comfort, yet the absolute in seduction and fantasy."

Suddenly, Tamson's hand fell away and she moved away from Erin, laying on her back an arm's length away from a startled Erin.

"I'm sorry," she whispered, an arm coming up to lie across her eyes. "I'm really sorry, Erin. I guess old habits die hard," she said with a rueful lay.

It took Erin a moment to catch up to what had just happened, her body screaming out for more attention, nipple straining against her t-shirt in search of the elusive touch. "What – " she tried, but her voice cracked. Clearing her throat, she tried again. "What do you mean, 'old habits die hard'?"

Tamson's arm flopped back down to the bed as she turned her head to look at Erin. "I just feel really close to you right now, through all this shit you've gone through with me, and I guess I just turned back to what I know in order to show gratitude or affection." She turned to face the dark ceiling again. "Sex." She looked at Erin again. "Honestly, at this point I'd be using the closest person to me to make me feel better, but I can't do that to you, Erin. I *won't* do that to you. You mean too much to me, now," she whispered before turning to her side, back facing Erin.

Erin was stunned at what she'd just been told, but didn't doubt a single word that came from Tamson's mouth. Gathering her wits about her again and getting her body under control, she turned to her side and scooted up behind Tamson, spooning their bodies together and wrapping a protective arm around Tamson's middle, even as she was careful not to push too hard so as not to hurt her wounds.

"Tamson," she said softly, resting her chin on Tamson's shoulder. Though Tamson didn't say anything, Erin felt she had her attention. "You can still feel close to me and know that I'm here and that I'm not going anywhere." She smiled when she felt Tamson's hand move to rest over her own. "And, though I don't really know what I'm capable of, I know I can give you this."

Erin moved back from Tamson just enough to give her the room to move to her back at Erin's urging. Tamson looked up at her, their positions affectively reversed.

"Give me what?" Tamson asked, searching Erin's eyes.

"This," Erin whispered, lowering her mouth to Tamson's.

This kiss began very soft, Erin barely brushing her lips against Tamson's. It didn't take long before their lips began to move together with the barest touch of their tongues before Erin moved away. She smiled down at Tamson and left a final kiss on her lips before she urged Tamson to move back to her side, where she resumed their previous position.

"Good night, Erin," Tamson whispered, pulling Erin's arm tightly around her.

"Good night, Tam. Sweet dreams."

※ ※ ※ ※

Erin watched small shops pass by the town car as she drove Charlotte into town. She had been shocked when she'd been asked to drive. Charlotte explained that she had her good days and her bad days with her cataracts, and today was a bad day.

"Go ahead and park on the street, honey," Charlotte directed, pointing to the store she wished to start with. Pulling the car to a graceful parallel stop, Erin pulled the break and cut the engine. "Ready to do some shopping?" Charlotte asked.

"Oh, sure." Erin smiled, though she hated to shop.

"Wonderful. We'll shop and I get to pick your brain." Charlotte got herself out of the car with a grunt of exertion.

"Oh boy," Erin muttered, also getting out of the car.

※ ※ ※ ※

Tamson sat cross-legged on the floor, surrounded by the contents of The Box. Tucking a long strand of hair behind her ear, she studied the loose pictures she'd found tucked into an album.

Spread out in neat rows, she studied them all. Smiling faces. Happy faces. There were pictures of two toddlers, maybe two, trying to waddle across the floor. On one end knelt a much younger version of Tamson's mother, all smiles and bright eyes. On the other – his back about three-quarters to the camera lens – stood a man. His shoulders were broad, thumb hitched in a belt loop. His hair was long with neatly shaped sideburns. Was that her father?

Another picture showed happy, proud parents with a swaddled baby in each of their arms. That *had* to be her father. Tamson studied him, a profile shot. He was grinning at Connie. He had a strong, squared jaw and his mustache was darker brown than the light brown hair on his head. He was thin, but looked handsome. Connie looked so unbelievably young. She still had the freshness of a young girl, not yet realizing what horrors awaited her. She looked at the man Tamson assumed was her father, and there was nothing but love shining in her eyes.

Tamson brought the picture up close to her eyes, staring into her mother's face.

"What went wrong?" she whispered.

❧❧❧❧

Erin was shocked at the amount of energy and gittyup Charlotte had. Erin loaded the last of the bags into the trunk with a tired sigh and slammed it shut. Sliding behind the wheel, she glanced over at the woman in question, who had a pencil between her teeth as she punched in a bunch of numbers on a small calculator.

"Where to?" Erin asked, inserting the key into

the ignition.

"Grocery store," Charlotte managed around the writing implement. She tucked the calculator back into her purse and scribbled something down in her checkbook registry. She gave Erin directions and they were off.

※※※※

Taking a long swallow from the bottle of water, Tamson turned her attention back to the new stack of pictures she'd discovered hidden in the old trunk. These pictures were so different from those found in The Box. Connie was either pictured alone or with Tamson in various stages of growing up.

She picked one up, feeling the glossy surface underneath her fingertips. Her mother was sitting on the couch, legs pulled up under her. Her chin rested on a fist and she was looking out into the distance. Tamson recognized the picture, as she'd been behind the lens. She'd found her mother's old Polaroid and had fooled around with it, snapping pictures of just about anything that would sit still, including Connie. Eleven years old and not understanding the pressures her young mother was under, Tamson had thought it all one big joke.

Now, looking into the profoundly sad eyes of her mother, Tamson thought about it clearly, sober and as an adult. Knowing now what she couldn't have dreamed then, she wondered how her mother had kept all her secrets so hidden for so long. How had she lived with the ghost of a dead child haunting her? How had she lived with shadows covering all the truths of her life, all the lies she'd told? How could she look Tamson in the eyes every day, knowing that an identical set were supposed to be looking back at her?

"Why, Momma?" Tamson whispered, her heart heavy. "Why not let me help you carry your burden?"

She caressed the glossy surface with her thumb before reaching up and wiping a tear from her right eye, amazed she had any left. In every picture she saw – after the death of Jenny – the light in her mother's eyes had died right along with her. There may have been a smile on Connie's face, but her heart seemed to have grown hard, filled with holes of guilt and loss, all of which Tamson had unknowingly been victim of.

Gathering all the pictures together, Tamson was tapping them into a neat stack when one fell out. Setting the stack aside, she picked up the lone picture. Dale Young stood next to her mother, both dressed for what looked to be Halloween. Tamson was chilled when she saw what their costumes were: Dale grinned obscenely from out of a dark hood, his face painted white with ghoulish circles around his eyes and lips painted black. He held a scythe to Connie's throat. She wore a white dress, torn and dirty, face a light bluish gray. Makeup had been used disturbingly well to show a slash across her throat, as though the scythe had indeed made its mark.

A shiver passed through Tamson in that moment, knowing in her heart that Connie was dead. She set the picture aside, putting the others back in The Box.

Blowing out a breath, Tamson stood, hands on hips as she looked around the room. She had turned it upside down, looking through all the boxes, some of their contents spread around while others were tossed into messy piles against the wall. She had yet to decide what to do with most of the stuff, part of her wanting to take it all back with her, and the other, bitter part of herself wanted to burn it all.

She wondered what her mother had become in the past eight years. All of the clothing was of a much larger size than Tamson remembered, with hugely oversized sweatshirts and t-shirts and cotton pants that could be filled with three Tamsons. There was so little that was personal or made any sort of personal statement about Connie. The colors were dull or washed out, nothing like the stylish, colorful woman Tamson had known.

In the boxes of books, Tamson had been shocked to find not one, but six different bibles. Each one had been well used, the pages dog-eared and covered with finger smudges. Tamson had never even seen a bible up close until she was a teenager, going to church with the Deacons'. Where had the bibles come from?

Tamson saw a hatbox that surprised her. She hadn't seen it before. Walking over to it, she shook the top free, even more surprised to see a greeting card-sized envelope, colored light purple, with the top left hand corner filled out by Connie Young, 362 Dillon Dr., Dallas, TX. The front center only had Tamson Robard scrawled with a flourish. Flipping through, there was greeting card after greeting card after greeting card, all addressed to her, the address left blank. There must have been more than fifteen in all. About to open one of the sealed envelopes, Tamson stopped, eyes rising to the ceiling at the sound of footsteps.

"Tamson? You home?" Charlotte called.

"Yeah," she called back, quickly pushing the cards away from her, hidden from view should anyone come in.

Chapter Nineteen

March 19, 2007
Happy Birthday, baby. I can't believe you're turning 20. Just blows my mind! Makes me feel old somehow. I'm really going to try hard to find out where you're staying so I can send this to you. I saw Mitchell the other day, and he said he was going to try and see what he could find out. Guess we'll see.
 Come see me soon, honey. You can call me at (214) 555-1493. I love you, Tamson.
 Mom

December 21, 2007
Merry Christmas, Tamson. I sure hope you're having a wonderful holiday season. I missed you so much at Thanksgiving this year. As every year. It just doesn't seem the same without you, Tamson. I promise, honey. I don't care what Dale says. You're welcome here.
 I love you, Tamson.
 Mom

January 3, 2008
I can't believe we're in a new year already.
 Honey, I'm sorry about what happened. It never should have happened. I never should have told you to leave, and well, there're lots of things I shouldn't have done.
 Mom

March 19, 2008
My baby is growing up. Happy Birthday, Tamson. I hope you had a good year, honey.
I miss you so much.
Love,
Mom

"Honey?" Charlotte called, her voice muffled behind the wood of the door.

Tamson glanced up, pulled from the sea of greeting cards spread all around her on the bed. Charlotte tapped again. "Come in."

The door squeaked lightly as it was swung open, Charlotte standing in the open doorway. "Did you want some cobbler, honey?" Charlotte asked, hopeful. She held up the flowered plate in her hand, the dessert enticing in all its peach glory atop it.

"Oh, uh, sure," Tamson lied. She gathered all the cards together, careful to keep them in order by the dates she'd found.

Charlotte walked over to the bed, handing the plate and fork to her granddaughter, placing a soft kiss on her forehead. With a gentle smile, the older woman turned to leave when the soft utterance of her name stopped her.

"Yes, honey?"

"Can I ask you something?" Tamson asked, poking around at the cobbler to avoid looking into Charlotte's eyes.

"Of course."

Tamson set the plate aside, her stomach roiling at the question she needed to ask. She was unable to meet her grandmother's eyes as she asked it. "Did you try and take me away from my mother when I was five or six?" As the silence stretched, she looked up to meet her grandmother's very troubled eyes.

Charlotte let out a heavy sigh as she sat on the side of Tamson's bed. "How to word this," she murmured then cleared her throat. "Honey, yes." She met Tamson's gaze, which was becoming clouded. "It was six months after, well, after we'd laid Jenny to rest. We hadn't seen you at all. I met your mom at the McDonald's and we had lunch." Charlotte smiled, though it was sad. "I watched you play on the minimal play equipment they had in those days." She met Tamson's gaze. "Nothing like what they have today. In those days, they had the little Burglar and Grimace characters on those big springs. Anyway, your mom and I got into an argument about you. About her not letting us see you, your dad's family, that is. She wouldn't even let you play with your cousins anymore. You and Jenny used to play with them a lot. It was wrong, Tamson. Of me. It was a stupid thing for me to do, and I've regretted it every day since, more than you know."

"Why did you do it?"

"Because I loved you. *Love* you. I felt you needed more support and love in your little life than just your mom, who was struggling so much."

Tamson studied Charlotte's eyes, seeing nothing but sad sincerity, and lots of regret. "She—" Tamson cut herself off, loyalty once again rearing its ugly head. Swallowing, she continued. *No more lies.* "She used to tell me you were a monster. We ran from you." Tamson's voice was soft, filled with confusion and regrets of her own. Looking up, she saw green eyes filled with unshed tears, Charlotte's painted lips trembling slightly.

"I'm not a monster, Tamson," Charlotte whispered. "Just a grandmother without her grandbabies."

Tamson felt something within her snap, the lock on her heart, perhaps. Leaning over, she took Charlotte in a tentative hug. It didn't take Charlotte long to gather Tamson to her.

"I'm so sorry, honey. So sorry you've had to go through so much in your short life. I know what you've been told about me, but I want you to know that you are loved, Tamson. You are *so* loved and always have been, by me and your granddad before he died. All we ever wanted was what we felt was best for you. I still do, honey. I hope you believe me," she whispered into her hair. "Please forgive me for not finding you earlier. Please."

Tamson's eyes closed as she snuggled into her grandmother's embrace. She nodded at Charlotte's words. Something inside her begged her to believe the older woman. She was shocked to feel fresh tears of her own leaking down her cheeks.

After long moments, Charlotte pulled away just enough to give her a huge smile.

"What say you come on down with us and have some cobbler and coffee?"

Tamson nodded. "Um, except I don't think my stomach could handle coffee right now."

Charlotte burst into laughter, tugging Tamson to her feet. "Honey, I'll make you anything you want!"

࿇࿇࿇

"I can*not* believe I let you do this," Tamson

growled, sitting in a well-covered chair in the center of the kitchen. The old, torn sweatshirt she wore waited to catch any droplets. She heard Erin chuckle from somewhere by the sink, the sloshing of liquids emphasizing the agonizing sound. Tamson growled again, knowing that the sounds were colors and chemicals being mixed together.

"Don't be such a whiner." Erin chuckled, carrying the mixed bottles to her friend, her plastic glove-covered hands crinkling with her every movement. "Hold still."

"Where *exactly* am I supposed to go?" Tamson muttered, making Erin's smile grow.

Erin squirted the entire contents of the bottle on top of Tamson's head, tossing the empty plastic bottle to the sink then began the saturating process. Using strong finger strokes, she made sure the smelly goop covered every strand, massaging it into her scalp and roots. Tamson's head bobbed slightly with the movement, her eyes closing at the process to make sure none of the noxious goop got into them.

"Okay," Erin said after nearly five minutes, "let's get you bagged."

Elastic plastic bag firmly in place, Erin set the egg timer for the thirty-five minutes suggested on the box, and stripped off her gloves. Sitting across from Tamson, Erin sipped from the glass of red wine she'd been nursing for the past hour and a half.

"Can I get you anything?" she asked, amused by the green daggers that shot her way. When Tamson shook her head, Erin got serious. "So did you find anything interesting today?"

Tamson sighed softly, nodding. "I think she was pretty unhappy. She looked awful in the pictures

I found." Tamson looked down at her hands, which played with the bottle of conditioner that came in the dye kit. "You know," she said, her voice soft. "I really feel like I should have been there. I should have protected her, Erin."

"Do you think you could have done anything *had* you been there? I mean, what's to say that you wouldn't have disappeared, too?"

"Nothing says that. I don't know." Tamson shrugged. "More than likely I'd be wherever my mother is now, too. But man," she let out a heavy sigh. "I don't know."

"What? What are you thinking, Tam?"

Tamson met Erin's eyes, hers dead serious. "I don't think she's alive anymore."

Erin felt her blood run cold. She didn't know a great deal about the situation, but had seen enough of the true crime shows on the A&E channel to know what could happen. She had tried to stay optimistic about things, but seeing the look in Tamson's eyes, she wasn't so sure.

"I'm so sorry, Tam."

Tamson shrugged, setting the bottle of conditioner on the table. "She should have known better. Dale was a bastard from day one." They sat in contemplative silence until Tamson spoke again, changing the subject. "Oh, hey, when you were gone today, your cell phone kept going off."

"Shit!" Remembering her brothers, Erin barked out quick instructions for Tamson for when the timer went off then dashed upstairs.

Erin's heart was pounding as she waited for someone to pick up the phone on the other end of the line. Her brothers Joel and Charlie had been calling her off and on for the past day and a half. No doubt they were worried sick when she didn't show to meet them at her apartment.

"Erin?!" Joel exclaimed as he answered his cell.

"Hey, Joely—"

"Where the hell are you?! Are you okay? Do you have *any* idea how worried we've been?"

"Joel, wait, I know. I'm sorry."

"Where the hell are you? Are you back in Northglenn?"

"No. I'm in Fort Worth, Texas."

"Texas!?!"

Erin winced as she pulled the phone from her ear, her brother's worried roar painfully shrill.

"Jesus, Erin! We've already contacted the goddamn cops!"

Oh crap. "Okay, Joel, shut up a minute so I can tell you what's going on."

"You better!"

❧❧❧❧

Tamson chuckled, not wanting to have to make the call Erin was making. No doubt her family was worried and angry. She glanced at the timer: seventeen minutes to go until she'd see the new her.

❧❧❧❧

"Yeah. Basically. She really needs me right now, Joel. I'm going to be here for her."

Erin's younger brother was silent for a moment, letting everything he'd just been told process. "So when are you coming back? And what about your job?

Aren't you supposed to start soon?"

"Yeah. I know. I talked to my boss. She was fantastic about it. She's giving me until next Monday."

"That was lucky."

"I know. I really thought I was out of a job." Erin looked up at the ceiling as she lay on the bed.

"Erin, is this woman worth all this? I mean, you don't really even know her, right?" Joel asked, voice soft and understanding, but his concern was there, too.

"Yeah. I don't know, Joely. It just feels right. This is the right thing for me to do. I've never done anything like this and I think that I would have hated myself for the rest of my life knowing I hadn't stayed to help Tamson through this. She had no one. I have no regrets. Even if I had lost the job."

There was silence on the other line for a long moment before, "Wow. That was amazing of you, Sis. And though you scared the hell out of me, I'm really proud of you."

Erin couldn't keep the grin of pride from her face. "Thanks, Joely."

※ ※ ※ ※

The timer dinged zero hour and Tamson knew it was time to see what the goop had done. Grabbing the conditioner bottle from the table again, she headed upstairs to the bathroom, hearing Erin's soft, smooth voice through her closed bedroom door as she passed.

Stepping into the bathroom, she looked at her reflection, wincing at the funky, shower cap look. The deep red dye on the sweatshirt collar didn't make her feel any more confident about this.

The water ran hard and hot, just how Tamson liked it. Erin told her to keep washing her hair until the water ran clear. On her third go round, she closed her eyes again, allowing her fingers to roam through the thick strands, digging into her scalp. It brought back the feel of Erin's fingers doing the very same thing little more than half an hour before. It felt wonderful, and she allowed her soft sigh to speak for her.

※※※※

"Hey there, honey," Charlotte greeted from the couch as Erin wandered in.

"Hey," Erin said, plopping down next to her. Erin blew out a breath. She felt tired but relieved that her family was consoled and the search dogs had been called off. "Do you think Tamson liked the clothes you got for her today?"

"I think so," Charlotte said, switching through various channels using the remote for the TV. "She didn't say much, but," she held up a finger, "she didn't seem angry, either."

"Well that's good." Erin laughed. "I think she'll be glad to get out of my clothes." Erin smirked.

※※※※

Tamson slid the frosted glass door shut behind her, stepping out onto the soft rug. After using the towel to dry an exquisite body, she wiped down the mirror, the steam giving way to her reflection. She was stunned, having not seen herself with her normal hair color in years. Before the pink, she'd been purple then blue before that.

Looking closely, she realized that she could easily pass for Charlotte, forty years younger. Shrugging off the notion, she quickly dressed, greatly relieved to have some clothes that fit.

Grabbing a brush, she began to run it through the long, dark strands. She couldn't believe how different it made her look. She was pale, but didn't look nearly as bad as she usually did. Why hadn't she realized that before? Leaning forward, she studied her eyes. They were clear and very green, today. She wondered what Erin would think.

Over the past couple days, Tamson had been fighting an internal war. Her body was craving, begging for, and needing some candy. Her head was too clear, too focused, and she was beginning to resent the reality that swirled around her. It was heavy and painful. Tamson would be lying if she said that hearing the fate of both her parents hadn't affected her. She had been fighting against the urge, knowing deep down that in order to get through this, she needed to keep a clear head. She silently told her body that it would be rewarded for it later. For right now, she had to keep it together and focus on getting this all over and done with and returning to her life in Colorado. But then again, half the reason she used in the first place was not to be present in that life in Colorado.

Tamson sighed at her own reflection. "I'm so fucked."

She could hear Charlotte and Erin talking from the living room as she headed that way. To her surprise, she felt suddenly very self-conscious. She hesitated at the top of the stairs for a moment before finally, with a deep breath, she headed down.

Mid-sentence Charlotte stopped speaking when

she saw Tamson step into the archway of the room. Erin slowly stood, eyes glued to Tamson.

"Wow," she whispered.

Tamson rolled her eyes. "Stop! You guys are making me feel stupid. Jeez." She felt like a bug, though – and she'd never tell Erin this – it made her feel good that the new look had her approval.

Charlotte's loud, off-key voice broke the sudden tension. "I feel pretty! I feel pretty and witty and gaaaaay!" She hurried over to her granddaughter, taking Tamson's hands in hers and led her around the room, singing. It wasn't long before Tamson was grinning, whipping around, and singing right along with while Erin stood back and laughed.

Finally, Tamson had to stop. She was laughing so hard that it was becoming hard to breathe, her bruised ribs making their presence known. She sat down, taking shallow breaths to control her breathing and rapidly-beating heart.

"A little too much excitement for you, huh?" Charlotte joked, not sure what was wrong.

"Yeah. Tell my ribs that," Tamson answered.

※ ※ ※ ※

Erin turned down the comforter on her bed then tugged on the t-shirt she'd been sleeping in. A soft knock on her door got her attention.

"Come in."

Tamson peeked her head around the door. The difference Tamson's natural hair color made still took Erin aback.

"Hey," Erin said, sitting on the edge of her bed.

"Hey." Tamson stepped fully inside the room,

closing the door behind her so she wouldn't wake Charlotte, who'd gone to bed an hour before. "I was wondering, when are we leaving?"

Erin stared at her friend for a moment, surprised by the question. "That ready to leave, huh?"

"Well, I know you need to get back. Erin, you've got a job and stuff waiting for you back in Denver. I can't keep you away from all that any longer than I already have."

Erin nodded, respecting the gesture immensely. She knew they had to get back but felt torn. "What about all your mom's stuff?" she asked softly.

Sighing, Tamson sat on the end of the bed, a bit of space between her and Erin. "There's nothing I can do." She shrugged. "The cops are doing their thing, and me sitting here disrupting your life, and Charlotte's life, well," she shrugged again, "it's just a waste of everyone's time."

"First of all, Tam, you're not disrupting *any*one's life. Certainly not mine." She placed a reassuring hand on Tamson's knee. "If you feel that you're ready to go, then we'll go."

Tamson nodded, looking down at the hand then smiled at Erin. "Okay. I think we should head out tomorrow."

"Alright. We'll head out."

"Okay." Reaching down, Tamson gently squeezed Erin's hand then stood. "Goodnight, Erin," she said, though looked at the bed with wistful eyes before she moved towards the door.

"Tamson?" Erin called softly after her. When she had Tamson's attention, she stood, sliding under the covers and patting the mattress beside her.

Tamson blushed slightly, but did walk to the

bed, hitting the light switch on the way. "I'm sorry," she whispered, lying on her back and pulling the covers over herself. "I know I'm like a five year old, right?"

Erin laughed, turning on her side to face her. "No. I don't see it that way at all."

Tamson mirrored her position, the two no more than a foot apart. "Can I tell you something without you getting mad and throwing me out again?" she asked with a twinkle of joking in her eyes.

"Oh boy. Sure."

"When you were sleeping on the bus, I read what you'd written in the notebook. It's really good, Erin. Fantastic, actually."

Erin fought hard to stop the blush from consuming her features, but wasn't entirely sure how successful she was. She was grateful for the darkness in the room. "Thank you. That means a lot to me." As her eyes began to adjust to the dimness, she was able to make out more of Tamson's features. "What made you decide to become a dancer?"

"You're quite generous to call what I do dancing." Tamson smirked. "And, I can make pretty good money at it. Men seem to like what I do."

"Well, you're absolutely gorgeous."

"Jeez." Tamson laughed. "What is this? Make Tamson embarrassed night or something? Between you and Charlotte …"

Erin grinned. "Just stating a fact, so deal with it."

"Have you ever been to a strip club?"

The question surprised Erin. "Me?" She laughed. "Consider who you're talking to, here."

"Right." Tamson grinned. "Miss 'I've never done a gosh darn bad thing in all my life'."

Erin laughed outright at that. "You know, a week ago I would have been utterly insulted by that, but it's true. Well, not that I haven't done anything bad in my life, but ..."

"Right. I mean, you *did* help tee-pee a house once."

"Hey now, I was the lookout. I didn't actually *do* it."

Tamson grinned. "Right. Silly me."

Suddenly, Tamson shoved the covers back and got out of bed, flicking the overhead light on.

"What are you doing?" Erin asked, sitting up.

"Come on, get out of bed," Tamson said, the radio alarm clock in her hands. She kept the volume low but tuned it to a station with R&B music. "Gonna give you your very own private dance so you can say you've been to a strip club." She shot Erin a saucy little grin.

Erin felt her stomach drop and palms begin to sweat. She had no idea what Tamson was about to do, and though she was nervous as all get out, she had to admit she was curious.

"Um, okay." She looked around the small room. "What do you want me to do?"

Tamson eyed the chair. "Sit over there. It should be big enough."

"Big enough for what?" Erin gasped, eyes huge.

Tamson gave her that same little smile again. "Big enough for the finale. Sit."

Erin sat, legs together and hands resting in her lap, looking ever-so-much the good little school girl.

Tamson's hips began to sway to the sultry beat of the music, her eyes focused solely on Erin, her body language dripping with sexual intent. She danced in a small space in front of the chair, hands running up and over her t-shirt-clad torso until she cupped her own breasts for a moment before her hands moved up and over her neck and finally into her hair.

"Sexy with a cast, huh?" She grinned, her body never losing the beat.

Erin smiled, which helped her body to calm a bit, but her heart was beating so fast she worried Tamson would be able to either hear it or see it pounding against her shirt. She nearly threw up when Tamson danced her way closer to her, teasing her with small touches to her face and hair. She turned and wiggled her behind, making Erin laugh when she began to slap her right cheek with a *woot woot* with each slap.

"Now is when," Tamson said, her voice a low purr as she grabbed Erin's hands and moved them to the arms of the chair. "I get to torment my customer."

Erin gasped softly when Tamson danced her way right onto her lap, Tamson's knees straddling her hips. It was a tight fit; the wingback was just barely wide enough to accommodate Tamson's dance.

"This is when you get to put your hands on me, baby," Tamson purred, taking Erin's hands once more and putting them on her hips.

Erin swallowed hard as her gaze fell to Tamson's breasts, which were almost pushed into her face, the nipples hard and pushing against the thin material of Tamson's t-shirt. She had to admit, watching Tamson dance was one of the most erotic things she'd ever witnessed in her entire life and was utterly stunned at just how affected her body was by it. For a moment, she felt very ashamed and deeply confused, but pushed it away.

"You see," Tamson said, once again taking hold

of Erin's hands. "When someone pays for a lap dance from me, they get to sample the merchandise just a little bit." She ran Erin's hands up her sides and finally cupped her own breasts with them, her hands still on Erin's. "However," she continued, using Erin's hands to squeeze her breasts, "I don't let the men touch these."

"Why not?" Erin asked, her voice barely above a whisper.

"Because these are reserved for the ladies." Tamson grinned, giving her breasts another squeeze before she released Erin's hands, sliding her own down Erin's arms before she rested her hands on the back of the chair, her dance finished as the song came to an end.

If Erin was honest with herself, she wanted to continue touching Tamson's breasts, which were so soft and absolutely gorgeous, like the rest of her body. But, she felt like Tamson was used and exploited enough, so allowed her hands to drop back to the arms of the chair. She was surprised when Tamson didn't move off her lap so looked up into Tamson's face to find that she was already looking at her, her expression no longer that of the seductress, but it hadn't fully left her eyes. Erin felt her heart begin to pound again at the hunger she saw there.

"So?" Tamson said, her lips curling up into a smirk. "You gonna apply at The Swagger anytime soon now that you know what the job entails?"

Erin grinned and shook her head. "No, not for me. Besides, I don't have a sensuous bone in my body."

"Oh, I happen to disagree with that statement," Tamson said, that little purr back in her voice. She ran a finger along Erin's jaw line. "I happen to think you're incredibly sexy and very beautiful."

"Thank you," Erin whispered, her gaze falling to Tamson's lips, which were so close to her own.

Of their own accord, her hands slid off the arms of the chair and onto Tamson's bare thighs. She was amazed at how soft the skin was, so vastly different than the gross hairiness of Mark's.

Erin's eyes slid closed when she felt soft fingertips caress her face, seeming to be tracing her features.

"So beautiful," Tamson whispered. "So very, very beautiful."

Erin's breathing grew shallow as those fingertips brushed across her lips, only to disappear and be replaced by Tamson's own lips. The kiss was very soft, very gentle, then all too quickly over.

"I'm sorry," Tamson said. "I just can't seem to stop doing that, Erin." She smiled shyly when Erin opened her eyes and looked at her. "I just feel so damn drawn to you." She moved off Erin's lap. "I better go before I do something I'll regret or get slapped for." She looked down at Erin, who still sat in the chair. She grabbed one of her hands and squeezed it. "See you in the morning."

Left alone, Erin took several deep breaths, desperately trying to get her body to calm down enough for sleep, as well as desperately trying to talk herself out of chasing after Tamson and begging her to do whatever she wanted to do.

Chapter Twenty

June 28, 2010
It didn't work. Remember I had told you Dale was going to stop drinking. Well, he managed to stay dry through the spring, and then I just don't know what happened. I'm trying to stay optimistic. I just don't know this time.
I love you, honey. Mom

March 19, 2011
Happy Birthday, baby.
Love,
Mom

September 25, 2011
Does it ever get better?

"'Does it ever get better'," Tamson whispered, reading the simple sentence once again. Shaking her head, she gently placed the greeting card back into its envelope. "Not for you, Momma."

Setting the card onto the small stack that she'd already read, Tamson rubbed dry, tired eyes. She wiped her hand across her forehead, feeling the heat coming on again. She was uncomfortable, jumpy, and *still* deeply horny, sleep eluding her. The clock ticked twelve past four in the morning. Pushing up from the bed, she ran her hands through her hair, grimacing at the moisture that came back. She dreaded the night and all the demons that lurked within. Especially in the past few nights.

Not for the first time in the last hour, her eyes flickered to her jacket and what she knew lay hidden in a pocket. Her tongue snuck out to race across her bottom lip, the bitter taste already in her mouth, her tongue swimming in memory-laden juices.

Turning away, she curled her hands into fists, looking at the snapshot of Connie and Dale from Halloween again and then the one sitting next to it, her father. His eyes were sunken in and his face pale and his body rail thin.

"Where are you now?" she murmured, looking into deep-set eyes, hooded, the pupils dilated to the point of no iris color. She looked at the condition of his skin, bruised-looking from the thinness of the unhealthy flesh.

Looking back to her mother, though she had a smile on her face, her blue eyes were dead. Tamson pushed up from the floor and walked over to the mirror that was anchored to the dresser. She looked at her own reflected face: pale, eyes a bit sunken, and the smattering of bruises and healing cuts that littered her features. She looked over at her mother once more, then down at her own arm, still in a cast.

Walking toward the window, Tamson brought a hand up to capture a tear which had made a stealthy trail over her cheek. The bruises no longer hurt and her arm was down to a dull ache. So why did she still feel so sensitive? Why did she still hurt?

Looking over at the floor next to the dresser, she saw the bags loaded with the new clothes Charlotte had bought for her, almost all still bearing their sales tags. Next to them was her jacket and shoes as well as half a pack of cigarettes and a comb. That was it, all of Tamson's worldly possessions.

A sudden feeling of failure and profound rejection of life washed over her, pushing her to sit on the edge of the bed. She thought of Erin's apartment with all of her nice things, swords, nice furniture, and a place to call her own. Erin wasn't much older than she was, a couple, few years maybe. Looking back to her bags of new clothes, Tamson felt more tears squeeze past the walls of her jaded heart. Where would she go once she got back to Denver? It was more than obvious she couldn't go back to the apartment. Maybe Hank would allow her to sleep in the back room for a few days until she could figure something out.

Charlotte had asked her if she wanted to stay in Fort Worth, live at the farmhouse with her. Tamson had to admit it had been tempting, but all in all, she knew she wasn't ready for that. Besides, she had a few loose ends that needed to be taken care of in Denver. Mainly Tanner. She needed to see where he was at, and what, if anything, he had done. If he'd betrayed her trust and opened his mouth …. Was there a warrant for her arrest?

Her conversation with Erin at the McDonald's came back to her, about that night and about her part in Josh's death. She hadn't been clear headed enough in the past three years even to allow herself to think about it, or *want* to. But now ….

Tamson sighed, her eyes begging to be allowed to close. She dreaded what she knew would be coming for her in the dark, but her body was rebelling, beginning to shut down. Gathering the scattered greeting cards, she set them gently on the bedside table and climbed under the covers.

※ ※ ※ ※

The bags of Tamson's new clothes were piled by the front door, along with bags filled with food to snack on during the long trip home. Erin counted the bags, trying to figure out how on earth they were going to manage them on the bus.

She didn't look up as Charlotte walked into the room, but instead saw another bag filled with food join its mates.

"Charlotte, how on earth are we going to carry all of this stuff on the bus?" she asked, finally putting voice to her worries. She glanced over at the older woman, genuine concern filling her eyes.

"Actually, I want to talk to you girls about something. Tamson!" Charlotte called, playing with something in her hands. Tamson hurried down the stairs, coming around the corner with a question in her eyes. "Okay, now girls." The older woman looked from one to the other before taking Tamson's hand in her own, putting something on her palm before closing her fingers over it. Looking to Erin, she explained. "You girls are *not* riding a bus back to Denver. Tamson," she said, grabbing her granddaughter's gaze. "I want to give you an early Christmas present, honey."

"Oh, Charlotte, no. I can't—"

"You hush now," Charlotte interrupted. "I know you're trying to work on some things back home and I want you to have every advantage you can." Opening Tamson's fingers, she held up the set of keys she'd placed there. "Out back, in the barn, is your granddaddy's car. I don't drive it and he certainly isn't going to be driving it anymore. It's a crying shame for it to just sit there and gather dust."

Tamson looked down at the keys, three all told. She was stunned, emotion beginning to clog her throat. "What's the third key for?" she asked softly.

"That key is to my door. This is your home, Tamson, any time you want or need it. You don't need to call, you don't need to ask. You just need to come. Okay?"

Tamson nodded, unable to speak. She wrapped her fingers around the keys for a moment, absorbing what the gesture meant before opening them again. She took a deep, calming breath.

Turning to Erin, Charlotte gently took the keys from Tamson's palm. "Honey, would you mind running and fetching the car?"

"Not at all." Erin hurried out the door.

Turning back to her granddaughter, Charlotte took Tamson in a gentle, yet firm hug. "I feel like I'm losing you all over again, honey."

"You're not," Tamson whispered into the hug that, not only did she allow, but welcomed. Stepping back, she smiled weakly at Charlotte, who cupped her face then let her go. They both turned at the sound of an approaching engine. Tamson's gaze landed on a beautiful old car, a little dusty from being stored, but otherwise, gorgeous.

"That's your grandpa's pride and joy," Charlotte said with a sad and wistful smile. "He picked me up for our first date in that car."

They headed outside, where Erin was already getting out, running her hand along the sleek curves.

"This, my loves, is a 1955 Packard Clipper," Charlotte explained, voice filled with pride.

"Oh, Charlotte, I can't take this." Tamson looked into the older woman's eyes.

"Yes you can," Charlotte said. "It's doing me no good sitting here, honey. I want you to have it. I prefer my Cadillac, anyway." She smiled at both women before squeezing Tamson's arm. "Come on, you two. Let's get you loaded."

The back seat was filled with all the bags of clothes and food Charlotte had so generously supplied. She hugged her granddaughter once more.

"I love you, honey," Charlotte said into the hug before letting her go with a kiss to the forehead. She then turned to Erin, taking her in for just as fierce a hug. "Thank you so much, Erin."

"I'll take care of her," she whispered back.

"You still have the directions I gave you?" Charlotte asked, holding Erin by her shoulders.

Erin nodded. "Yeah. And you said there's a coffee shop not far?"

"Yep. About a ten minute drive away."

"Okay, perfect."

Pulling back with a smile, Erin raised her hand in a small wave then climbed in behind the wheel. Charlotte crossed her arms over her ample bosom, watching as the old car pulled away from the house, blowing up clouds of dust in its wake.

"God speed to you, my love," she whispered, watching until the car was out of sight.

※ ※ ※ ※

The car drove smooth, the engine in pristine condition. Erin had never driven anything older than the 1988 Cutlass which had been her first car. She'd certainly never driven, or been inside a classic such as the deep midnight blue and white beauty she drove now.

Tamson's mind was on anything *but* the car. Somewhere inside she knew that it was hers, and her grandmother's generosity was beyond her comprehension. But right now, her thoughts focused purely on where they were headed. She watched the scenery pass, unfamiliar and strange. She'd lived in so many places in her life, not one of them truly feeling like home. She'd never had a home of her own, never lived alone, and never had a place where she could feel safe and secure. How she longed for that.

Resting her head back against the seat, she sighed, feeling tired and antsy. She just wanted to close her eyes in peaceful relief: no dreams, no noise, no images, and no ghosts. The weight in her jacket pocket felt heavy, her fingers itching to reach inside and relieve it of its burden.

As the car's engine droned on underneath them, Tamson thought about where they were headed. She hadn't been sure if she wanted to go or not, but had to make a decision this trip. Dallas was a lot closer to Fort Worth than it was to Denver. She had no idea when she'd get back down this way and if she'd want to head to Dallas next time. Or ever again.

"Are you nervous?" Erin asked, seeming to read Tamson's thoughts. She glanced over at her passenger, who had been quiet during the past thirty minutes of their trip. According to the directions that were splayed out across the screen of Erin's phone, they only had another twenty-five minutes to go.

Tamson heard the question and sighed, not really wanting to answer. Instead, she nodded.

"You know, we can turn around right now, Tam. You don't have to do this," Erin said, sparing a glance to Tamson.

Pushing herself up in her seat a bit, Tamson felt irritation clouding her mind, anger coming out of nowhere. "I know that, Erin. I'm not stupid," she snapped.

Erin glanced over at her again, but said nothing, instead turning back to the road.

Tamson swallowed hard, trying to keep her temper down. The taste in her mouth was getting stronger and stronger, hot and horribly bitter, but oh so tempting. She closed her eyes as her tongue slipped out, running over her lips, trying to wet them. She had been so dehydrated over the past few days. It almost felt as if only one thing could bring her back to life. Her hand lay on her denim-clad thigh, fingers spread over the expanse.

Seeing movement out of the corner of her eye, Erin glanced over again. Tamson's pale hand, which rested on her thigh, was on the move. She saw the fingers curling up, Tamson's fist pounding lightly onto her thigh. Erin's gaze roamed up to Tamson's face: her brows were drawn, eyes tightly closed, and tongue flicking out to cover parched lips. Erin's eyes flew back down to Tamson's hand, which was slowly making its trek up her leg, fingers opening to take the end of her jacket. The material was caught, pulled taught before let go. The fingers walked their way toward the pocket, the same pocket Erin had seen Tamson head to before, in Tamson's room.

Looking back to Tamson's face, she suddenly had an idea of what the problem was. Tamson's eyes had been clear, her demeanor quiet and gentle over the past few days, as the real Tamson had been allowed to take a breath. But how long could that last?

Tamson pushed her hand away, grabbing the flesh of her thigh. "God damn it all to hell," she breathed, taking in gulps of air.

Tamson's eyes slammed shut again, her brain conjuring up the picture of her mother, throat slit in stage make-up fun. Her hand inched up to touch the hard crust of the cast that wrapped around the base of her thumb and blanketed her knuckles. Taking several deep breaths, she forced her eyes to open. She felt warm fingers take those of her cast-laden arm. Squeezing the welcome comfort, she glanced over at Erin, returning the soft smile.

The silence stretched for a few miles, though it wasn't uncomfortable. Erin glanced over at her passenger from time to time, making sure she was okay. Tamson had grabbed a bottle of water from one of the bags Charlotte had loaded into the back seat. As she sipped from the bottle, she seemed a bit more relaxed, though fidgeted slightly.

"Tam?"

"Yeah?"

"What's your plan? Once you get back to Denver?"

Tamson sighed heavily. "I don't know. I've been asking myself that for four days."

"The thing that happened, with that person you hurt," Erin began, glancing over at Tamson, who said nothing, but nodded in acknowledgement of where this may be leading. "What happened?"

"Guess I went apeshit with a baseball bat," Tamson said simply.

Erin nearly choked on her own tongue. "What?!"

Tamson shrugged. "Tanner, Josh, and I crashed a party. They got into a fight over something while I was ... busy, and Josh and I ended up going home alone." She sighed as she fought the images of that night out of her brain. "I think I had a bad trip or something." Shaking her head, she looked out her window, looking at a family riding in a minivan as they passed. It made her think of Sam, Zea, and the triplets. Turning back to look out at the road, she continued. "Josh got hurt."

"Got hurt? What do you mean, 'he got hurt'?" Erin asked, sparing a glance at Tamson before returning her focus to the road.

"He died." Tamson's words were so quiet, Erin wasn't sure she'd heard them right.

"He died?" At Tamson's nod and solemn look out the window, Erin's brows raised. *Holy shit.* "How did he die, Tam?"

Blood covered the bat, blood splattered...

"Baseball bat," she whispered again.

Christ! Erin swallowed, looking to the road, glancing in her rearview mirror as she changed lanes. Knowing a baseball bat had *hurt* him and a baseball bat had *killed* him were two hugely different things.

"Tam, help me here," she said, "I've never done drugs, so, if you're high, are you capable of something like that?"

Tamson sighed, running a hand through her hair. "You're capable of a lot, Erin." She gave Erin a quick look then turned back to her window.

"What motive would you have had? Were you and Josh fighting? Was he beating you like Tanner does?"

Tamson sighed, shaking her head. "Amazingly enough, no."

"Was it just you and Josh there?"

Tamson thought about that, trying to remember. They were partying at home, having a good time. The front door had opened, but no one had come in. She had thought it was a trick of the acid at the time.

"I don't honestly know," she said, her brows knitting in thought. "I remember noise," she whispered, then shook her head. "I just don't know. I don't remember." A small smirk crossed her lips. "I just know that I was battling the stairs, trying to get up them. It was like they were melting beneath me. The next thing I *do* remember is Tanner helping me to my feet, showing me what I'd done."

"Tamson, that makes no sense," Erin said, shaking her head. "You don't know what Tanner and Josh were fighting about at the party?"

"Not really. Though I can guess, I think." She met Erin's brief gaze. *She has got the most beautiful blue eyes.* "See, Tanner had been living with us for awhile by that point. He had been a friend of a friend who needed a place to crash. He ended up staying, paying rent, that kind of thing. Either that, or he'd supply the candy and we paid his way. Anyway, Tanner made no secret that he was after me." She shook her head, rolling her eyes. "He was a real ass. Still is," she muttered. "Josh was getting a little pissed about it, but knew Tanner wasn't a threat. One night we all had some fun, had some good blow, and ended up having a nice little three-way party upstairs."

Erin's brows shot up at this bit of information.

"It was a mistake. Tanner tried and tried to get us to do it again, or at least for me to, but I wasn't interested. Josh certainly wasn't." She shrugged. "Tension started to grow."

"Enough for Tanner to strike out?"

"I doubt it. Tanner is a piece of shit with no balls," she scoffed.

"That may be, but Tamson, the guy is obviously violent as hell." She glanced at her passenger as they stopped for a red traffic light. Her gaze was met. "Look what he's done to you." She gently touched Tamson's cast. Tamson looked down, her hair falling like a curtain to hide her expression. "Don't you think?"

Tamson sighed, taking in several quiet breaths. She was so damn tired of her emotions escaping the tight reign she'd had on them for so long. Bringing up a hand, she discretely wiped away a small tear. Shrugging, she shook her hair free of her face. "I don't know."

Erin took in the defeated slump of Tamson's shoulders and the way she just seemed to sink into the leather seat of the Clipper. She looked so small, so young, so utterly conquered. Deciding to revisit this subject later, Erin put a smile into her voice. "Hey, hand me one of those orange juices, will ya?" She wasn't thirsty in the least after the monster breakfast Charlotte had fixed for them, but it acted as a great segue to another subject.

≈≈≈≈

Erin felt sick to her stomach as they passed through the arched, cement sign, welcoming them to Elkland Correctional Facility. The Clipper pulled up to a ten-foot sliding gate, topped by spools of barbed wire. She looked at Tamson, not even wanting to imagine what was going through her mind.

"I'm sorry I can't go in with you, Tam," she said, her voice soft.

Tamson sighed, glancing at her. "It's okay. I need to do this alone, anyway. You'll be at the coffee shop?"

Erin nodded. "Call my cell when you need me to come. I'll be here in ten minutes."

"Okay."

Erin leaned across the seat, taking Tamson in a warm hug and leaving a kiss on her lips. "Good luck."

Tamson rested her forehead against Erin's for a moment before murmuring, "Thanks."

Tamson took hold of the door handle, pulling until the door popped open. She quickly shrugged out of her jacket, tossing it to the front seat as she stepped out into the cold, windy day. The sky was heavy and gray, filled with pregnant clouds and the smell of rain. Tugging her sweater closer around her body, she pressed the red button on the box that the man at the checkpoint had told her to push. A tinny voice echoed out into the day, asking her business and name.

"Tamson Robard," she called back.

Within a few moments, a long, metallic moan filled the day, the huge gate slowly sliding open. Tamson stepped into the chain link sally port.

Erin watched, hand resting on the steering wheel. The fence slid shut behind Tamson's slight form, a heartbeat later the fence in front of her sliding open, allowing Tamson to step into the landscaped front yard of the imposing stone building, her hair blowing in the wind.

Erin let out a breath. "Good luck, Tam," she whispered, getting the car moving again.

Chapter Twenty-one

The female officer at the front desk was all business, instructing Tamson to empty her pockets and walk through the metal detector. Making it through without setting it off, she was stopped by the woman, who began to carefully examine her cast, shining a penlight down inside, making sure she wasn't hiding anything within its confines. She was instructed to walk through the sally port, past Master Control, and finally down the stairs and into the door to the right.

The visiting room was fairly large with round tables dotting the space, with a carpeted area for children tucked into a corner. Random vending machines lined one wall and a raised dais with a seated officer dominated another wall. She was told to sit at table fifteen. Spotting the placards with table numbers, Tamson spotted her table and nervously took a seat in the dark blue, plastic chair. Her stomach was roiling and suddenly she wished she hadn't eaten the huge breakfast Charlotte had prepared for them. She worried her eggs might make an encore appearance.

As she sat there, she heard a loud buzzer sound, which she realized was the sound of the door opening to allow an inmate to enter the visiting room. The heavy, steel door slid open and a man stood in the doorway, wearing the dark green scrubs-like uniform the inmates wore.

The man had short, brown hair, the sideburns long but shaped. His eyes scanned the room, stopping when they landed on her. He swallowed, visibly nervous. Various tattoos covered his forearms, all the same quality: dark gray in color, the edges just this side of clear. All tattoos done inside.

Tamson felt her heart pounding as he got closer, jumping slightly at the scrape of the chair across the tiled floor as he pulled it out from the table to sit. Tamson stared into deep-set eyes, forehead furrowed with the roadmap of a hard life, half of it spent behind bars.

"You sure did grow up to be a pretty thing," Vincent Robard said, a tentative smile caressing his lips, his trimmed goatee moving with the action. "Momma was right."

Tamson had no idea what to say to that. She had no idea what exactly her father would say, or what he would look like in person nor how she'd feel about seeing him. A tempest of emotions swirled through her heart and mind, and she wasn't sure which emotion to grab on to.

"I'm real sorry about your momma, darlin'. I hope they find her okay," he said.

Finally, Tamson snapped back to reality, and one word flew out of her mouth before she could capture it and think about it. "Why?"

Vincent cleared his throat and laced his fingers. "Well now. That's a mighty big word, darlin'." He smiled at her, though it was tentative. "Which why would you like?"

"All of them!" Tamson exclaimed, catching the eye of one of the officers on duty. Suddenly she felt her heart fill with anger and betrayal. Her beloved sister's face filtered through her mind. "Why did you do it? Why did you kill Jenny? Why did you beat the shit out of my mother? Why were you such a bastard?"

Vincent sat there, looking very stunned. Clearing his throat again, he nodded, as though resigned to his fate. "Alright. I'll tell you. It was an accident, Tamson. I never meant to hurt you or your sister."

1991 - Fort Worth, TX

"I'm sick and goddamn tired of you coming in here wasted, Vin!" James Roach bellowed, hands on his hips. He looked down his bulbous nose at the young guy who had been working for him at the factory for not quite a year and a half. Vincent Robard's eyes were red and dilated.

"I'm sorry, man," Vin slurred. "It was only supposed to be a beer at lunch."

"And the time before that? And before that?" James' voice got louder with each word. "I can't do this no more, Vin! I've covered your ass too many times."

"Man, I got a wife and kids—"

"You should have thought of that before you got stupid!"

It only took a second and Vincent was out of his chair, lunging at his boss. Both men grunted as James tried to use his greater size to get the drunken man off him. A crash echoed in the small office as the scuffle pushed one of the chairs, slamming into a metal filing cabinet. Another slam joined the crash as the office door was slung open, the knob embedding itself into the plaster behind it.

"Get the fuck off, man!" Byson Washington roared, grabbing the smaller man by the back of his shirt and throwing him across the room. Vincent tried to grab onto a small bookshelf to keep his balance but instead brought the piece of furniture down with him.

"You're fired!" Roach roared, tongue flicking out to swipe at the bit of blood at the corner of his mouth. "Get this loser out of here before I get his ass thrown in jail!"

Vincent cursed at a trashcan as he stumbled into it, making him drop the bottle of Jack he'd been carrying. "Mother fucker," he muttered, kicking at the shattered pieces of the bottle.

৵৻৵৻৸৻৸৻

"Girls, go to the living room and sit down. We'll watch some TV," Connie said, ushering the twins out of the kitchen, the dinner dishes still on the table ready to be piled into the sink until she got around to washing them. Hitting the power button on the TV, one of the characters' faces from *Rugrats* immediately filled the screen, the new cartoon twenty minutes into the episode.

About to hit the volume button to turn the show up for the girls, Connie glanced toward the hallway, her ponytail flicking her in the cheek at the sudden movement, after she heard a loud crash followed by another.

"You girls stay here and be good," she said absently, heading back into the darkened hall. She could hear the twins chattering to each other. "Vinny? What are you doing?" she asked. Her husband had been messing around in their bedroom since he'd stormed in from work an hour ago. He didn't answer as he shoved open another drawer, tossing clothes out behind him with both hands. "Jesus, Vincent! What are you doing?"

Ignoring her, he pushed past his wife, heading toward the tiny closet, on a mission.

"What's going on?"

"Fucker's gotta pay," he muttered, pulling the louvered door open. He shoved hung clothes from one side to the other, peering between garments before turning his attention to the shelf above them.

"Who's gotta pay?"

"Momma?"

"Go play, Jenny!" Connie called out, her gut telling her it wasn't going to be a good night. Vin had obviously had dessert before coming home, and he looked angry. "Are you high?" she hissed. "You promised you wouldn't do that with the girls home."

"Don't fuck with me tonight, Con," he growled, looking her in the eye, his own dilated and hooded. "I'm busy."

"Who's gotta pay?" she asked again, trying to get his mind back on whatever he was doing. "What are you looking for?"

"My gun. That fat fuck is going to pay for this. Fuck!" He yelled, not finding what he was looking for, Vincent pushed away from the closet and fell to his knees next to the bed to look under it. Still not finding it, he stood and shoved the top mattress off the box spring.

"James?" she asked, familiar with Vincent's nickname for his boss. "What did he do?"

"He fired me," Vin muttered, as if he had just told her he'd found a penny under the bed.

"What?! Goddamn it, Vinny!"

"Momma, don't say bad words!" the girls called

in unison from the living room.

Connie ignored them, her blood beginning to boil, though she did lower her voice. "Vincent, what are we going to do? We have rent coming up."

"Do you think I don't know that?" Vincent roared, placing large hands on Connie's shoulders and shoving her out of his way.

"Were you drunk again?" she asked, barely managing to stay on her feet. She saw it coming, raising her hands with a squeak.

"Don't fucking lecture me, Connie!" Vincent screamed in her face, hand stinging from the blow he'd just delivered. He shook it out, turning around in a circle, scanning the bedroom. *Where haven't I looked?*

Connie's world was momentarily an explosion of stars. She blinked against the harsh bedroom light, head beginning to pound already.

"Momma?"

Looking to the doorway, she saw Jenny and Tamson huddled together, both sucking on their blankeys.

"Come on, girls," she said, ushering them out of the room, wincing as she heard a loud crash at her back. Turning the volume on the TV ridiculously loud, she got the twins settled on the floor. Kneeling beside them, she cupped the back of both their heads in each hand, bringing them in one at a time to place a gentle kiss on their foreheads. "Stay here and be good, okay? Momma will be right back."

Getting to her feet, she hurried back further into the trailer, knowing she had to stop Vincent. In his state of mind, he was liable to do something really crazy, like actually try and shoot his boss.

"Vinny, honey, why not think about it tonight, huh?" she pleaded, grabbing her husband's arm as he hurried into the girls' room. "You know, me and you, we can shut ourselves up in the bedroom, maybe bring out a pipe, huh?" She tried to play off his weaknesses for drugs and sex.

Breathing hard from his search, he looked down at Connie, eyeing the goods she was offering him, his gaze settling on her breasts. For a moment, Connie thought she had him but then suddenly he shoved her aside again.

"Get the fuck out of my way," he growled, heading into the bathroom.

"Vincent!" Connie called after him, starting to feel desperate. She knew where the .38 was hidden and Vincent was getting close. Flying to the doorway of the small, avocado-green bathroom, she watched as he tore apart the cabinet under the sink. "Don't do this."

"You don't understand, Connie!" Vin roared. "I got two fucking kids to support, and your ass! What, are *you* going to get off your ass and get a job?"

"Get off my ass? Vin, who the hell do you think takes care of our daughters during the day? Huh? You want to start paying for daycare, fine! I'll go back to work."

Vincent stood. His heart was pounding, eyes more and more desperate, more anxious and paranoid. Turning to the cabinet above the towel bar, he pulled the door open, nearly ripping it from its hinges.

"Vinny, no," Connie whispered, seeing the gleam of the oiled, black metal.

Vincent howled in triumph. "Mother fucker is going to pay!" he crowed, raising the gun over his head, waving it dangerously.

"No, Vinny. There's another way. We'll get you another job. *I'll* get a job." Connie yelped as the gun was suddenly pointed at her.

Vincent grinned, waving the gun in her face. "It's not even fucking loaded, Jesus. Calm the fuck down"

"Vinny, please don't point that thing at me. You know how much I hate guns," Connie pleaded.

"Too fucking bad." He twirled it on his finger, just like the gunslingers he used to watch on TV.

"Vincent, put the fucking gun away!" Connie yelled, feeling more and more nervous. She watched in horror as his thumb flicked off the safety, his eyes daring her to do something about it.

"Don't tell me what to do, Connie! All fucking day all I hear is don't do this, don't do that, well fuck you! I'm the man here, and I'll do whatever the fuck I want! You got it!" He grabbed her face in his hand, squeezing her cheeks together, making her look at him. She tried to pull away, feeling humiliated and angry, but his hold was harsh and his grip was strong.

"Vin—" She grabbed for the gun, tired of the playtime. She heard the softest, sweetest little voice followed by the loudest popping sound she'd ever heard. "No!" she screeched, watching, dazed as Jenny's tiny body was slammed against the bathroom door, sliding to the floor, leaving a smear of red in her wake. She still clutched her blankey to her chest as her eyes slipped shut.

"Jesus Christ!" Vincent screamed, the gun falling from his hand.

Connie fell to her knees next to her daughter, pulling her lifeless body up into her arms.

"Call the doctor!" she screeched, looking

desperately for some sign of life, *any*thing. "Call the fucking doctor!"

Present Day

Vincent's head had yet to raise since he'd started his story. The shot from twenty years ago still echoed in his head, waking him from the dead of sleep almost every night, his daughter haunting him. There was the silence of the tomb across from him. He was terrified to look up and face those same green eyes that dogged his steps every day.

Tamson grabbed the edge of the table, her head suddenly feeling very light and wobbly. The screech of her chair echoed around the visiting room as she ran into the bathroom, slamming the door behind her. The toilet seat was barely raised before she was on her knees, tips of her hair nearly touched the water in the bowl as the remnants of her breakfast came to life.

Coughing as dry heaves took over, Tamson fell back to her haunches, forehead resting against the cool porcelain. The sting of tears weren't far behind, her shoulders shaking with her sobs as she clawed at the toilet.

The bang. The bang Vincent had spoken of had hit her between the eyes, something she felt more than remembered. For better or for worse, she didn't remember. But, god she *felt*.

Her tears dried, though her soul was still in shreds. She finally managed to get to her feet, running her hands shakily through her hair. After washing out her mouth with water from the faucet, she looked at her reflection. She was pale, sickly pale, and tired. So, so soul tired.

Vincent sat where she'd left him, his fingers tracing a scarred pattern on the table. He looked up as Tamson took her seat once more, unsure of what to say to this man who she could not see as a father. Looking into his haunted blue eyes, she felt nothing, just... nothing. No connection to him, not even to his DNA.

"Thank you for telling me," she said at length, her voice quiet, even, and emotionless. "I'm going to go now."

"Wait," Vincent begged, desperation in his voice. He reached across the table and grabbed her hand. Tamson said nothing, her eyes flickering to where his large hand encompassed her smaller, lifeless one. "I see it in you, Tamson." Vincent shook his head, "don't let it get you, too."

"I don't know what you're talking about."

Vincent smiled, though it was sad. "The drugs'll kill *you*, if not everyone you love."

Tamson snatched her hand away, standing. "I hardly think you're the one who should be judging me, Vincent. I'm not the baby killer." With those last words, she turned and headed out of the visiting room, leaving a shell of a man behind.

❧❧❧❧

Erin was almost startled when her phone chirped to life. Seeing a number she didn't recognize, she quickly answered.

"Hello?"

"I'm done," Tamson said, her voice emotionless and very cold. Without another word, the line was disconnected.

Tamson was sitting on the curb just outside the huge sally port when Erin pulled up. She grabbed Tamson's jacket and put it in her lap to make room as Tamson climbed in.

"How did it go?" she asked, unsure. Tamson looked awful. Her eyes were red and her face was incredibly pale.

"Just drive," Tamson whispered. She took the jacket from Erin, hugging it to her chest.

Nodding in acquiescence, Erin put the car in gear, grinding it a couple times – not used to the car – and got them going. The car was filled with silence as the Clipper pulled out of the prison compound, heading out into the city. It wasn't even quite noon yet, but Erin felt like they'd already had a full day.

She glanced over at Tamson several times, worried about her. She hadn't said a word, hadn't moved, had barely blinked, since she'd gotten into the car. Her body was slumped in the seat, weaving with the motion of the car.

Erin drove on, flicking the radio on, but keeping the volume low. Some local station pumped out hits of *"Today and yesterday, all day, every day!"* They passed any number of cars and people walking the streets. The buildings whizzed by, suburbs of Dallas and industrial districts.

Erin turned left onto the 34th Street Bridge, when she was nearly startled out of her mind.

"Stop the car!"

The Clipper came to a screeching halt, the car behind them slamming on their brakes and honking. Tamson opened her car door, ignoring Erin's pleas for her to get back into the car. She walked over to the railing of the bridge, looking down into the chaotic waters below. She held her jacket to her, almost like her blankey from so many years ago. Reaching into the pocket, she felt the smooth plastic of the baggy and pulled it out.

Looking at it and seeing the small crystals inside, she looked back out over the water. Chewing on her lower lip for a moment, she looked back out over the water again before she threw her arm back, grunting with effort as she pitched it forward with all of her might. She watched as the baggy spiraled into the air, absorbing the gray of the day before it began to plunge downward, a gust of wind catching it and sending it sharply to the right before it seesawed down with a tiny splash. It was a bitter/sweet moment as it was swept away in the turbulent waves.

Tamson smiled, eyes closed as she leaned her head back, feeling the chilled air on her skin.

Chapter Twenty-two

Erin brought her hand up, running a finger under her eye, looking at the moisture it had gathered.

"Are you okay, honey?" Janice Riggs asked, her voice soft over the phone.

"Yeah." Erin sighed, looking out into the Lubbock night as she leaned on the railing outside the motel room. "This has all just been unreal, Mom. I can't fathom what she's going through."

"Sounds like this girl has truly gone through hell."

"Yeah. I think she has. Sometimes I just look at her and am just in awe. I don't know what happened today, but from Dallas to here, she was basically like a zombie, just kind of curled up in the seat, you know?"

"What is she going to do once you guys get back to Denver? She has nowhere to go, right?"

"Nope. Nowhere. I'm more than willing to give her a place to stay until she can figure something out, but my place is tiny. I don't even know if she'd accept the help," Erin said with a heavy and tired sigh.

"Well, if, like you said, she's decided to try and kick this drug habit, she's going to need a lot of help, honey."

"I know. I have to start work Monday. I don't have that kind of time to dedicate to her, no matter how much I may want to." Erin ran her hands through her hair. "It's amazing how much you take for granted, how good our lives really are, Mom. I'll never look at life the same way again."

"Everything happens for a reason, Erin. Maybe this girl was put in your life now to teach you something. You both can help each other."

"I've thought a lot about that, too, funnily enough. I want so badly to help her."

"I think you already have, Erin. Probably more than you'll ever know."

"Yeah." Erin sighed, her body and mind exhausted to the point of passing out. "I'm going to go, Mom. I'm so tired. I really just need to decompress."

"Okay. Sleep well, baby, and I'm here, okay? Call any time."

"Thanks. I love you."

"I love you, too."

Erin snapped her phone shut, groaning as she pushed away from the railing and headed back into the room. It was nearly eleven-thirty, she and Tamson having arrived at the motel just after ten. Tamson was long asleep, heading straight for the double bed the moment they'd arrived at their room.

Stepping inside the dark room, Erin immediately went to the bed to check on her. Tamson was lying on her side, back to the rest of the room as she was curled up in the fetal position. Erin leaned down slightly, brushing a few strands of deep auburn from Tamson's face and brought the comforter up a bit further, tucking it under her friend's chin.

Satisfied that Tamson was safe and comfortable, Erin headed for the bathroom and began to run herself a hot bath. The tiny bathroom quickly filled with steam, and it felt wonderful as Erin stripped, letting her clothing fall where it may on the linoleum. Testing with a toe in the hot water, she hissed, quickly adding some cold water, watching as more steam billowed into the air. Finally at a comfortable temp, Erin climbed in.

A long, throaty moan escaped her lips as her tired body sank into the tub's depths. She rested her arms along the cool sides of the tub, a wonderful balance with the hot water that enveloped the rest of her.

She listened to the drip drip as the faucet cried into the water, the sound almost soothing, a lullaby of sorts. Erin sighed deeply, the rise and fall of her chest creating a brief wave pool, the water ebbing and flowing around her, caressing her skin. It wasn't long before she felt her body relaxing, her breathing evening out, and head gently falling to the side.

The night was dark, rainy, windy, and cold. The grass beneath her feet was slippery, the sky cracking open as Zeus' lightning bolt split the ground, leaving sparks, fire, and a gaping hole. Erin blinked rapidly, the fireworks burned to the backs of her eyelids. She held a hand up, trying to protect her eyes from the spectacle.

The smoke cleared, the smell of something burning still hung heavy in the air, clinging to Erin like a second skin. The rain mixed with the smoke that rose from the hole in the ground made the smoke dance as it wafted into the dark sky.

"Erin?"

Erin's ears perked, her name whispered and distant. She looked around to see nothing but endless wet grass and rain-filled night. Turning back to the hole, she felt compelled, pulled toward it. A loud clap of thunder overhead startled her, bringing her to her knees as her heart began to pound, fear gripping her. She stood, trying to steady herself on the grass, which was slick as ice and just as unforgiving.

"Erin?"

Steady, the writer began to walk again, making her way closer to that hole, and closer to the whisper. The edges of the ruined ground were cracked and raised, like the edges of a wound. Afraid to get too close, but knowing she had to, though not knowing why, Erin braced herself for what she might see.

"Erin?"

She opened her mouth, moving her lips to try and respond, but nothing came out, no sound, no reassurances, no promises of help.

"Erin?"

The voice was getting louder and more insistent. Erin felt her heart beat even faster, uncertainty gripping her in a powerful vise.

"Erin!"

Looking into the depths – blacker than black – Erin began to feel panicked, knowing that she must trust and dive. She took a deep breath, inching the toe of her shoe closer to the edge of the precipice.

Feeling suffocated and trapped, blue eyes squeezed shut, Erin turning her face away from the maw before her.

"Erin!!"

Another loud crack—

"Tamson?" Erin gasped, eyes popping open, her body thrashing in the cold water, which had risen almost to cover her lips.

"Jesus, Erin," Tamson sobbed, grabbing Erin's slippery body as she pulled her from the water into a sitting position.

Erin was shivering and disoriented, wondering why she found herself wrapped in the arms of a nearly-hysterical Tamson. She was cold and shivering badly. The warmth of Tamson against her felt wonderful.

"Don't do that again," Tamson begged, burying her face in Erin's chilled neck.

"What?" Confused, Erin allowed herself to be helped from the tub, a large towel wrapped around her, followed by Tamson's arms again.

"I thought something had happened to you," Tamson whispered, taking deep breaths to get her emotions under control. "I kept calling your name and knocking and you didn't answer ..." Her voice was cut off by new emotion.

Understanding filling Erin, she changed their positions, taking Tamson into her own arms, holding her close and whispering into her ear. "I'm fine, Tam. I'm okay."

"You were in there for so long, and no noise ..."

"Shhh. It's okay. I'm fine." As she held a badly trembling Tamson, Erin glanced back at the tub, realizing just how bad that could have been if Tamson hadn't broken into the bathroom and woken her up. A shiver passed through her as she thought about it. A shiver passed through her again as she thought of the dream, now just wisps of memory.

"You cold?" Tamson raised her head from Erin's shoulder, looking into tired blue eyes. Erin nodded, her lips beginning to tremble as she shivered. "Come on," she said softly, taking Erin by the hand. "Let's get you warm."

Erin was led to the side of the bed, allowing her towel to be removed. Tamson took the towel in her hands, starting with gentle strokes to soak up the excess moisture but soon, the touches began to turn into caresses. She met Erin's gaze, her towel-covered hands on her naked breasts, the nipples so hard she could feel them through the thick terry cloth. Without a word, she let the towel fall to their feet, her hands remaining on Erin's breasts.

Erin's eyelids became heavy, but suddenly it had nothing to do with being tired. She let out a soft sigh, her head falling to the side when she felt soft lips on her neck, her own hands feeling the softness of the cotton of Tamson's t-shirt-clad waist. Another sigh was released when a tongue ran up the length of her throat, a moment later lips meeting her own. Though deeply passionate, the tongue that met Erin's was slow and searching. She whimpered when she felt Tamson's hands leave her breasts and find her naked behind.

Erin knew in that moment that she had a huge decision to make, and she made it. Her hands reached down to the hem of Tamson's t-shirt, tugging up on the material as the kiss continued. The kiss broke just long enough for the shirt to clear Tamson's head before it continued with a vengeance.

Tamson pushed Erin to the bed, lying on top of her. Erin buried her hands in Tamson's hair, moaning as she felt their naked breasts pressed together, amazed at the warmth and softness. She opened her eyes when she felt Tamson pull back from the kiss. She met her gaze, fingers caressing the side of Tamson's face, a question in Tamson's eyes.

In response, Erin reached down and slid her fingers beneath the waistband of Tamson's panties, pushing them down. Tamson lifted her hips, allowing the material to be pushed beyond her hips. After a moment of her kicking them off, they lay completely skin to skin.

Tamson rested on a forearm, her other hand left free as she ran her fingers over the softness of Erin's face. She smiled when her gaze met Erin's before she left a soft kiss to Erin's lips then began to explore Erin's neck using lips and tongue.

Erin's eyes fell closed and let out a sigh of pleasure as once again Tamson's tongue ran across her throat. In just the few moments since she and Tamson had begun making love, she felt more than she had in four years with Mark. That very sobering thought left her stunned. Quickly enough, though, that and any other thoughts flew far from her mind as her right nipple was taken into a hot mouth.

"Oh my god," she breathed, hands burying themselves in Tamson's hair once more.

As Tamson's tongue flicked across an incredibly hard nipple, her fingers ran down Erin's side, fingernails grazing along the side of her raised thigh. She used her teeth to chew lightly on the rigid flesh in her mouth, moaning in response to Erin's soft whimpers. Her fingers dipped down between Erin's thighs, a long, sensual groan escaping her throat when she felt how wet Erin already was.

Leaving Erin's breast, she moved up to take her in a hard kiss, her fingers stroking Erin's hard clit. "You're so ready," she whispered against Erin's lips, leaving a final kiss before moving down Erin's body and settling her shoulders between Erin's spread thighs. Her mouth watered at the hot scent of Erin's arousal that met her nose.

Erin looked down her body and watched in nervous anticipation. Nobody had ever done what

Tamson was about to do. Mark, her only sexual partner, refused to perform oral sex on her, and she had no idea what to expect. She didn't have to wait long as Tamson's tongue sliced through the immense wetness. Erin's back arched and her thighs fell open wider, a long, languid groan falling from her lips.

Tamson took her time, exploring every single morsel of tantalizing flesh she found, enjoying Erin's unique taste, as well as how responsive she was to Tamson's touch. As she feasted, she used her fingernails to run along the inside of Erin's thighs, enhancing the sensations that she knew were running through Erin's body. From Erin's rising whimpers and moans, her hips beginning to buck against Tamson's face, Tamson knew Erin was close. She focused her tongue against Erin's clit, adding more pressure with each stroke.

Erin was lost, her body on full autopilot as her hips began to move faster and her moans and whimpers constant and high-pitched. Finally, with a loud cry, she climaxed, the bed beneath her vibrating for a moment with the intensity of her release. Her breath was stolen from her, as well as pretty much any ability to do anything, even think. She was vaguely aware of the fact that Tamson was kissing her way back up her body before taking her in a possessive kiss, which Erin was just barely able to respond to.

Tamson broke the kiss and rolled off Erin, tugging Erin with her until their positions were reversed. Her arm was beginning to ache horribly so she needed to get any pressure off of it. She ignored the rest of her body aching as they resumed their kiss.

Now, on top of Tamson, Erin's vigor returned as she was desperate to touch and kiss the gorgeous woman beneath her that she had to admit, her feelings for were growing by the day, which scared her to death, but she couldn't deny it to herself anymore. Breaking the kiss, she looked down into Tamson's flushed face, met by the intense hunger in her eyes.

"I want you, baby," Tamson whimpered, her thighs parting and her hands reaching down to cup Erin's ass, nudging to get Erin to move into the position she wanted her in, which put their bodies in perfect alignment.

Erin felt a thrill of sensation pass through her at both Tamson's words and the realization that she was pressed intimately to her.

"Move with me," Tamson encouraged, pressing up into Erin to give her the idea of what she was wanting Erin to do.

A bit nervous, as she'd never done anything like this before, Erin began to move her hips, her nervousness easing as the sensations grew. It felt amazing as she spread her own legs a bit, opening herself up more against Tamson's immense wetness.

Tamson cupped Erin's breasts as they kissed, their hips moving together. She spread her legs a bit more, raising her knees as her pleasure grew and intensified. She slid her hands around Erin's sides and down her back until she grabbed her behind in both hands. Their kiss broke as they began to breathe too hard to continue. Erin sped up her pace, pushing up to her hands and thrusting hard against Tamson, who was moaning loudly, her breasts heaving with her increased breathing.

"Fuck," Tamson groaned out between clenched teeth as her body began to burn and finally explode with a loud cry, followed quickly by Erin.

Erin collapsed on top of Tamson, who wrapped her up in a tight embrace, both trying to get their breathing back under control. Tamson cupped the back of Erin's head, leaving a loving kiss on her cheek.

Erin raised herself to her forearms and looked down into Tamson's face, so much emotion and feeling washing through her in that moment as she looked into Tamson's eyes. She caressed the side of her face before leaning down to initiate a slow, leisurely kiss, which Tamson returned. Finally, Erin moved off of Tamson, remembering about her badly bruised torso, and not wanting to hurt her anymore than she worried she may already have.

Climbing beneath the covers, Tamson curled up against Erin, resting her head on her shoulder. "Guess there is something to this cuddling thing," she said with a laugh and a yawn. She raised her head and looked down at Erin, her palm cupping the side of her jaw. "And, if you scare me like you did tonight again, I'll kick your ass."

Erin grinned and leaned up to kiss her before she pulled Tamson closer. "Good night," she whispered then closed her eyes and fell instantly to sleep.

❧❧❧❧

Erin sighed, readjusting her hips on the soft mattress while pushing the covers off her shoulders. She started, eyes still closed, yet brows knitting. A weight. On her back. Erin was lying on her stomach, the pillow hugged to her chest.

Turning her head, she saw Tamson's pillow was vacant, but then realized that was because she, herself had become the pillow. Tamson was curled up against her, head lying just to the left of her spine. As she became more conscious of her surroundings, she realized she was naked then her amazing night with Tamson came back to her.

Erin thought for a moment, trying to decide what to do. It was possibly one of the most uncomfortable positions she'd ever been in but she didn't want to disturb Tamson. Her bladder making the decision for her, she slowly scooted out from underneath Tamson's muttering self, then slid off the bed and padded over to the bathroom.

She pulled the stopper in the tub, the sound of the draining water making her have to pee even more. Relieved, Erin closed her eyes as her body did what it needed to do as she rested her head against the cool wall. She had noticed the light trying to seep around the heavy drapes they'd closed last night. Wondering what time it was, Erin reached over to grab her pants. Her phone and Chap Stik were carefully tucked into a pocket.

"Shit," she muttered, shocked to see it was after ten. Trying to decide what to do, Erin took care of herself, the toilet flushing as she padded out of the bathroom, stopping to examine the bathroom door. It had been ripped off two of its three hinges, the lock busted in Tamson's desperation to get to her. Shaking her head, she moved into the main room. Tamson had moved to her side of the bed again, lying on her side, her pillow aflame with the long strands of her hair.

Looking over at all of their stuff, brought in from the back seat of the car, Erin decided she really had *no* desire to load it all back up and get on the road again. Glancing back to the bed – and the woman lying in it – she decided that *that* was what looked good.

Climbing back in, she scooted over to Tamson and moaned softly at the feel of her warm skin against her. Her intention was to get back in bed and go back to sleep, but as her hand rested on a naked hip, suddenly she was very awake. She left a kiss on Tamson's shoulder, rubbing her cheek against the soft skin. She smiled when she felt a hand reach back and rest on the side of her thigh, which encouraged Erin to press her front a little more firmly to Tamson's incredible backside.

Tamson pulled away just enough to turn over and face Erin, both on their sides. She reached down to Erin's thigh and brought it up to rest over the top of Tamson's own and buried her face in Erin's neck.

"Mmm," she purred, leaving a hot trail of kisses along Erin's neck. "I think this is becoming my new favorite spot."

Erin smiled as her eyes fell closed and her head tipped back to give Tamson more access.

Tamson's hand slid to cup Erin's backside, pulling her in closer as her own thigh pressed against the gathering wetness between Erin's legs. "And this," she murmured, pressing harder and making Erin moan softly, "is definitely my new addiction.

※※※※

Erin popped up like a shot, looking frantically around the room for the source of the crash. Her eyes blinked as sunlight charged in through the swishing drapes. Tamson threw the bag across the front of the room, disturbing the drapes yet again.

"Fuck!" Tamson growled, grabbing another bag and ripping into it and stretching out the plastic.

Articles of clothing started to fly, blue eyes following their progress across the floor, a shirt landing on the lamp, its tag waving like a surrender flat.

"Tamson?" Confused, Erin pushed herself up all the way in the bed. Tamson ignored her, throwing the remnants of the bag at the wall with an inhuman roar. Getting out of the bed, Erin hurried over to her; Tamson quickly moved away from her.

"Where is it? Where the *fuck* is it?!"

"Where is what?" Erin asked, trying to put a hand on her shoulder.

"My fucking candy!" Tamson shoved past her. "Get out of my way."

Stunned and speechless, Erin watched in horror as another bag met the same fate as the others, including Erin's own messenger bag.

"Tam, you threw it out, remember? The bridge?" She fell to her knees, trying to grab up all of the things that had been flung from her bag. "Damn it, Tamson, stop it!" she yelled, ducking before a flying screwdriver from the toolbox hit her. "Stop it!" She lunged at Tamson before she hurt someone, knocking her to the floor.

"Get the fuck off me, bitch!" Tamson flared, using the superhuman strength of withdrawal to shove Erin off of her and into the table. Tamson was on her feet, hurrying over to the box, the only thing she'd taken from Charlotte's house. She ripped the lid from the cardboard container, sending it flying Frisbee style across the room, where it bounced off a wall.

"Tamson," Erin breathed, horrified as the tiny Mary Janes went flying in two different directions. "No, Tam," she cried, sniffling as she watched the baby blanket fly from the box. She scrambled over to her, grabbing her from behind, trying to get her away from the box. She knew that if Tamson were in her right mind, she'd die before she let anything happen to Jenny's things.

"Get off me!" Tamson raged, struggling to get out of her hold.

"Stop it, Tam! Stop it! Hit me, take it out on me, but don't take it out on Jenny."

Erin was stunned as suddenly she was shoved, hard. She was sent flying, knocking the chair over as she hit the table once again, her head banging against the leg. Tamson whirled on her, green eyes on fire and her chest heaving with exertion. Erin met her gaze, tears silently flowing down her cheeks. She watched as Tamson looked around, still panting. When she noticed the overturned box, her eyes landed on the baby blanket.

"Oh, no," she whispered.

Erin had no idea what to do, assuming withdrawal had set her off. She stayed where she was, trying to ignore the pounding in her head. Tamson looked at her again, eyes widening as if seeing Erin for the first time.

"Oh, god, Erin!" she breathed, falling to her knees in the middle of the room, hands going to her mouth, her fingers trembling. Her head fell, hair acting as an auburn curtain. "I can't do this," she cried, shoulders shaking as was her head. "I can't do this."

Erin grimaced as she pushed herself away from the table, her elbow making its presence known like a screaming banshee. Getting to her knees, she slowly crawled over to her.

"No!" Tamson shouted, moving away. "Don't touch me, Erin," she whispered, scurrying away on all fours until she was huddled near the bathroom door. "I can't do this," she said again, her crying harder, guttural. "I can't! I'm too fucking scared!"

"Tamson," Erin said, staying where she was, itching to go over to her. "Honey, you're the strongest person I know—"

"Don't you get it, Erin?" Tamson interrupted, her eyes red and puffy. "I hurt people! I'm not good enough for this," she said, indicating herself and Erin with her hand. "I deserve this shit!" she cried, touching some of her healing bruises and cuts.

"No, Tamson, that's *not* true."

"Fuck you, Erin! What do you know? You don't know *any*thing! I can't do this! I can't, I can't, I *can't!*" She beat her thighs with every declaration, finally setting her head on her knees, tears coming in earnest now.

Erin didn't care about anything. Tamson could hit her or shove her as hard as she wanted to. She scurried over there, taking her in her arms.

"No!" Tamson tried to fight her, but Erin held strong. "I can't do this," she whispered again, her strength finally giving way to profound torment.

"Shh, honey. Shh," Erin cooed, rocking Tamson slowly, cradling her head against her chest. "We'll get through this, Tam. You've got to believe me. We'll get through this. You and me."

"No."

Erin couldn't help but smile at the half-hearted attempt at rejection. She felt Tamson go limp in her arms, Tamson's tears making Erin's naked flesh wet with the tide. She kissed the top of Tamson's head, continuing to rock her.

"You've got so many people who care about you,

and love you. I promise, you'll never be alone again," Erin whispered, laying another kiss on Tamson's head, resting her cheek where her lips had been.

Tamson's eyes were closed. "I can hear your heart beating," she said softly, snuggling in even closer in the warmth of Erin's embrace. "Soothing."

Erin smiled and she ran her fingers through Tamson's hair. "What say you we get some breakfast?" she asked, not daring to pull away until Tamson gave her some sort of indication that she should. She felt the faintest of nods.

Disentangling herself from Erin, she looked into her face, eyes filled with the sorrow she felt. "I'm sorry," she whispered. "Of anyone in the world, Erin, you're the last person I'd ever want to hurt. I just ...." She looked away. "I just hope you can forgive me."

Erin smiled softly, shaking her head. She reached up and used two fingers to bring gently Tamson's face back to her. "Sweetheart," she said, caressing Tamson's face. "I'm not going anywhere, okay? I may not be able to relate to what you're going through right now, but I love... Well, I'm here, okay?" she finished lamely, stunned at what almost tumbled out of her mouth. Instead, she smiled and leaned in to give Tamson a kiss. Behind that kiss was her promise to see it through to the end.

"Thank you," Tamson whispered once the kiss had ended.

"Come on. Let's go get some breakfast – or – I guess lunch." She grinned.

Chapter Twenty-three

Erin looked over at her friend's plate, which was empty, just the glaze of egg yolk left. Tamson had quickly moved on to her plate of buttermilk pancakes, ravaging them and licking some butter off her thumb.

Sitting back, Tamson smiled with satisfaction. She looked at Erin's plate, which still had half of her breakfast of biscuits and gravy.

"What?" Tamson asked, meeting amused eyes.

"Hungry much?" Erin asked. She chuckled when Tamson's cheeks flushed slightly. "When do you want to leave?"

Tamson shrugged, watching as the afternoon light turned her glass of ice water into a prism. "I don't know. How much further do we have?"

"Not sure. I think probably about another eight or ten hours." Erin put a bite of food into her mouth, chewing thoughtfully.

"Well, it's already past two," Tamson said, looking at her friend. "Do you want to drive at night? It's going to be dark within a few hours."

"True." Erin swallowed the food down with a drink of her coffee. "Okay, how about we stay another night and leave first thing in the morning?"

Tamson nodded. "Works for me."

The store was huge and the smell of cut wood and home improvement stuff filled the air. Erin took a deep breath, loving that smell, though she had absolutely no idea what on earth most of the stuff was for. She followed Tamson as she scoured the store, finding an aisle with buckets of nails, screws, bolts, and washers. Almost as though an artist examining her brushes, Tamson reached into various buckets, collecting this piece and that, lining her palm with little bits of shaped metal.

"Okay," she said, scanning the other side of the aisle. "Now we need to find hinges." She walked over to a small display of them. "Do you have an electric screwdriver in your toolbox, Erin?" She glanced at her, catching the look of surprise. "What?"

"Nothing." Erin shook her head. "And yes."

"Good. Here we go." Taking a package from its peg, Tamson turned it over, reading the back. "This'll do it." Heading out of the aisle with the confidence of the most experienced carpenter, Erin followed like the anti-handy man she was.

Tamson held the extra screws between her lips as she stretched up to unscrew the last of the attached hinge. Handing the plate to Erin, Tamson grabbed the sides of the door, grunting slightly as she moved it to lean against the wall.

"Wow," she breathed, looking at just how badly the other hinges were destroyed. She whirled on Erin, pointing the screwdriver menacingly at her. "You do that again, I'll kick your ass, Erinbeth."

Erin's eyes flew open, hands flying up in supplication. "I'm sorry, I'm sorry! I'll never take another bath again."

Tamson smirked, looking at the doorframe. Luckily, there was no damage done to the wood or paint, at least nothing hugely noticeable. Turning back to the door, she began to remove the ruined hinges and screws.

Erin sat on the bed, watching Tamson work. She was impressed at Tamson's efficiency and seeming confidence with tools and carpentry.

"Do you like working with your hands?"

Tamson shrugged. "It's alright, I guess."

"My dad has this amazing workshop on their property." Blue eyes flickered up to gauge Tamson's expression. There wasn't one, save for her concentration on her task. "Yeah, it's great," Erin continued. "He goes out there just about every day, building, tinkering, whatever." She chuckled. "I think he's profoundly disappointed that none of his kids can do shit with our hands."

Tamson gave her a saucy look over her shoulder. "Oh, I don't know. You did just fine with your hands this morning."

Erin blushed, looking away. She glared when Tamson burst into laughter.

"And hey, as for tools," Tamson continued; she brought the electric screwdriver down to her crotch, the tool jutting out obscenely, "I'm sure I can find a tool or two that you could be good at using." She threw her head back and barked out laughter at the expression on Erin's face.

"Tamson!"

※※※※

Erin sat at the small two-person table by the

window, playing her tenth game of solitaire. Growling deep in her throat when she realized she wasn't going to win, she gathered all the cards and began to shuffle them.

Tamson had been asleep for hours already. After she'd finished fixing the door, Erin had seen Tamson's hands shaking, her demeanor fidgety and restless. Without a word, Tamson had curled up on the bed and fallen asleep. Maybe in the peaceful arms of sleep she could forget what she really wanted. Before she'd begun playing her game, she'd used the internet on her phone to read up a bit on addicts, and just what exactly Tamson was going to go through if she truly was going to try and stay clean. It wasn't pretty, and in truth, Erin prayed she had the strength to see it through with her. But then again, in truth, she had no idea what would happen once they got back to Denver and their crazy journey was over.

Turning back to her cards, Erin sighed deeply, tired, but feeling better to know that they'd soon be on their way home. It had been an adventure, but she was ready for the adventure to end and for a bit of normalcy to settle in its place.

Deciding against dealing another game, Erin set the deck aside and instead grabbed for her pad of paper and pen. She hadn't been able to write for a couple days, and missed it terribly. Re-reading where she'd left off, she began to write.

Lights. Twinkling lights. People walked, glancing at her, their mouths moving, but nothing coming out. Looking around, she realized she was at a carnival. Rides, moving in slow motion, mouths opening, releasing silent screams to the thrill of speed.

Walking along the midway, she looked from side to side, trying to make sense of where she was and why. She saw booths set up, cheesy games with even cheesier prizes, barkers trying to get the attention of the marks that strolled along, money burning holes in their pockets. She reached into her own pockets, feeling something inside one. Bringing it out, she found it was a ticket. To what? FUN HOUSE 'N GAMES!

Looking around, she searched for this fun house, seeing more booths, games, and food. Small clumps of people parted for her, like the red sea. They looked at her, some with a grin on their face, others outright laughing, that creepy wide-mouthed, silent laughter.

Up ahead, the giant face of a clown, his red nose a beacon. The wide, gaping mouth, painted just as red, invited the curious fun-seeker to enter. Looking once more at the ticket, she saw a man standing at the bottom of the stairs, his eyes on her. She handed him the ticket. The man took it, bowing in the slow-motion way of everyone else, watching her progress as she walked past him to enter into the attraction.

Unsure and nervous, she looked around, noting she was alone. Up ahead the floor buckled and fell, buckled and fell, making her rise and fall as she hung onto the ropes on either side to keep her balance. Stepping up onto a small landing, then another, she found herself spinning. Looking down, a disc of silver turned steadily, more little discs dotting her path until she was finally trying to walk over a rope bridge. Her hold was precarious at best, her legs wobbly, hands itchy from the rope she clung to, knowing that if she let go that would be it. She would surely fall and not be able to get back up.

It felt like days that it took her to drag herself

across that bridge, chest heaving and out of breath. On the other side stood an arched doorway, the room beyond black.

Curious, yet still timid and fearful, she moved on, scanning her surroundings. It was a hallway, long and narrow, black yet the further she went, the more tiny little stars began to pop up until it looked like she were walking through space itself. Touching the walls, she felt slickness, like glass, yet little hot spots where the stars twinkled.

Feeling at peace, and almost lethargic, she stepped out of the tunnel of space and into a room filled with mirrors. A maze of them – tall ones, shorts ones, wide ones, narrow ones. None showed a true image.

She looked into the first mirror she saw, gasping at the broken, bloody reflection that pleaded back at her, hand silently reaching out to her from the other side of the glass. Stepping away, fear and pain catching in her chest, she moved on. The next mirror showed a scene, lots of people. Men. As they parted, she saw herself lying on a table, skirt shoved up to her waist, legs dangling limply over the edge. Her own eyes that looked back at her were cloudy, unfocused, and half-hooded. She watched in horror as a man stepped up between her legs, lowering his pants just enough to do what he was in business to do. She watched her own image teeter up and down on the table with the force of each thrust. Again, a hand reached for her.

Shaken and feeling nausea begin to gnaw at her gut, she moved on. She was terrified to look in the next mirror, but had no choice. There was nowhere else to go.

A soft smile spread across her lips as she saw this reflection: she sat on the bench of a picnic table, leaning back on her elbows, which rested on the edge of the table. Her hair blew back in an unseen breeze, her eyes closed and face raised to the sun.

She stepped toward the mirror, reaching a hand up to feel the glazed surface, wanting so badly to step into that scene, so serene and calm. She had to move on. Nothing could last forever.

The mirror around the bin was darkened, a cloth hung over its visage. Slowly the curtain began to gather and raise, her shoes, jean-clad legs and her hands resting at her sides. She gasped, taking a step back and her hand reaching up to clutch her stomach. Before her stood herself, a small red spot like a bulls-eye dead center of her stomach. It slowly began to grow.

She didn't want to look up into the face, tears running down her cheeks. She didn't want to see it, but her eyes betrayed her, rising steadily until she looked into her own face, pale, ashen, eyes darkened and sunken. She almost looked skeletal.

"This should be you."

Tamson shot up in the bed, her scream still echoing through the room. She couldn't breathe, her hand going to her chest as she gasped, trying to suck in precious air.

"Tamson? Jesus, what's wrong?"

She felt more than heard Erin's frantic voice and felt her hands on her face. Tamson couldn't move; her eyes were wide and glazed, mouth open as her heart pounded in her ears.

"Tamson? Honey, talk to me. What is it?" Erin pleaded, sitting on the edge of the bed, hand still cupping Tamson's face. Her heart rate was beginning to slow, but her concern only grew as Tamson stared straight ahead, as though Erin weren't even there.

"Should've been me," Tamson gasped, not even realizing she'd spoken. Tears were still running down her cheeks, the hair near her ears soaked as the tears had puddled inside them.

Not sure what to do, Erin drew her to her, Tamson simply falling to the side, head resting against Erin's shoulder. Erin wrapped an arm around narrow shoulders, massaging the skin of Tamson's arm.

"Do you want to talk about it?" she asked, slowly falling back to the bed, taking Tamson with her.

Tamson settled against her shoulder, head slowly shaking back and forth. "I hate the dark," she whispered, barely audible.

Chapter Twenty-four

Erin glanced over at her chatty passenger for the fourth time in about as many topics. Tamson was animated, gesticulating, her eyes wide with the enthusiasm of her words. Erin had lost track of what she was talking about, her mind still somersaulting over the amount of words coming out of Tamson's mouth.

"You know?" Tamson finished, looking over at the driver expectantly. Erin nodded, trying not to look as confused as she was. Tamson turned back in her seat, watching the barren countryside pass by. She was exhausted, wanting nothing more than to curl up against the door and fall asleep. She couldn't. She must stay in the land of the conscious or she'd remember and have to see it again: her dream. No, her nightmare. "What's your favorite number?"

Erin's brows drew, trying to compute a whole *new* topic, yet again. "What?"

"Favorite number. What is it and why?" Tamson leaned against the door, looking at Erin's profile. She grinned, as yet again, Erin looked baffled.

"Oh, uh, guess I never thought about that."

"Come on, Erin. Think outside the box," Tamson pleaded.

"Alright. I guess it would have to be twenty-five."

"Why?"

"Well, it fits so nicely. It's like this perfect little square that fits neatly in fifty, one hundred, seventy-five..."

"Yeah, but it can't be broken up. It has to stay whole," Tamson pointed out.

Erin thought about that, turning it around in her head. "Hmm. True. Okay, what about you?"

"Eleven," Tamson said, no hesitation.

"Why?" Erin asked, playing Tamson's own game. And she was truly curious now. Favorite number. Who has a favorite number?

"Because it never gets used. Ten is used all the time, twelve is used because it's an even number. But eleven is just kind of," she paused in thought, glancing out the side window, "overlooked."

Erin glanced over at Tamson again, brows yet again dipping. Her first instinct was what??!! As she thought about it, a slow smile spread across her lips.

"I think that is one of the cutest things I've ever heard," she said. She met Tamson's gaze. "No, seriously. The underdog of numbers. That's great!" Erin gave Tamson a huge, face-splitting grin, which Tamson returned. "What's your favorite color?" Erin asked, settling into this game of questions.

"Red."

"Why? Does it have some humanitarian reasoning, too?" Erin teased.

Tamson rolled her eyes. "No, it's just a hot color." She gave Erin a grin that made Erin squirm in her seat. "It's a passionate color. What about you?"

"Hmm," Erin hummed, glancing in her rearview mirror as she changed lanes, allowing a speeding truck to pass on her left, tired of it inching up her tailpipe. "Orange and yellow. And," she held up a finger, "before you ask, yes there is a reason. I love sunsets."

"Cheesy, but understandable."

"Thanks," Erin growled, hearing the soft chuckle from her passenger. They rode on in silence for a few miles until Tamson spoke up again.

"If you won ten million bucks, what would you do with it?"

Erin chewed on her bottom lip as she thought about that, slowly roaming back over into the left lane, passing a small caravan of school buses.

"Well, I'd pay off my parents' and brothers' bills then buy me a house somewhere."

"Really? In that order?"

"Yeah." Erin glanced at Tamson, seeing the surprise on her face.

"Huh. My mom would just piss the money away."

"And you?"

"Probably." Tamson grinned, a bit of mischief in her eyes. "I know I'd get the hell out of here."

"Where would you go? I mean, if money weren't an issue, where would you go?" Erin studied the control panel, looking for the windshield wiper switch as the sky began to leak.

"Oh, jeez. Where *wouldn't* I go?" She leaned her head back, a wistful smile on her lips. "I'd love to see Europe. Alaska. Really anywhere. I just want to experience, you know?"

Erin nodded. "Yes I do."

"Have you ever been anywhere cool?"

"I've been to Burbank, California."

Tamson snickered, seeing the grin on Erin's face "Go you, you adventurous one, you."

"I know, right? Don't you wanna be me when

you grow up?" Erin grinned over at her. Her grin grew when Tamson reached over and rested her hand on Erin's thigh.

"Only if you'll be me," Tamson snickered. Erin grinned at her. It felt so good to smile and laugh.

"If you had three wishes, what would they be?" Erin reached behind the front seat, blindly reaching for the six-pack of Dr Pepper they'd picked up. Snapping one from the plastic rings, she popped the top.

"Three wishes, three wishes," Tamson murmured, thinking. She tapped a finger against her knee, head flying back to rubberneck a car they passed. "Holy shit! That guy was getting a bl—" She stopped herself, turning around to see Erin looking at her. "Well, fellatio."

Erin burst into laughter. "Tamson, I'm not as innocent as you seem to think. I won't break with the term *blow job*, honest."

Tamson looked away, face red. "Yeah, well, anyway, that guy back there was getting one."

"Okay, seriously. Three wishes." Erin took another long draw from her soda.

"Well, I'd wish for world peace, food for the hungry, and a woman President." She grinned big at Erin, who chuckled.

"Are you answering the question or practicing for a beauty pageant?"

"I don't know, won't I need to practice my wave, too?" Tamson raised her hand, fingers tightly held together as she gave her wrist a little twist.

Erin threw her head back, laughter filling the confines of the small car. She raised her own hand, giving her very own Miss USA wave to a Miata they passed, the passenger looking over at her like she had lost her mind. Tamson burst into laughter, clapping her hands together as she saw the Miata speed up.

"We're such bad people." Erin laughed, waving to the little sports car as she saw the driver glance back at them from his rearview mirror.

"He's no fun." Tamson chuckled. She reached behind them, grabbing the box of Ding Dongs. Tossing one into Erin's lap, she unwrapped her own chocolate cake treat. "Three wishes. Okay." She took a bite, chewing as she thought about her answer. "Well, world peace would be nice, but it's never going to happen, so why waste a wish?"

"Very true and very cynical." Erin did her best to steer with her knees as she unwrapped her Ding Dong. Quickly taking hold of the wheel once more, she took a big bite.

"I really wish my mom could know some peace in her life," Tamson said, head slightly cocked to the side in thought. "And I'd wish that I could talk to her again, ask her why, you know?" The air in the car had grown serious, unsaid suspicions flowing between them.

Erin smiled softly at her, placing her hand atop Tamson's, which had returned to her thigh, and squeezed affectionately. "Maybe you will, Tam. Don't give up yet."

"Yeah. Maybe." Popping the last bit of cake into her mouth, she chewed and swallowed. "My third wish would be for everyone to know such good people." She looked at Erin pointedly.

Finally, Tamson had given in to her need for

sleep, her head resting against the passenger window. The sun was starting to go down, the land around the old car sketched in gold and orange. Erin smiled, taking in the beauty of her home state. It was such a gorgeous time of day, that moment when day kissed twilight, bowing out gracefully for night to take its place.

The roads were becoming winding and straddled by mammoth rock faces, the red clay in the rocks making them look like a slab of steak, cooked medium rare, veined with tasty streams of fat. As pretty as it all was, she was definitely ready to get home.

≈≈≈≈

"That's the last of it," Tamson said, standing in Erin's living room with her hands tucked into the pockets of her jeans, all the new bags of clothes she'd helped carry in on the floor at her feet. She looked around, feeling nervous and unsure. She couldn't make herself meet Erin's gaze.

Erin walked over to Tamson and rested a hand on her arm. "What's wrong?" she asked.

Tamson shrugged noncommittally, chewing on her bottom lip. "I, uh ..." She looked down at her shoes. "I should go, Erin."

Erin's brows drew. "Why? Tamson, what's going on?"

Again, Tamson shrugged. "Erin, you've done so much for me, and I just, I can't keep dragging you through this shit." She finally met Erin's troubled gaze. "It's not fair. I mean, it was amazing, *you're* amazing, but I'm just a fucked up piece of shit stripper who can't get her shit together."

"Okay, whoa," Erin said, holding her hands up. "Time out. First of all, you're not anything close to a fucked up piece of shit anything. Going with you and discovering all that you've been through and why." She shook her head in amazement. "Honestly, I think you're one of the most incredible human beings I've ever met, Tam." She rested her hands on Tamson's arms again. "Honey, I want to continue to be in your life. I mean, yeah, there's a lot that needs to be done, and a lot of hurdles, but – "

Tamson stepped away from her, shaking her head. "No. It's too dangerous, all this shit right now, Erin." She looked down at her shoes again. "I don't want you to get hurt." She spared a glance to Erin. "By Tanner or by me."

Erin stared at her in stunned silence for a moment. "You know, I wasn't sure what was going to come of all this, if maybe everything happened simply because we were away from home and," she sighed and turned away. "And I don't know. Guess you needed comforting." She smirked and began to pick up the bags of clothing and toss them to the couch. "I don't know."

Tamson felt the sting of tears behind her eyes but refused to let them loose. This was for the best. "Erin – "

"No." Erin faced her, her jaw set and chin raised in stubborn pride. "It's okay. It is what it is." She reached into her pocket and removed the key to the Clipper. "This certainly needs to go back to you." She held the key out on her palm.

Tamson studied the key for a moment, frozen where she stood. Her stomach was threatening to revolt, and she wasn't entirely sure why. Again, not able to look Erin in the eye, she finally took the couple steps over to her and took the key, her fingertip grazing Erin's palm in the process. She ignored the jolt that sent through her. She watched as Erin walked away, disappearing into her bedroom, the door closing softly behind her.

"Fuck," she whispered, burying her face in her hands for a moment. Letting out a heavy sigh, she turned and looked at the bags from Charlotte. She considered leaving it all behind, but she'd imposed on Erin enough – so she was desperately trying to convince herself – and gathered everything up, making sure nothing of Erin's was in any of the bags.

With one final look around, Tamson headed toward the front door, passing the short hallway that led to Erin's bedroom on the way. She stopped, looking at the closed door. She heard a soft sniffle on the other side and literally had to fight the impulse to go to that door, fling it open, and beg for Erin's forgiveness.

Her own tears managing to escape, Tamson hurried to the front door and beyond.

Chapter Twenty-five

"Okay, so you think you've got everything?" Nancy Pierce asked her new employee, who sat at her desk just outside Nancy's.

Erin took a deep breath and looked around at everything she'd just been shown. She looked up at her boss and nodded with a smile. "Yes. I think I can remember all this."

Nancy grinned and patted Erin on the shoulder. "I have no doubt. I'll leave you to it." She started to walk away then stopped, turning back to her. "Hey, how's your friend doing, anyway? I mean, it sounds like it was quite the adventure, huh?"

Erin smiled as politely as she could and nodded. "Yeah, it sure was. And, she's fine. Just trying to get back into the swing of things, you know?"

Nancy studied her for a moment then returned the smile. "Glad to have you on board, Erin." With that, she headed to her office and closed the door.

Left alone, Erin looked at the list of notes she'd taken on current cases and order of priorities that needed to be done. She turned to the computer and typed in the username and password she'd been given for her new work email.

As she started to get settled into her day, she did her level best to keep Tamson off of her mind, but unfortunately, the moment Nancy had asked about her, all bets were off. She was definitely grateful for all the new responsibilities she had to master, as it did help somewhat to keep her thoughts on track, but it wasn't a complete success. It had been two days now since Tamson had left her apartment. Two very long days, and Erin desperately wanted to just forget and not lay in bed wondering where Tamson had gone and if she was still alive.

Letting out a heavy sigh, she literally shook her head, trying to shake out the direction her thoughts were heading and focus on her job.

⁂

"So, you finally get hot again with the red hair thing going on but you ain't in no shape to dance," Hank muttered, shaking his head. "How's the arm, kid?"

Tamson shrugged. "Aches, but it'll heal."

"Well listen, I'm glad you called. Maria get you settled in alright down here?" he asked, hands on his hips as he surveyed the small, basement bedroom in his house.

"Yeah, she was great, thanks." Tamson also looked around the tiny room, just big enough for a twin-sized bed, tall five-drawer dresser, and the doorway to the bathroom with a toilet and a shower stall, not even a sink.

"Well, you can stay here as long as you need to. Maybe teach Maria how to make a decent spaghetti."

Tamson laughed. "Be nice. You're lucky she was stupid enough to marry you."

Hank grinned. "Alright. See ya later, kid."

Left alone, Tamson sat on the bed, which squeaked under her weight. She wrapped her arms around her, in desperate need of a comforting hug, as well as in desperate need of so many things, which she was trying not to allow herself to think about. To her relief, a lot of the shakiness had begun to subside, but the craving was still strong, especially now. She felt so utterly alone, like not a soul in the world cared, though she knew that wasn't true.

With a heavy sigh, she fell back onto the bed and stared up at the ceiling. She had to admit, it was pretty strange being in the basement bedroom of her boss' house. She saw Hank every day, stole his drugs, taken his bullshit, and given some back in turn. She liked Hank, but he was just her boss. The thought of him having a life or home outside of the club just wasn't something that entered her brain. Sort of like being in school and seeing a teacher shopping and doing things that normal people do. Maybe that was it: seeing Hank as just a normal person, husband, father, and homeowner, was strange.

Tossing her musings aside, she sat up again. After spending a night in the Greyhound Bus depot downtown, she'd decided it wasn't safe and she needed to go underground for a bit – literally – until she figured out what she was going to do. She was terrified Tanner was going to find her or that she'd be outted by someone at the club, which was why she hadn't gone there, though that had been her first thought. She knew a few of the girls had slept on the cot in the back room more than once.

The one place she wanted most to be was the one place she could never allow herself to go again.

"I'm so sorry, Erin," she whispered, running her hands through her hair to get it out of her face.

Feeling lost and alone was certainly not a new

feeling for Tamson, but lonely, definitely a new one. The craziest part of that equation, however was that there was only one person on the whole of Earth that could wash that feeling away. Going out and looking for "company" wasn't going to cut it this time.

Pushing up from the bed, she walked into the bathroom to see the two neatly folded towels Maria had left for her, as well as a bottle of shampoo and body wash sitting on the back of the toilet. Thrilled to get a shower and not just a wash up in the bus depot bathroom, Tamson stripped and got ready for a hot shower.

❧❧❧❧

"So, what's the plan?" Hank asked, sipping from his beer as he gazed at Tamson, who barely picked at her food.

"Honestly, I don't know. It might just be better if I leave Denver altogether," she said, setting her fork down. She looked first at Maria then at Hank. "I'm not sure he'll stop until he finds me."

Hank nodded. "He's been at the club a few times this week asking around about you." He studied her for a moment. "What kind of hold he got on you, Tam? Why don't you just get that lousy bastard arrested for what he did to you and call it a day?"

Tamson shook her head. "Long story. I don't know. Maybe I'll go back to Texas. My grandmother offered me a place if I need it." She stared down at her half-eaten portion of lasagna. For all the world, she wanted to cry. It wasn't her arm that ached in that moment.

※※※※

Present Day, Houston, Texas

"Where the hell did she go?" Rhonda muttered absently, rhetorical as she knew her husband, Zane had no more of a clue than she did where their German Shepherd, Lulu was.

"Lulu!" Zane called out, the couple continuing on their hike, both scanning the area near the stream for their dog.

Just up the overgrown path stood a small copse of trees, a large rock jutting out of the ground next to it, the sound of the slowly moving water close by.

"Lulu!" Zane called again, this time getting a response. The dog popped her head up, tail wagging like crazy and something in her mouth.

"What the hell does she have?" Rhonda asked, bringing up a hand to shield her eyes from the strong rays of the overhead sun.

"Jesus Christ!" Zane yelled. "We gotta call the cops."

Chapter Twenty-six

"Oh yeah," Melissa whimpered, a hand whipping out to brace herself against the wall so her head wasn't bashed into it with each slapping thrust. "Fuck me!"

Tanner grabbed handfuls of the stripper's ass as his thrusts sped up even more, sending them both over the edge with a roar. He pulled out of her ass cruelly, missing the wince of pain on her face.

"Get us a beer, bitch," he panted, falling to the mattress and bringing up his hands to wipe the sweat from his face.

Without a word, Melissa pushed up from the mattress and padded to the kitchen in the apartment, which was a disaster and looked like a tornado had raged through it. She tried not to look at the blood that was still on the wall that Tanner had explained was because Tamson was a fucking cunt and deserved to be straightened out.

"Here ya go, baby," she purred, lowering herself back to the mattress beside him, handing him a can of Fat Tire. Without a word, Tanner snatched it from her fingers and popped the top, taking half the contents with just one gulp. "So, you still comin' tonight to watch me dance?" she asked, eyeing him.

Tanner didn't look at her as she shrugged. "Fuck if I know. Guess it depends on if there's somethin' better going on." He smirked at her.

"Damn it, Tanner!" she whined, smack him on the chest. "Don't be mean."

Tanner just grinned and finished his beer, crushing the can with a huge belch and tossed the crumpled aluminum to the corner of the room.

"So, I heard something the other day," Melissa said, running a polished red fingernail across Tanner's thigh.

"Yeah?"

"Yeah. Rumor has it she's staying with Hank."

Tanner pinned Melissa to the spot with a hard look. "You fuckin' shitting me? She's banging that grease ball?"

"I didn't say that, baby. Just said she might be staying there."

Tanner got to his feet, stepping over her to the floor. "Get the fuck out," he called, slamming the bathroom door shut after he entered the tiny room.

જાજાજાજા

"Okay, and then here's the deposition you wanted on the Steiner case," Erin said, laying another file folder on Nancy's desk, proud of herself that she'd gotten everything done on her list for the day. As the days went on, she was picking up more and more on Nancy's vibe, able to read her better so she could try and be anticipatory of her needs.

"This all looks really great, Erin," Nancy said, paging through the folder. She smiled up at her. "Good work."

Erin beamed. "Thanks. Well, if we're good I think I'll head out, is that okay?"

"Yeah, go, go," Nancy said, waving her off. "I've

still got hours before I'm out of here, but have a great night, okay?"

"You, too."

Erin headed back to her desk, able to hear her cell phone ringing as she got closer, so she hurried her steps. She'd be lying if she said she wasn't hoping for a particular person on the other end, and her heart sped up a bit when she saw it was a number she didn't recognize, but it wasn't a Colorado number.

"Hello?" she said into the small device as she leaned over her desk and shut down her email and computer. She stopped, brows drawing. "Yes, Detective Franklin, of course I remember you. Uh, Tamson isn't here … no, I'm sorry, Detective. I don't have a number for her—" Erin's eyes widened as a hand came up to her mouth. "I see. Um," she stuttered, hands trembling slightly as she sank down into the chair. "I'll see she gets the information, thank you. Goodbye, Detective."

Slapping the phone shut, Erin set it on the desk as she sat there, dazed. She glanced at the phone as though suddenly she'd get another phone call telling her it was just a joke and that Connie and Dale Young's remains hadn't been discovered four and a half hours away from their home.

"Oh, Tamson," she whispered, burying her face in her hands. Tears began to roll down her cheeks. "Where are you?" She looked up from her hands and grabbed for a tissue from the box on the corner of her desk. She dabbed at her eyes, rolling her eyes when she saw the black tell-tale signs of her smeared eye makeup.

"Thanks and have a nice day," Tamson said, leaving the shop with Hank's dry cleaning folded over her arm. He'd offered to toss her a few bucks if she did a few errands for him. She needed to earn money and save it so she'd have something to get herself to Texas with. She hadn't called Charlotte yet and make her intentions known, wanting to make sure it was ultimately what she wanted to do, first.

Tossing the bag-covered garments into the backseat of the Clipper, she climbed in behind the wheel and got the old car started, headed to grab a couple personal items she needed before heading back to Hank and Maria's place.

※ ※ ※ ※

Maria sang along with the music that blared from the docked iPod as she made her meatballs, her mother's recipe. Though Hank complained about her spaghetti, she thought it was fantastic. Swinging her plump behind around as she continued to serenade her kitchen, she didn't hear knock at the front door, nor the doorbell that followed. She did, however, hear the loud crash when the front door was kicked in.

※ ※ ※ ※

Erin sat behind the wheel of her car, fingers tapping as she tried to decide where on earth she'd start to find Tamson. Her stomach was in knots, not only because of the news she had to share with her, but because she was nervous to see her. No matter how many times she'd craved Tamson's presence with her or had dreamed about her or cried over her, she just wasn't sure what she'd actually get once she was in front of the woman again.

Finally deciding that The Swagger was the best place to start, she got her car started and headed out of the parking lot of her job.

☙❧❦❧

WHACK! "I *said,* where the fuck is she?" Tanner growled, the terrified fat woman held against the wall by his hand closed around her throat. He brought the gun up again and pistol-whipped her with it a second time. "Tell me or I fucking kill you bitch, you got me?"

☙❧❦❧

Hank sat in his office, rolling a pen between his sausage-like fingers as he read over the printed out schedule for the waitresses and bartenders. He lowered the writing utensil to scribble a couple changes but stopped when he heard a knock on the closed door.

"What the fuck you want?" he barked, irritated at the interruption.

"Hey, boss, some chick is here to see you," Luther, one of the bartenders said, peeking his head just inside the office.

"Yeah, what else is new?" Hank smirked. "Who is it?"

Luther stepped aside to reveal Erin standing just behind him. "Chick says she's got news or something for Tam." With that introduction, Luther walked away, leaving Erin standing at the opened door.

"Who are you?" Hank asked, turning the squeaky office chair so he could look at her.

"Um, sorry to bother you," Erin said quietly as she stepped inside. "My name is Erin and I'm a friend of Tamson's."

Hank eyed her up and down, wiggling the pen in the webbing between his thumb and side of his hand. "Yeah. Ain't you the chick she was staying with after that fuck got to her?"

Erin nodded, taking his offer to sit in a second chair. "Listen, do you know where I can find her? She left my place several days ago, and I really need to talk to her."

"You're her friend, why ain't she still stayin' with you?" he asked, not revealing that she was staying with him, as he wasn't sure about this chick. "You leave the message here and I'll see she gets it."

"Look, if it's all the same, I really, really need to speak with her. It's an emergency," Erin pleaded.

Hank looked into probably the most earnest set of eyes he'd ever seen then; with a heavy sigh, reached over and grabbed the handset of the desk phone. He used the flat end of the pen to punch in ten numbers quickly. "She better not have lost that fucking phone I'm lettin' her use," he muttered.

༄༅༆༇

With a growl, Tamson turned down the blasting volume on the car radio when she heard the first notes of the ring on the cell phone Hank had given her two days before. He was the only one who had the number, so she knew it had to be him, no doubt wanting her to pick something else up. She was turning onto Hank's street and just wanted to go to her room and relax.

Looking at the display on the phone, she rolled

her eyes as it was his office number. "Yes, I picked up your shirts. Yes, I picked up your golf clubs from the Pro shop. Yes, I picked up extra cheese for dinner tonight. Yes—"

"Tamson, shut the fuck up," Hank growled on the other end of the line. "Listen, I need you to come down here real quick. You got someone here who wants to talk to you 'bout something."

Tamson's brows drew. "Who?"

"Your buddy, Erin."

Tamson felt her stomach drop and palms begin to sweat. "I'm sorry, Hank," she said, voice quiet and filled with shame. "I can't."

"What do you mean you can't?" Hank bellowed. "She's your friend, for crying out loud! She says she's got something to say to you, so give this woman respect and come listen."

Tamson was quiet for a long moment, trying to decide what to do. "Alright Hank, fine. I'm on my way."

Tamson hung up the phone before he had a chance to say anything else. Tossing the phone to the seat next to her, she slowed the car and pulled into Hank's driveway. She sat there for a moment, contemplating going in and dropping off the cheese to Maria, whom she knew would likely already be working on dinner. Staring up at the house, something in her gut told her to get going. She couldn't explain it, but wasn't going to question it. Something was wrong and she just hoped Erin was okay.

Putting the car in reverse, she backed out of the driveway and headed back in the direction she'd just come.

❦❦❦❦

"Who's that?" Tanner muttered to himself, looking down at the front of the house from his vantage point in one of the bedrooms upstairs. He saw the old classic car pull into the driveway, sit there for a moment, and finally leave. He wasn't able to see the driver, nor did he recognize the car, but something in his gut told him she was getting away. "Fuck!"

Tearing down the stairs and over the body of the fat bitch who had tried to get in his way, he ran out the door and down the street to where he'd parked his truck a block away.

❦❦❦❦

Erin waited in the main room of the club, watching as some of the dancers milled around or worked on a routine. The bartender leaned on the bar, watching them. Erin had to chuckle at the immensity of her déjà vu, pretty much the exact same scene unfolding before her almost two weeks before. Even more ironic, despite everything she and Tamson had been through together, she was just as nervous this time as she'd been the first.

The front door opened, the darkened club briefly filled with blinding light as someone came in, the door slamming shut behind them. The person was Tamson and, it only took her looking around for a moment before she saw Erin and walked over to her.

Tamson tossed a wave in greeting to the few people who called out greetings to her, her gaze never leaving Erin's.

"Hey," Erin said softly, arms hugging herself.

She was amazed at just how much of Tamson's bruises and cuts had healed and disappeared, leaving just the ghost of discoloration in a few spots. She still had her cast in place, but other than that, looked beautiful. Erin cleared her mind of those thoughts, returning her focus to the fact that she had a very unenviable task ahead of her.

"What are you doing here, Erin?" Tamson asked, her voice even and somewhat calm.

"I need to talk to you. Is there somewhere we can go?" she asked, indicating the few stares they were getting.

With a nod, Tamson led the way back deeper into the club, leading Erin down the narrow, dim hallway that led to the room where the dancers got ready for their shows.

Erin stepped into the room ahead of Tamson, Tamson closing the door behind them and leaning against it with her arms crossed over her chest. She looked uncomfortable.

Erin took in the vanity top covered in various makeup implantation and used tissues, stained with a circus of colors from lipstick dabs. Finally, she turned to face Tamson, her heart beginning to race.

※※※※

Melissa walked casually to her purse, which sat on one of the tables. Her gaze was pinned to where the two women had just disappeared down the hallway. She dug out her phone and used the tip of a fire engine red fingernail to dial.

"Hey, baby. Your bitch is here."

Tanner felt rage breathing fire into his veins as he turned the wheel of the old truck hard enough to leave rubber on the street. He tossed his phone to the seat next to the .45.

"Look, Tam, I know you don't want to see me, but I just couldn't tell you this over the phone." Erin smirked slightly. "Not like I'd know where to call, anyway." She looked down at the shuffling high-heeled shoes she was wearing with her skirt suit, feeling quite out of place in her surroundings dressed that way. Letting out a heavy sigh, she met Tamson's guarded gaze. She so badly wanted to walk over to her and gather her in her arms. Pure will power kept her rooted where she was. "I got a call today."

Tamson remained quiet, her heart racing in her chest as she listened.

"A call from Detective Franklin."

Hank's heavy brows knit as he heard a loud crash towards the front of the club, from where he sat in his office. He tossed the pen to the desk and pushed up from the chair. Walking to the closed office door, he pulled it opened and glanced out into the hallway. Though he saw nobody, he heard a scream from the front of the house, which got him moving.

Erin and Tamson both looked at the wall, the dark hallway on the other side, then looked at each other.

"What the hell was that?" Tamson asked, already turning to grab the doorknob.

"Tam, wait," Erin said, her breathing increasing as a cold trickle began down her spine.

ふふふふ

"I asked you a very simple question, you dumb fuck," Tanner roared, standing over the man he'd just cold cocked. He bent down and grabbed the dazed man by the front of his shirt. "Where the fuck is she, Luther?"

Melissa stood back watching, a smirk smeared on her red lips. She said not a word, wanting to see how the drama would unfold. The heavy breathing of Hank, who ran into the room, looking around, caught her gaze. Melissa slunk back further into the shadows as Hank hurried over to the fallen bartender and Tanner, who glared at him.

"What the fuck you doin' in here?" Hank bellowed at Tanner, not noticing the handgun he held until it was too late and it was aimed at his chest. "Jesus," Hank breathed, gaze riveted to the sightless, cruel eye of the weapon. "Don't do nothing stupid, Tanner."

"Where is she?" Tanner growled, thumb pulling back the cocking pin. "You got five seconds."

"She's not here, man," Hank lied, praying he would be believable. He heard a snort coming from his left and saw Melissa enjoying the show. He returned his full attention back to Tanner and the gun. "Let's just everyone calm down, Tanner," Hank pleaded, his own voice lowering and calming. "Ain't no reason to get stupid, you know? Ain't worth it."

Tamson and Erin reached the end of the hallway, one turn to the left and they'd be headed right into the fray. Erin saw the gun first and grabbed Tamson, almost knocking her off her feet as she yanked her back into the hallway.

"Oh my god," she whispered, eyes wide in terror and chest heaving.

"Fuck," Tamson breathed, glancing back towards the end of the hallway again. "I gotta go to him, Erin," she said, her voice shaky. "It's me he's after."

"No!" Erin hissed. "We've got to get you out of here. *Now!*"

Tamson shook her head. "No. It's me he's after and I'm not about to let someone get hurt." She pulled out of Erin's grasp and headed back towards the end of the hallway.

"No!" Erin used her entire body weight to stop Tamson, tugging her back against her own body to stop her.

"Let me go!"

"Tamson?!" Tanner yelled, the gun still trained on Hank. "Get your cunt ass out here! I know you're here!"

Erin's eyes squeezed shut as she continued in her death grip of Tamson.

"Bridget," Hank said, his voice now dangerously low. "Call the cops," he said to one of the dancers.

"Enough of this fucking shit," Tanner growled, squeezing off two rounds. Hank's body jerked a few times before he fell to the ground. A scream in the hallway got Tanner's attention. He ran, barely missing stepping on one of Hank's hands as he did.

"Oh my god," Bridget whimpered, running over to her boss. She was relieved to see he was still breathing.

Erin hated herself for screaming, but the gunshot had been so unexpected, she'd lost it. Grateful that Tamson had bounced back first, she felt her hand grabbed in an iron grip and they were running down that very narrow, seemingly endless hallway. She saw a lit up EXIT sign at the end.

In Tanner's drugged up state and the dimness of the hallway, he could barely see the two figures running way ahead of him. He stopped and took what he figured would be good aim, squeezing off a round. He growled when he heard a small startled scream, but nothing more. He took off after them.

Tamson's chest was heaving from her frightened panting as they reached the end of the hallway to the emergency exit door, which would lead to the back parking lot and a maze of alleyways. That was also where she'd parked the Clipper, choosing to enter the club through the front door as the emergency door couldn't be opened from outside.

She used her free hand to slam the bar on the door, which allowed it to open. As the bright light of the afternoon hit her, another shot rang out and she found herself lying flat on her face with her legs still inside while her upper body was lying on the cement. Stunned for a moment and thinking she'd been hit, she realized Erin was lying on top of her and had knocked her down with her falling body. *Oh god, no!*

Using the incoming light from outside to help him aim better, Tanner raised the gun again, aiming at the two figures on the ground, one of which he could see was his target. Grinning like a madman, he squeezed the trigger but nothing happened.

"Mother fucker!" he yelled, looking at the gun, which had jammed.

Tamson took that reprieve to get out from beneath Erin and turn. She could see a red spot blossoming on the back of Erin's suit jacket.

"Erin," she whispered, shaking her shoulders, eyes never leaving Tanner, who was still messing with the gun. "Erin! Get up, baby, we gotta go. Get up!"

Erin groaned, her eyes blinking several times. Tamson got to her feet and used superhuman strength to pull Erin to her feet, as well. She knew she had to get them on the other side of that metal door; that would be their only survival.

Erin managed to get her legs under her and working as she was tugged out into the afternoon, the sun blinding from the dim insides of the club. She saw Tamson's car parked at the end of the small back lot, and she was being pulled towards it.

"We gotta get out of here," Tamson muttered, digging in her pockets for her car keys. "Fuck!" she cried when trembling hands dropped them. She spared a glance towards the emergency door as she reached down and snatched them from the ground. She was glad there were only two keys on the ring – one to her car and one to Hank's house – so she didn't have to try and find the right one. "Yes," she whispered when the key slid in. "Erin, get around to the other side of the car!" she yelled, getting her door unlocked, just as the back door was flung open, banging loudly against the brick wall of the building.

Before Tamson could get in, a ruthless hand

suddenly grabbed her by her hair, her head tugged back until she was able to see the much-taller Tanner looking down at her.

"Where the fuck you think you're going?" he leered, raising the gun and placing the barrel against the side of her head.

"Leave her alone!" Erin screeched, running around the front of the car as quickly as her injured body would allow. She grabbed at his gun arm, which got the gun pointed away from Tamson, but now she was faced with the most evil look in someone's eyes she'd ever seen.

"Cunt!" Tanner roared, bringing his arm back and using the side of the gun to plow into Erin's jaw, sending her sprawled to the pavement.

Erin landed with a groan, her body screaming in pain from every direction. She looked up when she heard distant sirens getting louder as they got closer. She managed to drag herself to her feet again, intending to go back over to Tanner and try again, but then she spotted something in the backseat of Tamson's car.

"You fucking whore," Tanner growled into Tamson's ear. "I'm going to splatter your brains all over this nice car just like I did with that faggot boyfriend of yours all over the carpet." Tamson cried out softly at the words, as well as the pain as her head was pulled back by her hair again. "Just too bad I don't get the joy of using that bat again."

"But I do," Erin hissed, swinging with all her might, the afternoon sunlight glinting on the metal of the golf club just before it made sickening contact with the back of Tanner's head.

Tamson saw the swing out of the corner of her

eye seconds before it made contact, managing to duck down and out of the way of Tanner's falling body, which fell on her legs.

Erin was panting hard as she held onto the club, looking down at the still body on the ground. Finally, she met Tamson's gaze, dropping the club as she hurried over to her, weakly helping her out from underneath Tanner's weight.

A loud cry tore from Tamson's throat as she clung to Erin, who held on just as hard.

≈≈≈≈

Erin slowly came to, realizing she was lying in a hospital bed with soft, gentle fingers brushing her hair back. She opened her eyes and turned to her left to see that Tamson was sitting on the side of the bed, her eyes red-rimmed and her face pale.

"Hey," Tamson whispered, smiling at her.

"Hi," Erin whispered back, her eyes slipping shut again at the pleasurable touches. Her head fell slightly toward them.

"You really scared me," Tamson said, her fingers running down a bit to stroke Erin's cheek.

"Why?" Erin asked with a soft, contented sigh, making Tamson smile.

"I thought I was going to lose you."

Erin's eyes opened and she studied Tamson's face. She saw so much love there and it made her smile. She shook her head, feeling weak and somewhat dazed from the painkillers she'd been given. "No."

"I'm sorry," Tamson said, tears welling in her eyes. "I was so stupid to leave you, Erin." She shook her head. "Never again." She cupped Erin's cheek and leaned in, placing the softest kiss on chapped lips. "I love you, Erinbeth Riggs."

Erin raised her hand, noting an I.V. was taped to the back of it, and cupped Tamson's jaw. "I love you, too."

They shared a kiss that was full of promise before Tamson pulled away a bit. "The doctor said you're going to be okay. They were able to remove the bullet. And, your family is on their way."

"You called them?" Erin asked, surprised.

Tamson nodded. "Yeah."

Suddenly, Erin looked extremely concerned. "Tanner?"

"He's gone. The police got a statement from me." She looked away for a moment, her jaw muscles working before she turned back to Erin. "He was wanted in four states for murder, Erin. Josh was just one more casualty."

"So were you," Erin said, brows raised in emphasis.

Tamson smiled sheepishly. "We both were. I'm so sorry."

Erin shook her head with a smile. "I'm not. Ultimately, he brought me back to you."

Tamson gave the first real smile she had since the day she'd walked out of Erin's life, fear and cowardice making her push away the woman she knew had changed her forever.

"Can I ask you something?" Tamson asked, moving off the side of the hospital bed and into a chair next to the bed.

"Of course."

Tamson looked down at her hand, which held Erin's, her thumb running over her fingers. "What did that detective have to say?"

Erin's face went even paler than it had already been. She turned away, unable to look into Tamson's eyes. "Um ..."

"Dale killed her, didn't he?" Tamson asked, her voice barely audible.

Erin took a deep breath before she turned back to meet Tamson's gaze. She nodded. "I'm so sorry," she whispered. "He's gone, too. A couple hikers found them."

Twin tears rolled down Tamson's cheeks, though she wouldn't allow a sob to escape. "You know," she said, looking down at her and Erin's entwined fingers. "I always worried this is ultimately what would happen to her." She shook her head in sadness. "Shame."

"Are you okay?" Erin asked, studying Tamson's face.

Tamson nodded with a brave smile and tears in her eyes. "Yeah."

Erin squeezed Tamson's hand, the two sharing a look of connection that would follow them for years.

Present Day – Greeley, Colorado

Tamson was extremely quiet on the trip, staring out her window the entire way. Erin glanced over at her from time to time, taking Tamson's hand in hers and squeezing to let her know she was there. Tamson smiled, returning the gesture then turned back to the passing scenery.

Lake Side Cemetery was beautifully appointed with rich, thick lawns, though they were winter gold at the moment. Trees dotted the property, shading the bone-white headstones. It was to be a graveside service, which Tamson was glad for. She had no desire to sit through a church service that she knew her mother wouldn't have appreciated or wanted anyway.

Erin pulled up behind a rented white Taurus, which Charlotte stepped out of, the skirt of her dress billowing slightly in the breeze as it blew out from beneath her heavy, wool coat. As soon as she realized who had pulled up behind her, she smiled, head cocking slightly to the side while raising her hand for a wave.

"Hello, my love," she said, taking her granddaughter into a tight, warm embrace, which Tamson fully returned.

"Hi, Grandma," she said softly, surprised to see the tears in the older woman's eyes as they parted.

Charlotte said nothing, allowing her emotions to speak for her. "Erin," Charlotte said as Tamson stepped aside, Erin stepping forward.

Together, Tamson in the middle, the three headed off the paved path of the cemetery, stepping over the curb to the grass, hearing it crunch under their steps. A dark green tent had been set up over Connie's final resting place, her casket above ground with flowers strewn across it. As each person arrived, they were handed a white carnation from a woman who worked at the funeral home. Tamson took hers, twisting it in trembling fingers. There weren't many people there, only the three of them, the preacher, and a man Tamson recognized as her mother's great-uncle.

The small crowd gathered beneath the tent, the minister said a few words, most of which Tamson didn't hear. Instead, she distantly felt Erin's shoulder against her own and she saw the casket. She could easily imagine her mother inside, though she didn't want to.

Finally, the minister finished and, as the casket began to lower into the ground and completely disappear into the earth, she glanced down at the page, fluttering in her trembling hand. It was filled with all the words and thoughts she'd written on the stolen page from Erin's notebook on the bus. She saw the words she'd written: *angry, how dare you, betrayed, I hate you*. Glancing back to her mother's grave, she suddenly knew it didn't matter anymore. An understanding swept over her like a wave of compassion, and she swore she heard the words *I'm sorry*, whispered on the breeze.

Raising her head, Tamson looked up into the blue sky above, not a cloud to be found. The sun reached down, kissing her skin and she felt at peace. Folding the page, she put it back into her pocket. Looking once more down at the wound in the ground, she gently tossed her carnation on top of her mother's casket.

"I forgive you," she whispered, a smile spreading across her lips. She turned to Erin, feeling her eyes on her. She extended her smile and opened her arms. Erin stepped into them, both holding each other tight.

"I love you, Erin," she said softly, feeling she'd lost one family only to find another.

"I love you, too, Tam. Everything is going to be okay. *You're* going to be okay," Erin whispered into the hug, placing a soft kiss on Tamson's neck.

Tamson nodded, taking a deep breath. "Yeah. I really am."

Tamson looked over Erin's shoulder, slowly pulled away as her eye caught on something. She walked around Erin, eyes unable to look away.

Erin turned to follow her with her gaze, seeing her fall to one knee before a stone.

BELOVED DAUGHTER, JENNIFER F. ROBARD
MARCH 19, 1987 – SEPTEMBER 9, 1991

☙☙❧❧

Wrapped in Erin's arms in her apartment, Tamson slept.

The day was bright, the sun high and the sound of laughter in the air. A park, filled with trees and green grass with a huge sandy area filled with equipment: swings, slides, and nets to climb on.

She sat on a park bench, watching the kids run around, yelling to each other. Somewhere in the distance a child was crying as she fell, skinning her knee only for her mother to hurry over to her, taking her in comforting arms.

One little girl in particular caught her eye. Her back was to her, and she was dressed in a bright blue dress that reached to her knees. Mary Janes dug into the sand to keep her footing as she climbed the ladder to a slide. The little girl climbed to the top of the slide then turned, looking at her, eyes of green boring into matching eyes. The little girl turned back around then slid down, her dress flipping up from the breeze her descent caused.

The little girl landed at the end of the slide then stood, turning to face her again. She stood there for long moments, a hand rising to play with a strand of auburn hair, the sun creating a fiery halo around her head. She slowly walked toward where she sat on the park bench, getting closer and closer. Finally, she stood three feet away, the freckles across her nose making a slight triangular pattern. She reached her hand out, waiting for it to be taken.

She reached out, taking the hand, small in her own adult-sized one. She felt its warmth and baby softness, the kind of softness that only a child can have, their skin undamaged by the sun and life. She studied the little girl's face, waiting.

The little girl looked into her eyes then suddenly the sun came out in all her grinning glory. The little girl smiled and smiled at her, showing tiny, straight, white teeth. The little girl, still smiling, backed up slowly, their fingers holding as long as they could until the little girl's shorter arm dropped to her side. One last grin, and she turned and ran back to play, only to be caught up in the arms of a beautiful young woman with blue eyes and golden blonde hair. Together, little girl and woman looked at her, love shining in their eyes.

From her park bench, she returned the look and the love.

"Goodbye," she whispered. "I'll always love you.

The End

About the Author

Kim Pritekel was born and raised in Colorado and still lives there today, in love with the Rockies and simple beauty of home. She began writing at age 9 and has yet to stop, as writing a novel is more fulfilling than therapy. Cheaper, too. Kim embraces all forms of creativity, including filmmaking, which she has done as a writer, producer and director, since 2006. She can be reached on Facebook or by email at XenaNut@hotmail.com

You can also find Kim's other books at - www.sapphirebooks.com

Check out Kim's other books.

After Shadow - ISBN - 978-1-939062-10-9

Clara always knew she was different, but just how different she was was to be seen. She will be forced on a journey to places that, though nightmarish to some, make perfect sense to her. While living a life in darkness and shadow, massaging the ghosts we all want to hide from beneath the covers, she will discover her own light of day. But, can she discover her heart?